Louisa Sophia and a Legion of Sisters

A Louisa Sophia Adventure

Russell Cowdrey

Acknowledgments

This book would not exist or be the quality product it is without the contributions of many people.

It begins with my personal cheerleader, Diana, my incredible wife. Thankyou for always being on my side.

To Professor Rogers, without your research, this book would not exist. Thank you for helping me bring this version of Eugénie's story to life.

A special thank-you goes out to the administration, the teachers, and the students of la Maison d'éducation de Saint-Denis for being so welcoming during my visit.

To the young women of the Rochambeau class at Saint-Denis who shared their stories, you inspired me, and Chapter 6 is dedicated to you.

Without the contributions of my fellow American historical author Alysa Salzberg, this book would be filled with too many French historical faux pas to count. Thankyou so much.

A big thanks to all the authors in my writing critique group for their input on my work.

To my stepson, Alberto, thank you for helping with the research.

I would also like to thank my editors, Brandon Purcell and Patti Waldygo at Desert Sage Editorial Services, and illustrator Alla Kholodilina for their invaluable contributions.

Contents

Author Forward

Thank you for reading *Louisa Sophia and a Legion of Sisters*. In all my writings, I strive to create fictional tales that weave themselves into the history of the story's time and setting. The inspiration for writing this book came from discovering the two-hundred-plus-year history surrounding one of the most unique schools in the world.

Founded by Napoleon in 1811, les maisons d'éducation de la Légion d'honneur, or the schools of the Legion of Honor in France, are a fascinating mix of female educational excellence, anachronistic militaristic administration, and unequaled student comradery.

Most of the characters in this book are 100 percent fictional, while some are fictional representations of real people or they are fictional characters whose backgrounds are taken from actual people. For the roster of characters and their backgrounds, please reference the "Historical Notes" section at the end of the book. For translations reference the "Translations" section at the end.

An epic journey follows, complete with bullies and villains, life-threatening situations, and historic destinations. But underlying it all, this is a story about a group of friends, sisters in the Legion, facing one of life's first major crossroads. Enjoy the adventure.

Chapter 1
Changing Grades

From the ridgeline of the Basilica, the distant lights of Paris called Louisa to adventure. Perched like a gargoyle so high above the rest of the world, she reveled in the liberating power of standing so tall.

A handful of times during the last four years, the staff had allowed her to visit the city's wondrous attractions. With each new experience, Louisa's understanding of the world and her list of future goals expanded. Now seventeen years old, she longed for her coming emancipation and stretched out a hand as if to touch the city that had shaped her dreams.

A strong spring breeze pierced her thin cotton school uniform, and gooseflesh sprouted in the cold's wake. She shivered, not wanting this moment to end. When her feet touched the ground again, this feeling would dissipate like the smoke wafting from nearby chimneys.

Most of the buildings in the suburban commune of Saint-Denis glowed with warmth, but a few were dark and showed damage from the Siege. Several had missing walls and cannon-disfigured facades, testimonials of a war whose loss still scarred the psyche of the French nation and its people.

Not my people.

Louisa had arrived at the Saint-Denis branch of Les maisons d'éducation de la Légion d'honneur in 1870, just a month before the Prussians surrounded the capital. Sixty years earlier, Napoleon had created the schools to educate the daughters of those who earned the nation's highest award for merit, the Légion d'honneur. They separated the girls attending the three schools according to each girl's family's status, with Saint-Denis being the topmost strata of social standing.

The first addition to Louisa's limited French vocabulary was the name the other girls gave her when the sisters were out of earshot. Even now, she wore "the Greek Bastard" as a badge of honor. For the first time in her life, she claimed her mother's heritage, something denied to her by the children back home in Corfu. There, they referred to her as "the English Girl," the words dripping with disdain.

If it had not been for the Clan of the Dissipated, she might have fled the school and the other students' constant derision. Like Louisa, the three girls who formed the rulebook-forbidden secret club were social outcasts for one reason or another. They had been the first ones to offer Louisa a hand in friendship. In truth, they became her first friends ever, and after her induction into the clan, they became her only real family.

As the wind whipped her raven-colored hair behind her, the building known only by its address of Cent Quatre captured her attention in the distance. Built during her tenure at La Maison de Saint-Denis, the monumental building's slanted glass roof sent a large beam of light into the heavens. It amused her that anyone would build a funeral home on such a grand scale. Given the building's purpose as life's last waystation, she imagined the light as a beacon guiding departed souls to their desired destination.

Louisa turned to her task and padded along the roofline toward the flying buttress at the side of the church and the squatting gargoyle that guarded it. After patting the creature's head, she slid down the pitched metal roof to the edge of the church with one hand on the arched buttress.

Saint-Denis's massive school, built during the seventeenth and eighteenth centuries, stretched away from the Basilica. France's oldest state-sponsored boarding school for girls was laid out like a giant "H," but the somewhat skinnier administration building created a cap at the top of the letter to form a boxy capital "A." Two beautiful courtyards containing four giant, starburst-shaped hedges, representing the Légion d'honneur medal, were in the middle, while extensive park-like grounds surrounded the school and the Basilica.

Closest to the Basilica, the administration portion of the building rose from the darkness, its outer wall and highest window separated from the church by a mere meter. Louisa only needed to climb ten meters down the column at the end of the flying buttress to gain entry.

Using the tips of her fingers, Louisa found the sloping beam and scooted hand over hand down toward the edge. She hung free at the bottom, thirty meters above the ground. She swung half her body around the column, then clamped her feet onto the flat end of the buttress. With her back to the administration building, she spidered down.

Her mind drifted to a time before Saint-Denis. In the dead of night, she had shimmied up a similar column on the side of the Holy Church of Saint Spyridon in Corfu City. Her uncle had waited below, acting as a lookout. It would be the second burglary for nine-year-old Louisa.

Six months earlier, Louisa's mother had sent the little girl's uncle to find her absentee daughter. That late afternoon, the young outcast had sought refuge by doing the one thing that made her feel in control in a life full of obstacles. Her uncle found her hanging by her fingernails on the side of a white limestone cliff with her feet dangling a hundred meters above the Ionian Sea.

A thief by trade, her uncle seized on the idea of using the little girl's unique skill to make some easy drachmas. Louisa's training began the next day and didn't stop until their last job. As soon as her private studies in languages and mathematics ended each day, her uncle drilled her on picking locks and pockets, hiding in the shadows, cataloging a room with a quick look, and escaping confinement.

At nine years old, she knew right from wrong. But from harsh lessons learned, she also knew the world would never make life easy for a bastard. Her decision to do as her uncle said came with no remorse. Louisa vowed she would take from the world more than the world would take from her.

The now teenage burglar used her free hand to pull a long metal file from her pocket. She leaned across the space between buildings and jabbed the sharp tip under the lip of the darkened window, then wiggled the file under the wood to use it as a fulcrum. She shoved the lever down, and the window popped open a few centimeters.

She returned the file to her pocket and strained against the window, working it upward a centimeter at a time. A lifetime of climbing had given her hands, fingers, and wrists incredible strength, so, less than thirty seconds later, the opening was a half-meter tall.

More than enough.

Louisa pushed off with a twist. Her body arched up and into the open portal across the gap. She landed on her stomach, half in and half out of the window. Her eyes adjusted to the near-total darkness after a long pause. The outline of the secretary's desk appeared in the small office. Each of the other three walls had a door. The one behind the small spartan table led to the headmistress's office. A place Louisa had visited too often and never on good terms.

There were no sounds but her heartbeat as she wormed into the room. She landed on all fours. Louisa rose, then turned from the desk and headed for the door to the records room. A lock stood between her and her objective.

She pulled several special pins from her hair and, with deft fingers, clicked open the lock. The scent of pine cleaner and aged, musty paper met her as she slithered inside. Louisa left a small gap in the doorway and repinned her hair. She retrieved a small candle and a match from her pocket. As she struck the match, its light bathed the small room in a soft glow. She touched the flame to the wick, which revealed floor-to-ceiling shelves piled with large record-keeping notebooks.

Louisa stretched the candle high to illuminate the spines of the notebooks. She tip-toed around the room, searching for the recently married Professor Marie-Catherine's Latin class grades and notes.

Dieu merci, she thought as she pulled the book from the lowest shelf. The volume opened near the middle to the leather-corded bookmark. She examined the format of several entries so that her "corrections" would match. After balancing the candle on the shelf, she produced a sterling silver fountain pen that she had "acquired" from someone's wealthy parent who had visited the school.

The sight of the writing instrument reminded Louisa how alone she was except for the handful of friends she had made at Saint-Denis. Her mother and uncle were gone, and she never considered her absent father to be family. His man Stevens had dropped her at the school with a promise that her father would see her again at her graduation.

With a shake of her head, Louisa refocused on the task. Due to her status as a social pariah, Louisa, along with Saint-Denis's other rejects, was slated to participate in the school's most despicable tradition, the Last Chance Tour. She could think of nothing worse than to be dragged across the continent and paraded before eligible bachelors from minor nobility or the wealthy merchant class.

Louisa sneered as she put pen to paper. With penmanship matching that of the teacher now living in Florence with her Italian husband, she detailed how Louisa, the best Latin student in class, had called Professor Marie-Catherine a horse-faced spinster. With a flourish, Louisa added the teacher's recommendation to punish Louisa by depriving her of the privilege of taking part in the Last Chance Tour.

Satisfied, she returned the book to its shelf and blew out the candle. Muffled words and the distinctive clacking of button boots––the source of the headmistress's apropos nickname, Buttons––followed by the softer tap-tap of a student's shoes, echoed in the hallway outside the office.

Skatá.

Louisa pulled the door closed, hoping no one noticed the loud click of the latch.

The hallway door opened, and Headmistress Madame Le Ray said, "Mademoiselle Chanzy, I do not have much time. Please be brief."

"Yes, Headmistress."

The door behind the secretary's desk opened, and the footsteps faded after it closed.

What the hell is Gabrielle up to?

Louisa cracked the door open. Lamplight peeked from under the door leading to the headmistress's office. After closing the records room door without the loud click, Louisa crossed the secretary's office and stuck her ear to the keyhole.

"As I was saying, Headmistress, my father, the general, has given me permission to accompany this summer's tour," Gabrielle said.

"But why would you want to go? You have countless suiters waiting on you."

"I would just like one last adventure, and since Joséphine must go, Julie and I would like to go to advise her. I'm sure Mère de la Nativité would welcome some help keeping an eye on the Greek girl and her *friends.*"

That witch wants to go so she can torture us. Louisa's thoughts raced at the implications.

"I don't think it's a good idea."

"My father will cover our expenses and a little extra to help offset the costs of replacing the old kitchen stoves."

"Well, that would be welcome."

The sounds of someone running came from the hallway outside the secretary's office. Louisa dove to the side and slid behind the secretary's desk. The door burst open, and Joséphine Maneval, Jeton Deux, rushed to the headmistress's door. She knocked twice and bounced from toe to toe.

And here comes one of Gabrielle's slimy shadows.

The headmistress opened the door, the light spilling into the office. Louisa closed her eyes, stilled her mind, and held her breath, becoming a shadow.

"Yes, Mademoiselle Maneval?"

The girl curtsied. "Headmistress, Mère de la Nativité sent me to tell you that the Greek girl was not at bedtime roll call."

Louisa stayed a statue as she winced inside.

"That girl will make me lose the ball." The headmistress sighed. "Let's see what she's up to this time."

The two girls trailed behind her as the headmistress marched out of the office.

Exclaiming to the heavens, Louisa thought, *Sapristi!*

Chapter 2

The Race

Louisa's eyes darted to the half-open window. It would be a close call for her to reach the dormitory before the headmistress did. *I can't get caught again.*

She grabbed the bottom of the frame and shoved it as high as possible. Clamping her hands on the building wall, she high-stepped onto the windowsill. She angled her head and shoulders outside with both hands pressed into the inside wall to hold herself in place.

Louisa pictured the jump in her mind. *Hope I don't tear my dress.*

She brought her hands forward, bunched her knees, and hopped across the meter of open air. Her fingers and knees clamped onto the column. Her stomach flipped, and a burst of energy shot through her as she slid down, her dress ripping. She gripped tighter, hands and thighs burning until she reached the end of the drop.

Each climb held the possibility of injury or death, and Louisa shook her head at the almost fatal mistake. *Stay focused.*

She reached high, straining to pull herself up using the strength in her arms, then locked her legs back onto the stone to repeat the process. At the top, she glided along the flying buttress back to the tiled roof using only her hands.

After regaining her balance on the incline, Louisa wiped the coating of stone dust off her scuffed and sweaty hands onto her dress. Then she fast-bear-crawled up the cold metal to the ridgeline on the Basilica's cross-shaped roof. She hopped to her feet, then sprinted to the middle intersection. She turned toward the top of the crucifix and her emergency route.

The sixty-year-old headmistress had to go down three flights of stairs and walk to the far end of the school to reach the dormitory. Even if the other clan members enacted their stalling tactics, Louisa had only minutes to reach the lavatory next to the vast sleeping hall. Her uncle's advice rang in her mind. *Hurry and you die. Think before you move.* His sage advice tempered her urge to rush.

Each time Louisa climbed the Basilica, she carried a long, black silk rope attached to a column inside a first-story classroom in the main building. On the first level of the Basilica's roof, she would secure her escape route by knotting the rope around the waist of a gargoyle with a long serpentine tongue.

On reaching the top of the cross, Louisa angled to her right and stumble-ran down the slanted roof. With the edge approaching fast, she grabbed the statue's hunched back and swung to a stop.

The thin black rope stretched from the gargoyle down to the last top window of the square A–shaped building. From there, Louisa would need to race the headmistress along the length of the school to the last classroom on that floor. The finish line lay a floor below inside the ground-floor lavatory.

She pulled on the rope to test the ties and picked up a long, five-centimeter-wide strap of greased leather with loops on each end. Louisa tossed the leather over the rope and grabbed both hand stirrups.

A candle appeared inside the large French window on the far side, and Virginie's head popped outside. After several frantic one-armed waves, Pleasure, Virginie's clan name, disappeared inside, leaving only a tiny glow as Louisa's target.

I never get to enjoy this.

She took a deep breath through her nose and stepped back. Exhaling through pursed lips, she sprinted down the slanted buttress. Twenty centimeters from the edge, she jumped. The rope dipped under her weight, and the leather whirred as the belt zipped down the line. Louisa tightened her biceps and tucked her legs, aiming for the opening.

Her feet crossed the threshold. She let go of one hand stirrup and dropped toward the floor at breakneck speed. When her toe tapped the ground, Louisa used her forward momentum to tuck her head and shoulder-roll over the marble flooring, taking out the jolt as her uncle had taught her. She came to her feet and flew toward a plastered wall. Virginie wrapped her arms around Louisa's waist, pulling her to a stop.

Virginie's eyes bulged inside her gold wire-rimmed spectacles. "It's bad. You have to hurry. Buttons was on the stairs, and Gabrielle has Jeton Deux looking for you." She shoved Louisa toward the door. "I'll take care of the rope."

Mon Dieu. I'm an idiot. The mention of the bully and her minion made Louisa realize that as much as it disgusted her, she needed to go on the trip to protect the Clan of the Dissipated from Gabrielle's foul plans. Later tonight, she'd have to go back and destroy the forged page.

With a nod, Louisa tossed her friend the leather strap and ran into the hallway. She pictured the headmistress's button boots clapping down the corridor a floor below her and lengthened her strides.

As Louisa raced toward the room, she forced her eyelids open and thought about yawning. About now, Marie—clan name Joy—would be intercepting the headmistress. Their agreed-upon story required a rare item from Louisa. Tears. With her eyes starting to water, she ran into the classroom and toward the open window.

Louisa vaulted the windowsill and twisted as she started to fall. She caught the lip with her fingers and glanced down at the ground-floor window. She trusted that Eugénie, clan name Gaiety, had opened the lavatory window below.

With a slight push away from the wall, Louisa released her hold. She fell three meters. As she passed the arched molding, she grabbed the stone and kicked inward. Then she let go and flew through the window at an angle, feet first. She landed in the center of the huge lavatory.

Chapter 3
The Fortune Teller

"**N**o, you cannot come in!" Eugénie yelled through the half-open door. Wearing a white nightgown, she blocked entry into the lavatory and kept her back to Louisa. "She needs a moment. Here, use this." She thrust a large-handled chamber pot out the door and waggled it.

"That's not fair."

"Life's not fair." Eugénie retracted her empty hand and slammed the door. With a quick spin, she pushed her back against the door as more knocks came. Through disheveled hair, she glared at Louisa. "We need to change your clan name from 'Daring' to 'Idiot.'"

Louisa yawned and winked at her friend. "It wouldn't be daring if it wasn't scary." She pulled her eyelids apart, forcing more tears to form. "Slap me."

Eugénie's eyes lit up, and she took three quick steps toward Louisa while raising her hand. "With pleasure." She smacked Louisa's cheek.

Louisa's face stung, and the tears came for real. "Dang, Gaiety. You enjoyed that."

"Serves you right." Eugénie blew a loose strand of hair from her face. "You forget that the rest of us can still get kicked out of Saint-Denis even if you can't."

Louisa nodded. "You're right." She put her hand on Eugénie's shoulder. "Merci." Then she pushed her friend, who stumbled backward. "Hit me like that again, and I'll break your nose."

"Whatever. You said that the last time, too." Eugénie turned toward the door. "Good luck."

With a *tsk*, Louisa walked to the far stall. The long room had twenty semi-private areas along the inside wall. With hundreds of girls in the adjoining dormitory, the room bustled with activity just before and right after lights out each night. As Louisa entered the doorless cubicle with its short walls, several girls came into the lavatory.

"About time."

"I'm about to burst."

"Stupid Greek Bastard and her band of low-lifes."

Louisa spun and glared at the mousy brown–haired Suzette Defoye from behind the wall. The sour Defoye was one of Gabrielle's hangers-on, and Louisa was not sorry that this would be the last month she had to deal with the students from the *terminale* class who were in their final year at Saint-Denis. Suzette jerked an arm up with a closed fist, her other hand in the crook of her elbow, forming the vulgar gesture. Then she ducked into the closest stall.

With a shake of her head, Louisa pulled up her dress. She yawned to keep the tears flowing before she sat on the wooden commode with its chamber pot under a round opening. She waited with her eyelids stretched wide and thought of the one thing that always made her sad.

In a low voice, Louisa sang a Greek song about lost love and remembered the day her mother had died. A former taverna singer in Corfu City, her mother had sung the same song every day after Louisa's father abandoned them. On the day her mother lost her fight with consumption, Louisa sang that song as her mom breathed her last.

The ambient sounds from the dormitory died down, signaling the entrance of one of the *dame surveillantes*. These zealous young nuns took their job of monitoring student behavior to an extreme. Louisa suspected that this particular silence instead portended the appearance of the headmistress.

"She's in the lavatory."

A loud voice yelled into the room. "Louisa Sophia!"

"Coming, Madame!" Louisa yelled back. She stood, fixed her dress, and rushed to the tall mirror near the door.

She ran her hands down her bodice, straightening the black material. She would do what she always did when she faced discipline for breaking a commandment in the school *rulebook*. She put on a contrite face while emptying herself of any emotion and, in particular, pride. That way, she could take the most egregious blows to her ego without response or lasting effect. With one final vision of her mother's face, she made sure a tear puddled on her cheek before entering the dormitory.

A small crowd of onlookers waited behind the headmistress near the lavatory exit. A hundred other girls stood or propped themselves up on their wire-frame beds, straining to listen. A meter behind Madame Le Ray, Gabrielle frowned. A couple of steps behind the blonde, blue-eyed beauty scowled Joséphine and Julie, Gabrielle's token followers whom the clan nicknamed Les Jetons.

You're too stupid to catch me, Louisa thought. She laughed inside while keeping her face disconsolate.

Louisa curtsied to the headmistress, who waved her forward.

Madame Le Ray grabbed Louisa's chin, inspecting one of her cheeks and then the other. "You missed roll call. What happened, child?"

Louisa let her eyes drift to the ground. "Nothing, Headmistress."

With a gentle tug, the headmistress raised an eyebrow and lifted Louisa's chin to look her in the eye.

Louisa bit her lip, getting into character. "I had a small disagreement with one of my friends."

"Who?"

Louisa shook her head.

"In a month, you will receive your *terminale* sash. Are you trying to earn a gray sash?"

"No, Headmistress," Louisa whispered, struggling to put as much regret as she could into her voice. From getting in trouble often, Louisa had worn a lower grade–level sash color many times and a gray sash more than once. Unfazed by the disciplinary tactic, she had always thought the punishment silly.

The headmistress leaned close and whispered into Louisa's ear, "No matter how much trouble you cause, you *will* go on the tour."

Louisa cut off her gasp of surprise. *Is she a gypsy?*

"Wash your hands. They are starting to bleed. Again."

Madame Le Ray straightened and raised her voice. "Tomorrow, instead of Chapel, you will find Mère de la Nativité and recite forty 'Hail Mary's while kneeling on beans."

The headmistress turned to the exit, shaking her head and muttering to herself until she was out of earshot.

Chapter 4

A Pyrrhic Victory

S itting at her desk, Louisa put her hand in front of her mouth to hide a yawn she couldn't suppress. She blinked several times and tried to clear her head. With only two hours of sleep the previous night, she needed a nap. Despite the headmistress declaring there was no amount of trouble Louisa could cause that would keep her from going on the tour, Louisa could not risk it. After the near escape, it had taken her most of the night to sneak out of the dormitory again and back to the Basilica roof to retrieve the altered page of records.

It would not have been such a long night except for Père Chomel. The insomniac priest had been pacing the hallway that led to the roof. Louisa had wasted too much time waiting for him to return to bed and regretted not retreating to climb the church wall from the outside.

Several students hurried into the classroom, trying to beat the bell. It would be hard to tell them apart without the girls' different body types and hair colors. The school's bland uniform of a black cotton dress with long sleeves and a small white collar suppressed individuality. A student's colored sash, the medals pinned to her chest, and any association insignia sewn onto a shoulder were all she could call her own.

Unless I'm working, I never want to wear black again.

Gabrielle and her brood spoke in hushed tones as they huddled in the far corner.

Like a gang of thieves, Louisa thought.

The irony of her calling anyone else a thief wasn't lost on Louisa, and she started fantasizing about her planned vocation in life once she was free of Saint-Denis.

Those thoughts disappeared when Mère de l'Adoration walked into the classroom, and everyone scattered to her desk. One of a handful of teaching nuns at the school, she wore her traditional habit, adding more black and white to the room. She waited to take her seat until every student had found her desk.

Louisa had complete faith in the results of the coming academic contest. Eugénie––the clan's leader and strategist––would lead them to victory as she had all year.

"Mademoiselle Savant, as battalion commander of the current *Garde impériale*, you may go first. Have you drawn up your order of battle?" asked Mère de l'Adoration.

Eugénie shot to her feet next to her desk, and her lucky charm––her father's Honour Medal of Foreign Affairs––with its silver medallion and blue-white-and-red ribbon bounced against her chest. "Yes, Professeure."

Louisa loved Mère de l'Adoration's classes. The nun's passion reverberated in the lessons she gave. On a one-woman crusade to steer as many students as possible into the teaching profession, she also worked hard to pass on the knowledge they would need to succeed at the vocation.

The weekly academic battle was one of the most ingenious learning tools employed by the determined teacher. At the beginning of Louisa's *première* year, the year before *terminale*, Mère de l'Adoration divided the sixteen students of her history class into four battalions. In most other courses, the other teachers, as dictated by the *rulebook*, separated friends and kept them from working together.

To her credit, the nun ignored that dictate, and the four members of the clan formed a fearsome unit.

After tapping twice against her father's medal, Eugénie moved with athletic deftness to the blackboard at the front of the room and picked up a piece of chalk. Under the first of the ten subject titles written on the slate board, she wrote a name. Marie went under *The Revolution*. She added names under topics until she had placed each of her battalion's soldiers' names on the board twice. Then she wrote Louisa and herself under the last two open subjects, *Athens vs. Sparta* and *The Eastern Question*.

A battalion commander must know her soldiers' strengths and weaknesses if she were to lead them to victory.

Each battle consisted of four unknown questions grouped under ten topics. The topics ranged from ancient philosophy to modern politics. Each girl in a battalion had to answer two questions, and no one member could answer more than three. In most battles, Louisa answered three questions, but not always. It depended on the topics covered. Like a grand strategist picking the best terrain for her army to engage the enemy, Eugénie had a sixth sense about which subjects suited each soldier's line of attack.

With a flourish, Eugénie spun and puffed out her chest in her usual challenge to the enemy commanders. She dropped her stick of chalk into the small wooden cup on the sister's desk with a clunk as she returned to her seat.

"Mademoiselle Chanzy, as battalion commander of the Chasseurs, it is your turn."

Gabrielle sneered at Eugénie as she stood. With haughty elegance, the tall blonde floated down the aisle of desks toward the front until she almost reached Marie. Louisa bit back a growl as her nemesis "stumbled," bumping into Marie's elbow. Marie lost hold of her slate tablet, which bounced off her desk with a loud bang.

Every head in the room twisted toward the sound.

Mère de l'Adoration stood and leaned forward, placing her hands on her desk. "Is everything all right, Mademoiselle Coffinières de Nordeck?"

With her freckled cheeks turning a splotchy red, auburn-haired Marie lowered her green eyes. "Yes, Professeure."

Gabrielle hid her snicker as she began to write the names of her battalion on the board.

With the witch's back to the classroom, Louisa fought the urge to let that extra nub of chalk fly. Nothing good would come of it. Then again, the headmistress said nothing would keep her from going on the tour.

Is it worth wearing the gray sash until the end of the school year? Probably, but some instinct told her otherwise, and she almost always listened to her intuition.

Louisa sighed as she put the chalk pebble down.

When all the commanders had written the names on the board, Mère de l'Adoration held a piece of paper as she walked to the slate and picked up a long, thin, pointing stick. "Let's begin." She tapped the seventh topic.

The first two-question skirmishes ended in draws. All the participating girls gave correct answers. After each success, a girl's teammates acknowledged their appreciation with small raps of their knuckles on their desks. When Marguerite became the first student to stumble on a question about the Crimean War, the raps came from her opponents. She shook her head as she sat down. By the fifth topic, Eugénie's and Gabrielle's battalions had a one-point lead on the third- and fourth-place teams.

The last question approached with the score still tied at seven apiece. Louisa rubbed an eye with her knuckle as she stood to answer her third question.

Mère de l'Adoration squinted at her paper before looking up. "Mademoiselle Sophia, please describe the events that led to the Second Peloponnesian War."

"Not fair," Gabrielle hissed.

Following protocol, Louisa curtsied and turned her head to address her answer toward Gabrielle. "I won't bore you with all the details, but when Athens took full control of the Delian League, they used their power at sea to stifle Sparta's commerce."

She paused and grinned at Gabrielle.

"Tensions did not boil over between the two city-states until Athens signed a mutual protection treaty with my home of Corfu. The island was known as Corcyra and was Greece's second-largest naval power. By bringing Corcyra into the League, Sparta became surrounded by league members. The Spartan ally, Thebes, struck the first blow, but it was the harsh response to the Theban attack that led to the inevitable. Sparta withdrew from their treaty with Athens, and the war began."

"And why was it inevitable?"

"If the Spartans did not respond, the Athenians could have eventually blockaded all of Sparta's commerce and forced them to capitulate."

"Correct." Mère de l'Adoration picked up the chalk to mark another point for Eugénie's battalion.

With a glance to ensure the teacher was preoccupied, Louisa mouthed, "That's not fair," and dabbed an imaginary handkerchief at the corner of her eye before sitting down.

Gabrielle snorted and crossed her arms.

"Mademoiselle Paley, your turn."

Julie––Jeton Un, a tall, skinny girl—stood and curtsied. Louisa had always considered her a hawk with her sharp cheekbones and bird-like nose. If Julie answered correctly, the battle would end in a tie, and Louisa hated ties.

"Your question on the same topic is to describe the differences between the forms of government used by Sparta and Athens. Also, tell us what these types of government are known as today."

Talk about not being fair. Even Jeton Un should get this one.

Julie wrung her hands together at waist level. "Yes, Professeure." She gulped.

Not possible. Does she not know the answer? Louisa thought.

Julie's eyes darted to Gabrielle, who glared back and jutted her chin at the floundering girl.

"Ummm," Julie whispered, "one was a republic, and the other was a democracy."

"Go on." Mère de l'Adoration rolled her open hand before her, urging Julie to continue. "Which one had a republic?"

Gabrielle's face grew ashen, and Louisa bit her lip not to laugh. She knew Gabrielle wouldn't dare try to help her underling answer the question, no matter how much she wanted to. The rulebook was unflinching about cheating, even for a favored student like Gabrielle.

"Athens," Julie whispered, glancing at Gabrielle.

Mère de l'Adoration shook her head. Gabrielle hissed and glared at Julie with disgust.

Julie's chin fell to her chest. She hurried to sit and buried her head in her arms.

"Victory!" With a wide grin, Eugénie half-stood and began knocking on her desk.

Louisa, Virginie, and Marie added their wooden claps to the celebration while the rest of the class squirmed in their seats, making sour faces.

As Louisa turned toward Gabrielle to gloat, she stopped short. The mean girl sat back in her chair, drumming her fingers on her desk. She grinned at Louisa as if she knew something Louisa didn't.

Chapter 5
Sour Stew

Louisa hurried down the refectory's center aisle, carrying her tray past Napoleon's huge portrait and his ever-watchful eyes. Even with the rule-book-mandated whispering, the lunchtime conversations of five hundred students bounced around the dining room's enormous medieval-style hall and its tall, rounded ceiling.

The clan's table sat in the far corner, to the right of the painting of the school's first headmistress, Madame du Bouzet.

After placing her tray on the brown-and-white-speckled marble table, Louisa sat facing the wall with the school's matron and thought for the thousandth time, *She really should have smiled.* Virginie––a slim, pale-skinned brunette with bespectacled brown eyes and lips hinting at a mischievous grin––passed a baguette to Louisa, who glanced down the table.

The other six students sitting at the far end of the table kept their eyes away from Louisa and her friends. The first-year students abided by Louisa's demands with fear-driven purpose.

What was said at the Clan of the Dissipated's table stayed at the table.

As Louisa tore the crusty bread in two, Eugénie, who sat beside Marie, leaned over the table. The tall, boyish-figured young woman used a finger to tuck her thin brown hair behind her ear. "Mère Sainte Adeline said we should pack a ball gown. My aunt's bringing my new one over before we leave." Eugénie smiled at Louisa as she continued. "Daring, you can have the one I wore last year to the Légion d'honneur Ball. I was only two or three centimeters taller than you back then."

"No, thanks." Louisa wrinkled her nose as she stared down at the bowl of matelote. She dodged a chunk of potato and a piece of white, flaky carp to dip the bread into the fish stew's broth. Bile rose in her throat as she took a bite of the softened bread. She couldn't wait until she no longer had to eat fish stew for lunch on Tuesdays. For the last four years, the vexing rulebook had dictated every part of her life, even codifying the school's breakfast, lunch, and dinner menus.

Fifty-three weeks to go, Louisa thought.

"You must take a dress." Eugénie's voice rose a smidge above the appropriate level. A young nun, standing nearby as a *dame surveillante*, raised an eyebrow toward the table while tapping a long stick against her palm.

Marie nudged Eugénie with her elbow. Eugénie nodded but turned a stern face back to Louisa. She whispered, "What do you plan to wear?"

Between chews, Louisa said, "My uniform."

Gasps came from Eugénie and Virginie.

Louisa lowered her bread to the table and sighed. "I won't be groomed like a prized sow and auctioned off to a bunch of slobbering gluttons."

"The Good Sisters are not going to like that." Virginie adjusted her gold wire-rimmed spectacles.

"This school and the nuns' job might be to make us suitable wives for some captain, major, or general, but that's not for me, and I'll convince the Good Sisters otherwise." Louisa batted her eyes at Virginie. "Mère de la Nativité, I'm scared. I want to wear my uniform in front of all the gentlemen. Please let me preserve my modesty." She tried to pout, but, try as she might, Louisa could not.

Virginie laughed. "Needs work."

Eugénie said, "You may not want to be there, but this is a fantastic opportunity for some of us. We're going back to Portugal."

Marie interrupted in a low whisper, "First time for me. What's so great about Portugal?"

Louisa's mind flew to the misadventures she had encountered when she, Virginie, and Eugénie accompanied Eugénie's aunt and Eugénie's older brother, Sébastien, on the pilgrimage from Porto to Santiago de Compostela in Spain.

Eugénie frowned at Marie. "Right now, the only thing that matters is that the men there won't be poisoned against us." She tapped her finger against the medal on her chest.

"I told you that going to the ball was a waste of time." Louisa pushed her bowl to the middle of the table.

Marie, almost as short as Louisa but more curvaceous, half-stood to reach over her tray and take Louisa's bowl. Marie scraped the remnants of her bowl into the new one. With her auburn hair pulled into a bun, her twin ringlets hung on either side of her face.

Eugénie pointed her spoon at Louisa. "You do this every Tuesday. You should be grateful for that fish soup."

Not again. Louisa blew out a long breath.

"During the Siege, you would have sold everything you had for that soup. Instead, we had to eat . . ."

"Gaiety, stop. I would like to forget about eating cat stew." Virginie looked down at her bowl with disgust.

"We ate a lot worse things than that. But back to more important matters. How could I know Gabrielle had spread rumors about us before we went to the ball?" Eugénie sucked air between her teeth. "It shouldn't matter that my family's in Algeria. Am I not enough as I am? Is love not enough?"

"Of course, you're enough. Any man would be lucky to have you beside him. You're smart, and you're beautiful." Virginie nudged Louisa's elbow.

Louisa swallowed the bread she was chewing and said, with as much sincerity as she could put into her voice, "They should be so lucky to find a woman like you." Then she said in earnest, "But I think you need to love yourself most of all. Remember what Euripides said."

In a snickering whisper, the other girls finished her sentence in unison, "*I feel no shame in loving myself above all.*"

Louisa frowned.

Marie waggled her spoon at Louisa. "If anyone could use a man, it's you, Daring. Someday, you'll understand that everything is not about you."

Conversations about boys tested Louisa's patience as much as the refectory's stale menu did, but she endured them because she loved her clan. She had no intention of ever tying herself to a man. In her experience, they were either simpletons without ambition or just wanted to use her. Maybe Louisa would think like her friends if she didn't have the ability to support herself, but she did and had no intention of wasting time on the lesser sex.

After Louisa was inducted into the clan, several times a week the other girls engaged in a kind of ritualistic discussion about boys. Louisa found it frivolous but endured the conversation to keep the peace. When Marie smuggled one of those inane romance books into the dorm, the topic dominated every conversation for a month. Out of boredom, Louisa tried to read it but couldn't stomach such a spineless, helpless woman as the lead.

Until the last two months, the topic had seemed like some faraway fantasy. Other than the summer breaks when the girls spent time with their families, none of them had a chance to speak to boys. There were no young men at Saint-Denis, and, without romantic distractions, the students focused on their studies. Not that the rulebook or the faculty gave the students more than a couple hours a day to think about anything else.

With their *terminale* year staring them in the face, fantasies about boys had become real-world discussions of men and plans for the future. Virginie had it all figured out, while Marie worried she'd never overcome her family stigma, and Eugénie obsessed that she wasn't good enough.

"This trip is a Godsend. What are you doing?" Eugénie pivoted her spoon toward Marie. "You should watch your figure. The Portuguese won't care who your father is. This might be your last chance to find a man."

With a large lump of fish balanced on the spoon halfway to her mouth, Marie frowned, her eyes sparking with green fire. She turned the spoon upside-down, and the carp plopped back into her bowl. The auburn-haired girl turned her freckled, cherubic face toward her heckling friend. "At least, *I have a figure.*" Her eyes became slits as she shoved the bowl of stew in front of Eugénie, whose eyes went wide. "You eat it. Add a little more weight, and you might develop some curves."

While a wave of red surged up her neck to her face, Eugénie moved her mouth up and down without a sound.

"Besides, think of the Siege. We wouldn't want to waste it." Marie's every word dripped with sarcasm.

Louisa started laughing as Virginie said, "That's enough. Both of you are being rude."

Marie took a deep breath as if steeling herself. "You're right. I'm sorry, Gaiety."

"I didn't mean to say that you're——" Eugénie shook her head. "I'm sorry, Joy."

"Forgiven." A melancholic smile touched Marie's lips. "I've been wanting to talk to all of you about a decision I've come to."

An ominous chill ran through Louisa as Marie made eye contact with each clan member. "I'm going to become a bride of Christ."

Louisa covered her mouth in shock. *Mère de Dieu,* she thought, and then, realizing she had blasphemed, she crossed herself.

"A nun!" Virginie exclaimed in a normal voice.

A long stick slapped the marble between their trays. All heads twisted to the dame *surveillante*, who jabbed the end of her switch toward Virginie and shook her head.

Virginie lowered her gaze and whispered, "Yes, Good Sister."

Louisa took a drink of water to give herself time to think. Marie had never said anything like this. She'd dreamed of being a mother more than anything. Louisa waited to speak until the *dame surveillante* returned to her post. "Your father's not a coward. He was a brave general in the war. Why should you sacrifice yourself because of a lie?"

Marie shook her head. "My brother and sister are each married with children. I'm the only one who can pay the penance the mob's demanding." She nodded. "You had a great idea. I'll wear my uniform to the dances as well."

"The mob be damned," Louisa hissed as she squished the bread in her hand until she formed a fist. "Fight."

Marie's freckles turned up as wrinkles formed near her eyes. She reached over and patted Louisa's fist. "Merci, but I'll fight my battles my way."

"Not to change this depressing subject, but I'm bringing my gown," Virginie said with a dreamy expression on her face. "Even if I don't need to find a husband, I'm going to enjoy dancing."

The other three girls grinned at one another. Louisa added a heavy dose of sarcasm when she joined Marie and Eugénie in saying, "Oh, Simon."

"You're the only man for me, Simon Jupin." Eugénie poured it on thick. "I've loved you since we were children."

Louisa was grateful that Virginie had doused the shock of Marie's news with some levity because Louisa could not accept Marie's decision. She thanked God that she was going on the trip. It would take a collective effort from the clan to save Marie from herself.

Virginie chuckled and said, "It's not my fault I have a plan. I'm getting my teacher's certificate, and then I'll marry Simon."

"Does he know that?" Marie asked, picking up a piece of bread.

"We made a promise."

"As ten-year-olds." Eugénie snickered. "You need to keep your options open during the tour." She laughed. "No one knows the will of God. Some man might even win Daring's heart."

"My destiny is my own." Louisa narrowed her eyes at Eugénie. "Don't worry about me. You need to watch your backs on this trip." Even Marie stopped chewing as Louisa paused to ensure she had their attention. "Gabrielle and both Jetons are coming with us."

Eugénie's expression twisted with fear, and Virginie went from pale to ashen.

Marie laid the bread on the table. "I've lost my appetite."

Chapter 6
Chicken Number Two

During the last week of the school year, the worst girls in the *terminale* class did everything possible to make the clan's life miserable. Led by the low-life Suzette Defoye, the group of six soon-to-be-graduating girls tripped Virginie, spilled a drink on Marie, and even put wet paint on Louisa's desk chair. All told, Louisa lost two school uniforms to their pranks.

Usually ready to fight at any insult, Louisa agreed with Eugénie and tried for once to take a road she'd never traveled before, that of a pacifist. Why not? The nasty girls would soon be gone from the clan's life for good. There was no use getting in trouble for such unimportant people. The self-imposed, one-sided truce ended when Marie woke one morning to find her hair tangled with glue. With revenge on the agenda, Louisa called the clan to war.

"These cowards deserve to be paid back tenfold," Louisa demanded of the girls forming a semi-circle in front of her.

"But don't you think this is going too far?" Marie tilted her head at Louisa. The uneven bun on the side of her head did a poor job of hiding how Virginie had butchered her attempt to cut out the glued hair.

"Before she passed, my mother told me to *never let your emotions rule your actions.*" Virginie pushed her spectacles up her nose. "They're not *all* guilty."

Louisa glared at them. "Really. If Gabrielle were torturing someone in the younger class, we'd put a stop to it. They're guilty for looking the other way. Same for the staff."

Eugénie laughed. "I'm with Daring. They deserve it. I can live with a little collateral damage."

Virginie shook her head. "I'll only help if you wait until the end."

Louisa frowned and then flashed them her most sinister smile. "Fine. Suzette is giving a closing speech. We'll do it then."

The following two days passed, and Louisa took their enemies' insults and attempted pranks in stride. She would get her payback. Virginie purchased what they needed from a kitchen cook and hid their weapons in the school's walled-in cemetery.

With every seat filled by students, prominent citizens, or proud parents, this graduation, like the other ceremonies Louisa had attended, droned on for way too long. After all, the self-important government dignitaries and retired generals, chests covered in medals, had to have their say. Most of which was nothing of significance. As the *terminale* girls began receiving their certificates, Louisa sneaked out of the auditorium with Marie. They raced to the cemetery.

Louisa reached into the cage and grabbed the black hen. She tucked the big bird under her arm while keeping the chicken's legs in a firm grip. Marie did the same with the rust-colored hen. They jogged back to the auditorium and opened the back door to the building just wide enough to listen.

It wasn't long before Grand Chancellor Vinoy said, "Mademoiselle Defoye has been chosen by her peers to give the closing remarks. Mademoiselle."

Louisa and Marie pushed the birds inside and shut the door. They dashed to the front, trying to hold in their laughter. That morning, Virginie had prepped the floor from the back door to the podium with two thin trails of the tastiest chicken feed. With her most nonchalant stroll, Louisa returned to her seat. Her posterior hadn't yet warmed the wood when she heard the first cluck.

On stage, in a chair next to the grand chancellor, Madame La Ray swiveled her head at the sound. A smattering of laughs came from the students seated in the audience. The black hen pranced down the aisle between the sitting *terminale* students. The bird clucked and pecked her way into view. By contrast, using more stealth, the reddish-brown chicken on the far side of the stage ate her way forward without a sound.

Suzette's face turned a deeper shade of red as the laughter grew. She stuttered through her next words, not understanding what was happening. Madame La Ray walked to the podium, button boots booming on the wood floor. She put her hand on Suzette's arm, and the girl stopped, tears in her eyes.

She directed Suzette toward the black chicken a meter behind the podium. "It's all right, dear. It's not you."

On seeing the farm animal, Suzette spun and searched the gathered students until she found Louisa. Her red face twisted with rage. Louisa made sure Buttons wasn't looking her way and winked at Suzette. The girl's eyes bulged.

The headmistress turned to the youngest soldier on stage. Young was relative, in this case. The colonel was fortyish and not in his sixties like the retired generals next to him. "Please help."

He inclined his head as he stood and bent toward the black hen.

Fly! Louisa screamed inside, urging the bird.

As the colonel grasped for the chicken's wings, the hen squawked and ran forward. The soldier lost his balance and fell to all fours. On the far side, a graduating student lunged for the red bird. That hen flapped its wings and jumped. It landed in the second row on the heads of parents and visiting citizens. A woman wearing a hat made from a pile of red ribbons screamed and swatted at the bird. The rust-colored chicken released a high-pitched cry of distress and flapped several rows away, loose feathers flying.

The Clan of the Dissipated sat in their chairs, reveling at the next twenty minutes of chaos as Parisian socialites and city-raised students failed, time and again, to capture the wayward birds. At last, one of the youngest students, wearing a green sash and a broad grin, held the brownish-red hen to her chest.

The colonel who had made the first unsuccessful capture attempt snatched up the black bird. Holding it high, he yelled, "I have it!"

The mayhem in the auditorium seemed to settle down, some participants looking around with wild eyes while others were more wary.

Eugénie turned to them. "Watch this." The tall, rangy girl strolled down the aisle toward the stage and yelled to Buttons, "Madame La Ray! Where's number two?"

The headmistress turned to Eugénie. "What?"

"I saw three chickens." Eugénie pointed to the black one. "That's number one." She pointed toward the young girl with the rust-colored bird. "That's number three."

Louisa covered her mouth as Virginie stood up and pointed toward the far side of the audience seating. "Over there, I saw a white one."

Near that location, a woman in a bright yellow silk dress let out an ear-splitting scream. Flush with terror, she shoved people out of the way and ran to the exit. Pandemonium descended again, and Louisa bent over, attempting to catch her breath between loud guffaws.

Chapter 7

Into the Underworld

With the tour's eight participants lined up in the courtyard, Buttons's inspection started at the far end with the mysterious Catherine Denault. A pair of mésange birds held Louisa's attention as they flitted among the branches of the huge starburst–shaped shrubbery. The small, showy, yellow-chested birds trilled, bobbing their blue-crowned heads and chirping in agitation at the garden invaders. While Louisa memorized the birds' calls, she blocked out all other sounds, including the nearby crunch of boots on the cinder path.

"Mademoiselle Sophia, did I say something funny?"

Louisa bit her lip and focused on the frowning headmistress standing before her. "No, Headmistress. I'm sorry. I didn't hear what you said."

Madame Le Ray sighed. "The next month will be a welcome respite for both of us. Mademoiselle Sophia, I hope you come back with renewed respect for the incredible opportunities given at this school." She shook her head and glanced down the line. "No matter. As I was saying, Colonel Theuvez, who retired recently, will be the leader of this expedition and shall be afforded the respect he is due as both a winner of the Légion d'honneur and the Médaille Militaire." Her voice was tinged with sadness as she said, "The war took most of his family, so please be considerate."

Poor man, Louisa thought.

The headmistress stood straighter, and her tone changed to that of a concerned mother. "I believe the cornerstone of an egalitarian society is the family, and the backbone of the family is a strong wife and mother. Like many other opportunities at our institution, this tour is provided to help our students make the most of their lives."

Madame Le Ray lowered her voice to imitate a man. "*Bring up for us believers and no thinkers.* The Emperor Napoleon wrote those words when he founded the school."

Louisa had never heard this quote and thought, *Pompous little donkey.*

The headmistress chuckled. "But luckily, despite the Légion d'honneur's military association, women—and not men—have always run this school. Each of you has been blessed with an education that allows you to think better than most men. For over half a century, our graduates have left us to become the wives and mothers of France's leading families."

With her hands clasped behind her back, Madame Le Ray walked down the line. "Unfortunately, each year, there are young women who graduate but have fewer opportunities to shine once they leave these protective halls." She stopped and turned to address them all again. "However, many students who attended similar tours found their place as wives of nobles and community leaders in other parts of France or other nations."

Not this woman. Let's go already.

Madame Le Ray locked eyes with Louisa. "While on the tour, I expect you to comport yourself with the same honor, dignity, and discipline representative of demoiselles of the Légion d'honneur. You are to exemplify the best of not only Saint-Denis but France. I will pray for your safe travels and for each of you to find your place to shine. Godspeed."

"Merci, Headmistress." Gabrielle curtsied.

While the other girls followed suit, Louisa mumbled, "Merci," and bent her knee. Afterward, she looked for her avian friends, but the little birds must have decided to skip the speech and were nowhere to be found. She tried whistling the same little chirps she had heard earlier, but they stayed hidden.

"Come on." Virginie tugged at her elbow.

Louisa looked up to see the rest of the group enter the school building and hurried after her friend. They crossed one of the grand hallways and exited the building into an enormous semicircular courtyard. The long, rounded building enclosing the garden housed the administrative offices of the Légion d'honneur organization.

Three carriages waited on the other side of the main gate. A broad smile stretched across Mère Sainte Adeline's plump, ruddy cheeks. She pointed each student toward her transport and said, "Hurry along, girls. We are going to have so much fun."

When the nun directed Louisa away from her friends toward the carriage last in line, she suspected the worst. With the door to the cabin open, Louisa floated up the two steps and paused at the sight of her traveling companions.

Ugh. It's going to be a long trip, she thought.

Louisa sat next to Mère de la Nativité. From the bench opposite her, Gabrielle's blue eyes sparkled as she smiled with false sincerity. "*Louisa.* Isn't this wonderful? We never get to spend time together."

Before answering, Louisa glanced at Mère de la Nativité. She thought the sister must have been a true beauty in her youth, but the woman's constant fasting had stolen her color. The nun seemed to ignore the two teenagers and kept her stern eyes locked on the Bible in her lap.

Louisa raised an eyebrow toward her nemesis. "I didn't know you *knew* my name."

"Stop being silly. What *other* name would I use?" Gabrielle flashed a sly smile.

The cabin lurched, and the carriage bounced over well-worn cobblestone streets heading toward the nearby Seine River. Due to an ongoing railway worker strike, they would board a barge to travel downriver to the port city of Le Havre, where a steamship to Porto awaited them.

Louisa leaned back into the leather seat. "We'll be at the docks soon. Let's just enjoy the view."

Gabrielle shrugged and opened a bag to retrieve a small book. "If that's what you wish." She became as silent as the nun.

As Louisa watched the buildings pass by, she thought about the nickname implied by Gabrielle's smile. How she, the Greek Bastard, longed for Corfu and the cliffs she loved. There must be seaside cliffs on the way to Portugal. Maybe she could find a chance to climb. That alone took the sting out of spending so much time with Gabrielle and her tokens. With hope in her heart, Louisa began to sing a song from the famous French opera *Orpheus in the Underworld*.

She thought it fitting to begin the tour, whose sole purpose was to bind her and her friends in marriage, by singing a song as Eurydice, a Greek woman murdered by her husband and his lover. As Louisa sang the happy stanza in her clear soprano, from the corner of her eye she thought she saw the nun's tight lips turn up.

Woman that dreams, sleeps not;
She rises with the dawn.
Early flowers appear finer; the meadows are embroidered;
But these flowers, who are they for?
You wish to know. For whom?
Say nothing of it to my spouse.
They are for the pretty shepherd who dwells there.
Louisa chuckled at the thought of her picking flowers for a man and switched to singing Eurydice's death aria. The nun frowned.

When it strikes me near thee, it attracts, it tempts me—Death!
I call thee. Take me with thee. Death! Thy charm penetrates me;
Thy cold brings me no suffering. It seems as if I were to be born again,
Yes, born again, instead of dying.
Adieu! Adieu!

Chapter 8
The Devil and Job

A gust of alkaline-tasting wind flowed through the carriage window, followed by a puff of fine gray soot. Louisa coughed and covered her mouth with her sleeve. Gabrielle and the nun put handkerchiefs to their faces. As her eyes watered, Louisa gave thanks that the greenish-brown river was far enough away from the school at Saint-Denis that the waste billowing out of smokestacks from factories lining the Seine seldom reached them.

Their carriage jerked to a stop, and Louisa hurried outside, hoping to find relief. Like a mist, the ash and the dust diffused the mid-morning sun behind a haze of gray. Louisa's cotton sleeve could not block the smell of dank water, smoke, and something biting and pungent like rotten eggs. Her eyes watered as her feet touched the ground.

She had disembarked from the carriage beside a long wooden dock paralleling the shoreline. Two narrow, keel-bottomed barges of considerable length were moored to the pier. Workers carried boxes of goods off one barge while another line of men rolled barrels onto another.

Louisa found her friends, and they huddled together without daring to speak. When she opened her mouth to say something, a foul, acrid taste soured her tongue. To her amazement, the longshoremen and the riverboat sailors seemed impervious to the pollution, bantering away as they transferred the tour's luggage to the barge.

"Let's go to Rosalie's Potluck for lunch."

"But Addy makes the best stew."

"Don't care, I've rotten luck there. The last three times, I got nuttin' but broth."

The men's conversation drifted away as they moved to the barge. Behind a handkerchief, Eugénie squinted as she gave Louisa her "See, I told you so" look.

Louisa turned away from Eugénie.

You won't make me feel guilty about that darn fish stew.

Still, Louisa felt a tinge of sorrow. The soup she hated would have been a treasure to these dock workers. It wasn't her fault they gambled for their lunches at potlucks. For all his faults, her uncle had given her skills to provide for herself. Never would she need to wager a meager salary for a chance to be the first to dip a ladle in a pot of soup in hopes of getting some of the prime bits.

A trim older gentleman stood near the gangplank wearing a fine wool suit and a tall gray top hat. By his ramrod posture, manicured imperial beard, and sharp eyes taking in every detail around him, Louisa deduced this to be Colonel Theuvez. At her recognition, she had to push against her training.

She had been taught by her uncle to identify men like the colonel with a glance, but he had also tried to instill in her a fear of such men's immutable sense of justice. Because she wasn't working, Louisa had nothing to fear. She promised to learn as much as she could, to better understand the thinking of men like him.

A sailor wearing a heavy blue peacoat and a straw boater's hat spoke to the colonel, who nodded. The colonel waved to Mère de la Nativité, and they exchanged nods. The nun, still holding a cloth to her nose, motioned for the girls to begin boarding. With the nuns in the lead, everyone lined up at the gangplank. Despite the soot-generated haze and the foul-smelling air, the colonel introduced himself and gave a slight doff of his hat to each girl, who curtsied and introduced herself before proceeding.

Last in line, at the man's tip of his cap, Louisa stuck out her left hand and waited, instead of dipping into a curtsy. The colonel raised an eyebrow but clasped her hand, returning her vigorous handshake.

As they shook, the colonel said, "You must be the infamous Mademoiselle Sophia. I am Colonel Theuvez. It is a pleasure to meet you." He chuckled. "Madame Le Ray must have been mistaken."

Louisa squinted. Several hands shorter than the colonel, she tilted her head back to meet the man's intense brown eyes. She put on her prettiest smile and squeezed his hand harder. "The pleasure is mine, Colonel, and I assure you, the headmistress did not exaggerate." Louisa wanted to spit as some ash settled on her tongue, but she stayed in proper form.

His eyes twinkled, and the lines around them grew more pronounced. "Are you sure? I should have found the horns by now if what she said were true." His grip grew more vigorous.

A devil? Does Buttons really see me that way? Louisa thought.

To hide that his words had left her nonplussed, Louisa hurried to say, "I save them for the true sinners."

He laughed and disengaged from their handshake. In less than a heartbeat, the light in his eyes faded, and melancholy filled his voice. "As with Job, the devil has already done his worst."

The hurt in his words pricked Louisa's heart as she thought, *How sad.*

He sighed. "You should go to your cabin and out of this mess. In a few hours, we shall have clear skies again."

Louisa bobbed her head and hustled down the wooden plank. When she reached the ship's edge, she hopped to the deck, ignoring the sailor who held out his hand to help her down from the gunwale. She navigated the narrow walkway against the railing and headed to the stern. Dodging the barrels lashed to most of the main deck, she headed for the cabins jutting up from the last third of the boat.

With long poles, the crew pushed away from the dock. Louisa skipped to steady herself on the shifting deck. When she was sure no one could see her, she spit over the side, trying to get the foul taste out of her mouth. She paused at the door leading to the quarters and turned toward a loud racket coming from the middle of the river.

The strangest and loudest ship Louisa had ever seen moved through the water using a very unusual system. A large chain rose from the river and ran over a blunt metal-covered bow to wrap around a giant winch in the middle of the boat. The chain continued over the ship's metal deck and dropped down past the sawed-off stern, disappearing under murky river water. Black smoke puffed out of the vessel's small smokestacks, powering an engine that turned the winch. With each crank of the big wheel, metal screeched and banged as the chain pulled the ship forward. *Clang! Bang! Screech!*

Three barges similar to hers followed in the chain boat's wake. With the first barge tethered to the floating winch, ropes tied the three together. The last ship's crew tossed a giant rope to two sailors at the bow of her barge, adding them to the river caravan.

As fascinating as this means of propulsion was, Louisa ducked through the door leading to the cabins. A coughing fit overtook her. She entered a narrow hallway to the sounds of chattering girls. She coughed a few more times and gasped, trying to catch her breath. Though the stale air was musty, her lungs found it a welcome relief. There were four doors in the hallway, two to a side. Marie's snorting laughter led Louisa to the last door on the right.

"There she is."

Chapter 9
Sunny Above, Cloudy Below

"Isn't this just wonderful?" Mère Sainte Adeline said, using a wet brush to scrub soot from her habit. Several hours after leaving the outskirts of Paris, the tour participants, minus the colonel, emerged from their quarters wearing clean clothes. To provide a space for the girls to lounge, the crew had built a makeshift second level by tying together several long boards and placing them on top of wooden barrels lashed to the deck.

While everyone else found a spot on the "sun deck," Louisa scrubbed her dusty, smelly uniform by the doorway. Finished, she tossed the wet dress onto the cabin roof. She used one leg to launch herself off the gunwale toward the cabins. With her hands on the top, she hauled herself up and onto an open roof in front of the taller wheelhouse. The captain chuckled from behind the wheel.

"Do they have monkeys in Greece?" Julie--Jeton Un—asked, snickering.

"She gets the monkey from her father's line," Joséphine--Jeton Deux—answered.

Louisa glared at the pair as Gabrielle laughed while everyone else, including Mère Sainte Adeline, chuckled.

With a cough, the nun cut off her laughter. "Girls, let's enjoy the sunshine and beautiful countryside."

Louisa frowned for a long second at Marie and Virginie, who had also laughed at the jest. She turned her back on her hecklers and spread her dress out on the roof to dry. She lay beside her damp uniform and took the nun's advice, though she had to block out the distant clanging of the chain boat ahead of them.

The fields near the river were green and lush from spring rains or filled with sprouting plants in plowed rows. The spires of churches heralded the coming of sleepy hamlets and bustling towns nestled along the river's banks.

Louisa ignored the rest of the ship while watching the world go by. After counting the tenth cross atop a church's tower, she decided to practice what her uncle called active listening. She tilted her head to the sun, closed her eyes, and concentrated on the conversations below.

"Julie, fetch my parasol. I have to protect my complexion," Gabrielle commanded.

"Joséphine, bring Gabrielle's parasol." Julie passed the order downhill.

Joséphine tossed back her sarcastic reply, "Sure, I'm not doing anything," but hustled off the sun deck and into the cabins.

She should make a stand.

Louisa considered Joséphine Maneval's, situation. From a once-powerful family, she attended the school as the great-granddaughter of some general who had served in Napoleon's Grand Army. Cursed with aging family connections and without fortune, the tall, solidly built brunette with a pretty smile employed a calculating demeanor to try and better her situation. Although Louisa could appreciate her way of thinking, she couldn't agree with the girl's decision to cozy up to Gabrielle in hopes of getting one of her throwaway suitors.

"Catherine, are you excited for the dances?" Marie's voice carried above the water slapping against the hull, the mews of the seagulls overhead, and the never-ending clang, bang, screech.

She'll give you nothing, Joy. Like always.

The girl's sing-song words came to Louisa like a distant nightingale. "I'm a little apprehensive."

That's new. As the only neutral party in the ongoing battle between the Dissipated and the other three girls on the tour, Catherine was an enigma. The slender girl with a soprano voice that rivaled Louisa's had arrived at Saint-Denis only two years ago. Shy to the extreme, the new student kept to herself, never divulging details of her past.

With a mystery afoot, the school's many gossips turned into sleuths as they sought clues to Catherine's history. After two years, there were only a few revelations. The month she'd enrolled, Catherine's medal-winning father had died from a lingering wound he'd received during the war, and her mother had died years earlier.

"Do you want to get married?" Eugénie tried to ease the girl into revealing more information.

"What are your plans after school?" Eugénie asked, following what Louisa assumed to be Catherine's usual evasive shrug.

In the pause that followed, Louisa pictured another silent lift of the girl's shoulders.

Louisa detected a hint of exasperation as Eugénie said, "You *have* considered your options. *Right?*"

"There's one thing I want to do," chirped the songbird.

After an even longer pause, Eugénie asked, "And that is?"

More silence before she said with defeated resignation, "Never mind."

The door to the cabin opened, and two quite different sets of footfalls were heard.

"Merci." The pop of a parasol opening.

"Where is Mademoiselle Sophia?"

At the colonel's voice, Louisa opened her eyes. She blinked for several seconds, then looked over the edge of the roof.

"There you are." The former soldier beckoned her to come down.

Louisa nodded. She scooped up her now-dry uniform in one hand, and, with her other pressed flat on the roof, she rolled off to hang by one arm. She dropped the last twenty centimeters to the deck beside the colonel. The man shook his head and turned toward the gunwale.

Louisa smiled, opened the door, and ducked inside the cabin hallway. In the clan's room, she placed the dress back in the small suitcase with her two casual dresses and another spare uniform. She'd brought the only three she owned.

Louisa paused. Muffled sounds came from beneath a hatch at the end of the corridor. With the stealth of a church mouse crossing a sleeping cat's den, she crept over to the hatch and lifted it a centimeter at a time.

"Set your main, Pierre," a gruff voice commanded.

"One décime on eight. Hand 'em over."

A small light came from the direction of the bow, and Louisa poked her head inside the open hatch, taking in the upside-down scene. Less than ten meters away, the three other barge crewmen squatted toad-style in the yellow glow of a kerosene lamp.

"Come on, Descartes. Make a bet."

The man with his back to Louisa said in a slow stutter, "Stop-p calling m-me that. M-me name's Lé, Léon, and I, I, always loo, lose."

The gruff-voiced man said, "You'll never win with that attitude, Lé, Léon, an' it's no fun with jus' two. Bet for him or against." He gave the stuttering man a light punch on his arm.

Léon stuttered, "I bet five centimes that he don't."

"Good." Gruff nodded. "Nothing else to do with them princesses on the deck."

The third man's voice squeaked, "Did ya see the tall blonde an' the short brunette?" He whistled. "I'd bet me *couilles* for a chance to lie with either of 'em."

Her nose wrinkling, Louisa thought, *Disgusting pig.*

In a slow stutter, Léon said, "D-don't say that ab-bout the young ladies."

Gruff stuck his hand in a pocket and passed dice to the pervert. "Lé, Léon's right. You best shut yer trap, or the capt'n 'll crush those tiny balls of yours."

Not before I cut 'em off, Louisa thought, her upside-down face growing more flushed from anger than from blood rushing to her head.

The pervert shook his fist and flung two white dice against a box. He exclaimed, "Zut, deuce-ace."

"I, I won."

"Your luck's turned, Lé, Léon." Gruff held his palm out to the pervert.

Despite feeling lightheaded, Louisa spotted his move. Gruff's other hand snaked into his pocket as the pervert handed over the dice.

He cupped his hands and said, "Got to make up for my losses. Two décimes on nine."

The others called their bets, and while they watched Gruff's throw of the dice, his free hand once again moved to the pocket that only Louisa could see.

Need to remember that move.

Until her discomfort threatened to become a full-on headache, she watched the cheater take his marks' money a little at a time. He never won more than two rolls in a row to keep them on the hook. The longer she watched, the angrier she became.

Louisa never made the mistake of judging a person's intelligence based on a speech problem, but after a few more exchanges between the men, it became apparent to her that the stuttering man was also slow. Twice, Gruff had taken advantage of the man's inability to count simple sums.

The thought of stealing from the poor or the disadvantaged disgusted Louisa, and she hated those who did. Besides the moral implications, her philosophy on practicing her arts lined up with one of her uncle's favorite sayings: "Why steal one drachma a hundred times when you can steal a hundred drachmas once?"

She closed the hatch and blinked away the spots in her vision as her circulation returned to normal. With her mind made up, she began to plan. Before Louisa left the barge, she would settle Gruff's burgeoning account.

Chapter 10

Savages and Scoundrels

"Again," General Eugénie commanded.

One by one, the clan members detailed their parts in the plan that Louisa had devised and refined.

Louisa had spent two nights spying on her mark. With her friends' help, she'd been able to sneak into the hold while the sailors were up top and to conceal her absence at evening roll call. She hid in the dark underbelly of the ship behind several crates and watched Gruff, the cheat, lock his belongings, including his loaded dice, inside his footlocker.

The end of the river chain remained only a few hours away at the town of Tancarville, and the Dissipated were on a war footing. Virginie would serve the role of the blocking force, while Eugénie would be the reserve, ready to enter the fray on several fronts. The best actress, Marie, had the hardest role as the distraction. If needed, she would cover for Louisa's clandestine activities and at the right time would bring the enemy to the battleground of the clan's choosing.

Eugénie nodded her approval of the plan and tapped her father's medal. "We're as ready as we can be."

Time crawled for Louisa as she sat cross-legged on her bunk. Everyone else seemed deep in thought while waiting to reach the pier. This wasn't the first time Louisa had recruited the clan to correct an injustice, but their silence reminded her that not all her schemes had been successful. To keep from fidgeting, Louisa practiced her lock-picking techniques as, in her lap, her fingers danced an intricate pattern with all its variations. The skill enabled her to bypass any standard lock in seconds.

Everyone jumped at the knock on the door.

The clear, stern voice of Mère de la Nativité followed one last rap on the wood. "Ladies, check your room, and bring your luggage to the deck. The captain wants us to disembark quickly." The nun's voice grew muffled as she roused the occupants of the next cabin.

Marie handed her small suitcase to Virginie and hurried outside. Louisa held open the door as Eugénie picked up her own suitcase, along with Louisa's. The two without luggage waited until the other rooms emptied before they stepped into the crowded passage. Louisa scanned the narrow corridor before entering behind her friends and scooting backward to the rear hatch.

Marie's voice carried through the doorway and over the chattering girls filing out onto the deck. "Look, a toad is in the water."

At the signal, Louisa tossed the hatch open and crawled through head-first so she did not have to hold her dress. Her hands went down several rungs while her thighs kept her from plunging to the floor below and held her skirt in place against the edge of the hatch. She tucked her knees and flipped over the rung to land on her feet in a crouch. Above, the hatch banged shut.

The barge shuddered as it made contact with the pier. Louisa raced down the narrow path between boxes and sacks toward the sailors' sleeping quarters. She pulled the special hairpins from her bun.

She squatted before Gruff's footlocker, and her fingers blurred. At the count of three, she pulled on the padlock, and its shackle popped free. A musky cloud made her shrink back as she threw open the lid. She lifted the tray that held the man's odds and ends to reach his clothes.

She rummaged through Gruff's belongings and placed each item in a pile next to the tray. Louisa ran her finger into the four corners. Finding a slight slope in one, she poked down, and the thin board popped up on the opposite side. She wedged a finger under the false bottom and lifted it.

Eight pairs of white dice formed a line beside a bulging burlap purse. Louisa pocketed the dice and the coin bag. Thirty seconds later, the lock clicked with everything in its place.

The mental clock in Louisa's mind tolled midnight, but she still had one thing to do. She frog-hopped over to Léon's locker. Its lid flew open even faster. She opened Gruff's purse, removed a twenty francs note, and replaced it with a brief letter she had written in advance. She dropped the coin sack on top of Léon's possessions.

Light suddenly poured into the hold, and the cargo hatch banged against the deck as the lock clicked.

Skatá.

Louisa bear-crawled along the path away from the light and dove behind two crates as boots padded down the small stairs. She curled into the darkest corner and controlled her breath, becoming a shadow.

"Get your hands off me!" Marie's shrill command bounced into the hold, and the boots stopped.

The captain yelled, "What the hell's going on?"

"I didn't do nothing," came the trembling reply of the pervert.

Marie's voice rose to new heights. "By the Blessed Virgin, this man grabbed my bottom!"

The boots clattered up the steps as the pervert squealed, "I did no such thing!"

Louisa ran toward her exit. After reaching the ladder, she pushed hard on the lid and raced up.

Virginie stood in the hall with her two suitcases, hiding Louisa's entry. "Took you long enough." She flattened herself to the wall.

"Justice takes time." Louisa skipped sideways to the door and burst outside.

"Captain, what kind of savages do you employ?" the colonel roared.

The captain stood with his palms outstretched. "Sir, I can assure you, he will be punished."

"Oh, my. Oh, my," said Mère Sainte Adeline, wide-eyed, while Gabrielle and the Jetons snickered.

"Ladies. Off. Now." The finger at the end of Mère de la Nativité's straight arm directed them to the gangplank.

The other girls shuffled toward the dock with their luggage while Louisa fought against the tide of black. Marie locked eyes with Louisa, winked, and burst into tears.

How does she do that?

Louisa popped free of the fleeing girls. Gruff stepped between the pervert and the captain, with his back to Marie. "Sir, don't be hasty."

Gruff stumbled forward from Marie's hard shove, and Louisa stepped into his path. They collided and went down in a pile. With arms tangled, Louisa said, "Excuse me, Monsieur."

The captain held out his hand to help her up, and as she reached for it, she let go of all eight dice in her other hand. White cubes scattered around the deck.

"Wha- What?" Léon said behind Louisa.

The dice had settled around the small open area. The flustered faces of the crowd soon changed to confusion.

"Ch. Chea. Cheater!" Léon yelled.

Louisa mimicked their confused expressions and suppressed a laugh.

Léon bent down and picked up one of the dice showing a single dot. He squinted at it and then at the rest of the gaming pieces. His eyes narrowed at Gruff, who wobbled on his feet in bewilderment. Léon's right hook caught Gruff on the cheek, and the man sprawled backward.

Louisa snatched Marie's hand and pulled her toward the gangplank while the captain yanked Léon's arm. Full of rage, Léon snapped his head around and said with nary a stutter, "He's a cheat, Captain. He stole my money."

Still holding Marie's hand, Louisa laughed as she bounded down the plank. The colonel bellowed, "Savages! Savages and scoundrels!"

Chapter 11

A General Buffoon

Louisa offered the open tin of Boissier's hard candies to their chaperone, the colonel.

"Well, I don't mind if I do." The older gentleman took a moment to circle the assortment of treats before plucking a blueberry-flavored hard candy and popping it into his mouth.

Mère de la Nativité shook her head at the proffered tin while Mère Sainte Adeline's eyes lit up. "May I have Ana's?" The jolly nun helped herself to a cherry and a lemon ball as Mère de la Nativité frowned at her.

Ana? Hard to imagine de la Nativité as a real person.

Louisa smiled and moved toward the dock where the clan sat with the quiet girl, Catherine. All the tour participants waited to board a water vessel while the crew filled its holds with supplies and cargo.

After the clan's resounding victory on the Seine, the barge captain had little choice but to fire the cheat and punish the pervert. The girls enjoyed a silent celebration, exchanging grins and winks. They boarded carriages that took them to a small abbey in Le Havre to spend the night.

Despite her sore lower back from sleeping on a hard bed in a drafty, spartan cell, Louisa woke in a cheerful mood. The colonel had promised to allow the girls an hour to shop before boarding the ship to Porto. While the other students gawked at expensive dresses, Louisa found a general goods store where she used the cheater's twenty francs—a week of a sailor's wages—to purchase gifts for each clan member.

For herself, Louisa found her favorite lemon- and lavender-scented perfume and a tin of the master confectioner's treats. Eugénie, the artist and architecture dilettante, who had complained since they'd left Paris about forgetting her sketching kit, would receive eight Staedtler pastel pencils and a drawing journal. Virginie's gifts included a ribbon and a fancy feather matching her ball gown. The romance novel Louisa picked for Marie took some sleight of hand to sneak past the tour chaperones. Louisa bought it hoping that the silly book might help change her friend's mind about becoming a nun.

"Did you forget us, Greek Girl?" Julie Paley said in disgust.

Mid-step, Louisa stopped and forced her smile to widen as she addressed Jeton Un. "No. Just like you didn't forget my name."

"Weren't you taught to get enough for everyone?"

"Of course. I just don't consider you anyone." Louisa turned her back and held out the tin to her friends and Catherine, who sat on their upright suitcases.

"Don't worry, Julie. Let the Bastard and her friends eat all the sugar candy they want. It will be the highlight of their trip," Gabrielle said, her voice just loud enough to carry to Louisa.

Mágissa. Louisa's shoulders tightened, and her lower back spasmed, but she refused to respond. When each girl had chosen a candy, she put the tin in her baggage and pulled out Eugénie's drawing pad.

Virginie jumped to her feet, eyes wide enough to fill the oval lenses of her spectacles, and whispered, "Simon?"

Louisa looked over her shoulder. A man in his late sixties with an outlandish silver walrus mustache strutted like a peacock in front of a strapping young man. The youth struggled to keep pace as he balanced a large suitcase on top of a big travel trunk. With each pompous stride, the older man swung his silver pommel cane. He wore the finest black wool suit with a matching top hat, while the younger man's well-worn pants, jacket, and bowler were a step above a common laborer's.

Is that THE SIMON?

Louisa glanced at Virginie, who appeared rooted in place, her eyes glued to the servant.

"I say, Colonel Theuvez, well met," said the gentleman walrus.

The colonel sighed. "Brigadier Etienne Gerard, what a surprise."

"I was speaking to Major General Vinoy last month. Have I told you the story about when he and I served in Algeria?" The brigadier pointed his cane at the colonel. "Remind me. I'll tell you over dinner."

"Brigadier Gerard, sir. May I put these down?" The young man's face was red, and sweat dripped from his dark hair into his blue eyes.

The brigadier turned with a frown. "If you must." He looked back at the colonel.

The servant set the luggage on the ground and leaned on the trunk, his chest heaving.

"Adolphe, do you remember how strong you were after the academy? When I joined the Hussars, I could have stood at attention holding that trunk for hours. I would never have hired such a dullard had I known he was so weak."

The ridiculed man's face and neck turned a darker shade of red, and his eyes narrowed.

Kópanos. Louisa added another name to her list of jerks.

"Then you were stronger than I. I could not have done the same. By the way, why are you here?" asked the colonel.

"Right. You were always a man to stay on mission. As I said, I was speaking with the grand chancellor, who mentioned your little expedition. It happens that I have business to attend to in Porto and Lisbon."

Louisa stopped listening to the retired military men because Virginie had become unstuck. In a daze, she walked toward the handsome man and tapped him on the shoulder.

Sweat flew from his nose, and his eyes widened as he turned.

Virginie said, "Simon Jupin. It's really you."

"Virginie," he murmured in a raspy breath. He wrapped his arms around her waist in a bear hug, lifting her off her feet while Virginie laughed with delight.

Gasps came from the crowd of women staring at the couple.

The familiar shrill voice of disapproval, which had often targeted Louisa, shot from the supervisor of the *dame surveillantes*. Mère de la Nativité yelled, "Young man, unhand that girl!"

He's done for.

In two heartbeats, the nun floated across the distance to the hugging couple and smacked Simon on the back of his head.

His brown bowler hat flew away. Turning ashen, Simon put Virginie down and backed away from the snarling nun.

"Ma Mère, please stop," pleaded Virginie. "Simon's my childhood friend."

"By the Little Corporal's ghost, what have you done now, buffoon?" bellowed Brigadier Gerard.

All the blood in Simon's face drained at the rebuke, his ashen color turning milky white. Virginie stepped between her beloved and his attackers. "Sir, I can explain." She directed her words to the brigadier while her eyes pleaded with the nun.

The nun's face softened, and she stopped her response.

Simon stepped beside Virginie and wrung his hands at his waist. "I'm sorry, sir. I haven't seen Virginie for many years. I got carried away."

Under the walrus mustache, the brigadier scowled. "I have faced death on many occasions, and never once did I lose my dignity. You serve a general of France. If you are to continue as my manservant, you must rise above your lowly birth and purport yourself with decorum."

Simon bowed his head. "Yes, sir."

The colonel said, "Brigadier, Ma Mère, it appears that no harm has been done, and the ship has signaled that we may board." He looked at the two chastened teenagers. "I'm sure Mademoiselle Ghesquiere and the gentleman will be on their best behavior the rest of the trip."

Virginie and Simon nodded.

"Please follow me." The colonel pointed at a sailor standing on the steamship next to the gangway. There, passengers entered from the large gangplank that rose from the dock to the deck of the *SS Lafayette*. "The chief mate will direct you to your quarters."

"Very good, Theuvez. See you at dinner. Come along, boy." Brigadier Gerard marched toward the ship without waiting.

Simon hurried to pick up his hat and plopped it on his head. "Virginie, we'll catch up later." He hoisted the trunk, struggling under its weight, and shuffled bow-legged after the brigadier.

The colonel let them get a good lead before he directed the nuns to follow. Louisa and the rest of the clan swarmed Virginie, everyone trying to ask her question louder than the others.

After seconds of confusion, Eugénie said, "Enough." Louisa and Marie went silent as Eugénie continued, "Let's talk in our cabin."

Gabrielle and the Jetons marched past them, and the blonde said, "Nothing but common rabble."

Joséphine sneered at Virginie and cackled, "More like common harlots."

Louisa stepped toward the much taller girl with a clenched fist, but Eugénie grabbed her elbow and pulled her back. "Leave them." Then, draping her arm over Virginie's shoulder, Eugénie said, "It must be destiny."

Chapter 12
The Deceiver's Chaperone

Louisa stepped from the passenger cabin hallway onto the deck. With her roommate Marie out of commission, she ignored the chaperones' command to stay inside unless two other girls accompanied her. Besides, what could the Good Sisters do? They were each busy filling a bucket.

Louisa moved to the railing, giving the three girls leaning against the wall a wide berth. She grimaced and fought to control her gag reflex as she walked past the trio.

Like dominos falling, first Marie, then Catherine, and then Gabrielle retched, spewing bile into the bucket between their knees. Louisa wrinkled her nose and hurried away from the temporary infirmary arranged along the outdoor passage. The seasick students had been sent outside to remove the stench from the small first-class staterooms, each shared by two girls.

Most of the first-class passenger areas near the gunwale had covered walkways, while inside were sumptuous sitting areas, smoking rooms, a library, and even a puppet theater. Yet all the girls agreed that the most lavish rooms on the ship were the shared lavatories with the amazing flush mechanisms.

As lovely as the accommodation was, Louisa had one destination in mind. On reaching midship, she found a stairway leading up. The sunshine warmed her face as soon as she stepped onto the uncovered upper deck. To either side of her, funnels belched smoke from the engine room's coal-burning furnaces located deep in the ship's belly.

A couple of crewmen on deck gave her a cursory glance before returning to their duties. Straight ahead, one of the ship's two main masts stood tall, its sails furled and unused. With her eyes drawn to the crow's nest at the top, Louisa sighed.

In the same calm manner that she might approach a pick-pocket victim, Louisa walked toward one of the rope ladders tied to the top of the mast and anchored to the deck. She put her hand on the rope and swung as if playing. With her peripheral vision, she noted the placement of the four nearby sailors. No one paid her any attention.

With a jump and a pull, she bounced her feet onto the second rung, a meter off the ground. As fast as she could manage, Louisa pulled and stepped higher, all while working with the sway of the rope and not fighting it. The lack of anyone sounding an alarm assured her she hadn't been discovered, but still, a third of the way up, she paused to locate the men on deck. With the sailors still oblivious, she climbed.

Meters away from the opening into the nest, she saw movement above and heard voices.

"You have one of those chocolate treats?" A loud yawn floated down to Louisa.

"Even if I did, I wouldn't share with the likes of you." Another man laughed.

Disappointed that she couldn't reach the top, Louisa took in the scene while clinging to the ropes as the ladder swayed with the rolling waves. The coast of France was not visible to port, but to starboard the clear day allowed her to see a hint of her father's England. Though she'd never set foot on the island kingdom, her future after Saint-Denis lay there. Since finding out about Girton, Mère de l'Adoration hadn't stopped talking about the college for women founded near the men's college at Cambridge.

"Come on, give a guy a break. I need something to keep me awake."

If Louisa wished to continue her education, Girton appeared to be the best of the limited options for European women. A few years spent gaining knowledge and honing her other craft seemed like a sensible plan to Louisa. In addition, college would give her more opportunities to socialize with a higher class of marks to help fund the independent lifestyle she desired.

"You always were a stingy bastard."

"I am."

The overhead conversation pulled Louisa out of the future and back to the present. Reluctant to start climbing down, she scanned the ship. Near the stern, where the second-class passengers sunned themselves, she glimpsed a Saint-Denis school uniform. The dark-haired girl sat on a wooden lounge chair, and then a man in a brown jacket and a matching bowler sat down in the next chair over.

Pleasure needs a chaperone. Or she might earn that nickname. Hah.

Louisa swung around the ladder on the underside of the lattice rigging so that her legs hung free. She flew downward, a chimpanzee swinging from one wooden rung to the next.

"Oi, miss! You can't be playing on that."

A meter from the ground, Louisa let go and bent her knees on contact before racing toward the ship's rear. "Sorry!" she yelled with a wave over her shoulder.

At the companionway, she bounded down the steps two at a time to the main deck. The few passengers strolling along the covered passage gave her odd looks as she ran by. Reaching the aft deck became a puzzle as she had to wind her way through several internal hallways and up another set of stairs.

At last, she could see through a door window with a sign above it that read, *2nd Class Promenade Deck*. A steward just outside opened the door as Louisa spotted the pair.

"Mademoiselle, may I help you?"

Louisa smiled at the young man and pointed toward Virginie. "I'm here for my friend." She marched past and headed toward the couple but slowed when Simon took Virginie's hand. Louisa sat on the long end of a lounger, a row behind and to the side of the sweethearts but close enough to listen.

Simon jutted his chin toward Virginie. "When did you get spectacles?"

Virginie touched the side of her glasses. "Shortly after I arrived at Saint-Denis. I had trouble reading the blackboard." Her face turned red. "You don't like them?"

"I do. They make you look intelligent." Simon chuckled before growing serious again. "What do you want to do when you graduate?"

"Once I have my teaching certificate, I'll settle in Paris. I love the idea of teaching."

"That sounds like a wonderful plan."

Virginie nodded. "I'm sorry about your father's store. What is he going to do?"

"He took a job designing hats with one of the big factories," Simon growled. "He hates not working for himself, but it lets him use his skill and make enough money not to lose the house."

"Is that why you're working for that awful man?"

He nodded. "It's the best-paying job I could find without an education. I had been apprenticing under my father. When we were little, I never imagined being a milliner, and just when I came to want that life, God had other plans."

"I couldn't put up with his insults," Virginie said.

"At times, I get angry, but it could be worse. At least, he doesn't beat me." Simon chuckled.

"It's nothing to laugh about. The man made me so angry this morning. He has no right."

Still holding her fingers in one hand, Simon caressed the top of Virginie's hand with his other one. "His rank and his money give him the right. It's as it always has been and always will be."

Virginie snorted. "We'll see if he can keep his dignity when I come for him."

Simon laughed. "I've missed you."

"And I, you." Virginie's voice had a husky tone.

Control, Pleasure. Stay in control, Louisa thought as she scrunched lower in her chair.

"I will put up with his insults and save every centime I make. Then, when you finish at Saint-Denis, you can keep your promise."

Virginie's voice held a slight tremble when she asked, "What promise is that?"

"Don't feign ignorance." A hint of concern came with Simon's next words. "You didn't change your mind, did you?"

"The goal of this tour is to find us husbands."

"What?" squeaked Simon.

"Didn't General Ass tell you? We're going to Portugal to see if we can find a man willing to take on a tarnished woman like me."

Simon let go of her hand. "A husband? Tarnished? What are you talking about?"

Even looking at the back of Virginie's head, Louisa could see her mischievous smile in full bloom as she said, "Some of the girls on the trip are here because they're orphans like me. Others have families who live out of the country or have lost their power and money." She grabbed Simon's hand and laughed. "Don't worry. I have no intention of finding a husband on this trip, but now I've changed my mind." She drew him closer. "Now that the man I promised to marry when I was ten is on this trip with me."

Simon whispered, "You didn't forget."

"Never."

Their heads came together, and all Louisa could hear were the sounds of kissing. With each passing second, Louisa's chest tightened at the thought of what might happen if a chaperone discovered them. Fear for her friend forced Louisa to fulfill the unlikely role, and she stood. As she reached out to break up the kiss, an impish thought took hold, and Louisa said in a shrill imitation of Mère de la Nativité, "Get behind me, Satan!"

Virginie jerked her head back and shoved Simon in the chest. He toppled from his chair, crashing to the floor, his arms and legs sprawling. Virginie jumped to her feet and spun, her face glacier white.

Louisa doubled over laughing at the two lovebirds.

Chapter 13
No Good Justice

The waiter held the chair while Louisa sat, and he helped her scoot forward. At the head of the table, Captain Larent stood between the colonel and the brigadier until each female member of the tour was seated. The captain sat in his oversize chair, followed by the other two men.

"Sir, if you would like your man to eat with us, there is one more seat." The captain waved toward the other end of the long table where a place setting remained unused.

"Merci for the invitation, but I'm afraid the young man's lack of breeding might cause embarrassment." Brigadier Gerard shook his head. "No, he can stay where he is, in case I need something." Simon stood at attention behind the brigadier, trying without success to keep calm as a slight frown touched his handsome face.

Virginie had lucked out with her future husband when it came to looks. Not that Louisa would ever settle down, but if she did, she didn't need anyone as handsome as Simon. Character, then intelligence, would top her list of the most prized qualities in a man. But, after a moment's self-examination, she admitted that any man impressive enough to win her heart would also be pleasing to the eye. *Where will I ever find a ruggedly handsome intellectual with impeccable integrity?*

The staff served the guests red or white wine from the bottle—a welcome change from the watered-down whites they drank in the children's dining hall.

The ship had only a third of its total complement of first-class passengers, so the captain had graciously invited the chaperones and the students to eat at his personal table on the second night of their journey. The luxurious dining room, with its vaulted ceiling, flowery muraled walls, and velvet-cushioned chairs, resembled an opera house more than any dining room Louisa had ever been in.

Since first boarding, much to her disappointment, the students had eaten each meal in the much less impressive children's dining room. Tomorrow morning, the ship would dock in Brest, and another third of its passengers would board before leaving that afternoon for Porto. Louisa suspected that after tonight, they would be back at the kids' table for future meals.

The captain stood with his glass of wine. "Good Sisters, Mademoiselles, Brigadier, and Colonel. I've been privileged to share my table with passengers from around the world, but I do not believe I have ever run across an entourage such as yours." He raised his glass. "Merci for giving me such unique company tonight, and good luck on your expedition. Please enjoy the meal. Santé."

"Santé." Louisa raised her wine and clinked her glass with her neighbors'. Rolling her eyes, she touched her goblet to Gabrielle's as the blonde signaled her own distaste at doing anything with Louisa by a cluck of her tongue.

The captain sat, and conversation picked up while soup was ladled into the high-quality but not too fancy bowls. *A practical compromise to account for rough seas*, Louisa thought.

From her place in the center of the captain's dining table, between Mère de la Nativité and Marie, Louisa had a clear view of the captain, the brigadier, and Mère Sainte Adeline. With years of practice, she blotted out the existence of Gabrielle and her underlings from where they sat across the table from her. Her attention stayed locked on the adults at the end, as she studied every interaction and personal nuance. In a mental catalog, she stored and updated her understanding of each individual to predict his or her future actions.

"Brigadier Gerard, I take it that you have different goals than the colonel and the mademoiselles on this trip."

The brigadier used his napkin to wipe soup from his walrus mustache. "Yes, Captain. I'm acting as a buyer for several noble families. Securing quality wine has become increasingly difficult, with the blight destroying more European vines. While the rest of the participants are busy socializing, I shall be meeting with port wine distributors in Porto and establishing connections with vineyards in the Douro Valley."

The captain took a sip of his wine. "We have two good ports onboard. A white from Cockburns and a red from Wares." He waved the waiter over. "For dessert, please serve the brigadier both of our port wines."

The waiter nodded and stepped back.

"Merci," the brigadier said before slurping a spoonful of lettuce soup.

Louisa tasted the creamy green liquid and thought, *At least, it's not fish stew,* before reaching for the pepper.

The captain buttered a piece of bread and asked, "And, Colonel, given the history of animosity between our nations, why did you choose Portugal as your destination?"

The colonel put his spoon back into his bowl. "I'm not sure. I wasn't consulted."

Mère de la Nativité said, "I'm at fault, Colonel. My family resides in Lisbon, and my mother is ailing. Madame Le Ray arranged our destination to allow me to see her."

As she updated her catalog, Louisa contemplated which was more significant news. That Ana de la Nativité had a family, or Buttons was such a softy. Louisa took another spoonful of soup.

"Sorry to hear about your mother. Are you Portuguese?"

"My mother is. My father was a diplomat. He passed from illness after I came to France."

From across the table, Mère Sainte Adeline added, "Was that when you were a student at Saint-Denis or after you married?"

Gabrielle's eyes bulged, and Louisa's soup went down wrong, causing her to cough. Taking a sip of wine, she collected herself in time to feel Mère de la Nativité's leg move.

"Ow," said Mère Sainte Adeline as she reached under the table. "Ah, never mind. I'll pray for your mother."

A new entry on the nun's ledger read, *a student of Saint-Denis and married.* Louisa went on to add, *probably widowed.* So much now fell into place when Louisa reevaluated the austere, melancholic disciplinarian of the nun. At the same time, soup bowls were whisked away and replaced by plates of prime rib bookended by potatoes and carrots.

"Captain, have you ever been to Algeria?" asked the brigadier.

"I have not had the pleasure."

"Well, the colonel and I have. When we were young officers, isn't that so, Adolphe?"

The colonel sounded like he'd eaten something sour. "Yes. The Siege of Constantine was my first deployment."

The brigadier settled back in his chair. "My first action as a cavalry officer was a few years before you in '30 when we took Algiers. I won't bore you with the details, but during that time, I won my first commendations for bravery." He appeared lost in thought for a moment before continuing. "The real excitement came after the fighting, when I battled and eventually won the affections of a young *indigène* woman." He leaned toward the captain and lowered his voice. "Cupid's arrow struck me as soon as I entered her presence. She smelled of jasmine, and her piercing brown eyes made my knees shake, even with her face veiled. I knew then that I must have her."

"Oh, dear." Sister Adeline's cheeks flushed as she stared at her plate with intensity.

The captain chuckled as the colonel raised his hand. "Etienne, I recommend you finish this story after we retire to the smoking lounge."

The old walrus blinked and looked around the table. "Right you are, Adolphe. Right you are." He motioned over his shoulder. "Simon, run fetch my smoking jacket and those Cuban cigars for after dinner."

"Yes, sir." Simon moved behind the captain, navigating around the table. He hopped to the side to dodge a waiter who stepped backward into his path, but he still bumped the man. The waiter stumbled forward, and two empty glasses fell to the floor. The wine bottle teetered before clanging to the metal tray, its contents spilling for a second before the waiter righted it.

A chunk of bread struck Simon in the back of the head. "Damn it, boy, watch yourself." The brigadier shook his head. "Stop making a fool of me."

Virginie's gasp sounded almost like a sob.

Enough! Louisa's face grew warm as she moved Brigadier Buffoon from the Jerk List to her Skatá List. She pushed back her chair as she stood and wormed her way free of the table. With fiery eyes, she glared at the walrus on her way to the accident. On his knees, Simon chased after a glass that had rolled under another passenger's chair. Louisa squatted beside him and blotted at the stained carpet with her napkin.

"Miss, I can do that," Simon and the waiter said almost in unison, their voices full of concern.

With a pat on Simon's arm, Louisa did not attempt to lower her voice or hide her disgust, but she did temper her words when she said, "Go get the braggart what he wants. I'll take care of this."

Simon rose and hurried toward the exit.

"Well, I never!" the brigadier bellowed as he stood and marched after Simon, his cane punctuating each step.

The waiter took Simon's place and began cleaning up the spilled wine. Louisa came to her full height and pulled back her shoulders, looking the walrus dead in the eyes as he stomped past her. "Really? I believe you were just about to tell us how you once did in Algiers."

An iron grip took hold of Louisa's arm, and Mère de la Nativité hissed into her ear. "Go to your room. Now."

Her ire still being stoked, Louisa snapped her head around to see the nun's icy stare. A chill ran down Louisa's spine, dowsing her fire. She nodded, curtsied to the table, and exited the main doors. At the enormous winding stairway with brass handrails, she paused. On the next level down, she could hear the brigadier yelling, "This will cost you!" The handrail rang from the slap of something solid, and the walrus shouted, "A week's pay!"

Chapter 14
Pangs of Liberté

Taking a deep breath through her nose, Louisa relished the salty air while pushing down her revulsion at the stench from the nearby city. The selective nature of her mind amused her. Vivid details of her previous visit to Porto came flooding back, but the smells also came, much to her chagrin, as if she were experiencing them all again for the first time.

She stepped onto the uncovered deck and soaked in the warmth of a sun she hadn't felt for days. Seventy-two hours in solitary confinement had been trying but productive. With only Marie's trifling romance book to read and onion soup for sustenance, she had literally climbed the walls to keep her sanity at the start of her confinement.

I can never go to prison, she thought. Her stomach growled as she shuffled behind her friends in the long line of passengers headed toward the gangway.

The hours alone made Louisa remember her uncle's thief's wisdom. Whenever she had resisted his grueling training regimen, he always reminded her, *Even good thieves get caught, but great thieves do not remain imprisoned.* Then, they redoubled their training to work on breaking free from different restraints, travel trunks, and locked rooms. Had she wanted, she could have been free from the cabin in seconds, but she knew that doing so would court disaster. She needed to take her undeserved lumps and move forward.

One good thing came from her imprisonment: she was able to put all the hours spent doing needlepoint at Saint-Denis to good use. Reflecting on her most recent adventure in the hold of the barge, Louisa realized she needed to make her dresses more like the work clothes she wore on her real jobs.

By the time Mère de la Nativité had unlocked her door a few minutes ago and given her a stern warning about future behavior, Louisa had finished her sewing. Into her three uniforms, and her best blue silk tea gown, she'd sewn an intricate harness system. With limited supplies, she'd used material from the fancy maroon drapes that framed a landscape painting on the wall of her windowless cabin.

Now, with a simple pull on two hidden strings at her waist, the middle of her skirt, both front and back, would rise to her inner thighs. Other strands wrapped around her ankles and could draw parts of the skirt closed. After she tied the belt at her waist, the black uniform's lower half could become a set of pantaloons. Even better, with a quick pull of the knot, the outfit dropped into a demure dress.

If she had time on the trip, Louisa would acquire some black cloth to make a face covering big enough to cover the white collar. Then her improved burglar outfit would be complete.

Virginie looked over her shoulder and whispered, "Simon wanted to thank you."

"He shouldn't. I cost him a week's salary." Louisa had worried that Simon would hate her for making his situation worse.

Flashing Louisa a wry smile, Virginie said, "He said he would lose another week's pay just to have seen the brigadier's face." She chuckled.

"I'm glad he's not mad, but let him know I'll pay him for what he lost."

Virginie shook her head. "You don't need to." She turned and spoke to Gaiety ahead of her.

I will, anyway, Louisa thought. She hated being indebted to anyone.

The sounds of the busy wharf where the ship was moored drew Louisa's attention to the city of Porto. They had docked near the mouth of the Douro River on the right bank. The pier at the bottom of the ship's gangplank stood where two large hills met. Four- to six-story tenements, painted a patchwork of colors and topped by the city's ubiquitous red-tiled roofs, sprouted from every open space on the rise.

Halfway up the hill to the right sat a sizeable two-steepled church, but it was dwarfed by an enormous rectangular building at the top of that hill, commanding the most prominent position. More towers with crosses peeked from behind the giant box, hinting at another church. To her front, at the top of the other hill, stood a large, prominent tower. Louisa merely gave it a cursory inspection before focusing on buildings close to the ship.

Many of the tenements were in a state of decay, but several had muraled facades of blue-and-white tiles, while others were covered in multicolored patterned or solid tiles. With all of the activity around the wharf, the city had an aura of aged industriousness, as if it were trying to regain heights long past.

The pier swarmed with workers dressed like any Louisa had seen in other countries, but here, more Africans were working along the docks. Similar to her last visit, she found the Portuguese language strange to her ear as the men yelled and called to one another while hauling goods to and from the ships.

On the narrow streets that wound up and away from the water, the populace wore a mixture of work clothes, modern suits, and outfits that she assumed were traditional clothing. Some women wore dresses with flowing sleeves and layers of colorful skirts. The styles reminded her of the traditional garments worn back in Corfu.

It still bothered Louisa that her mother had never allowed her to own or wear a Greek costume to any of the frequent festivals. Her mother insisted on dressing Louisa in modern styles and told her she was destined for more than Greece.

"Merci, Colonel," Virginie said as he helped her onto the gangplank.

"Mademoiselle Sophia, good to see you again."

"You, too, Colonel. It's a beautiful day."

Holding his hand out to her, the colonel asked, "Did you find your internment worth the indiscretion?"

Louisa shook her head. "Yes and no." She put her hand in his.

The colonel's eyebrows rose. "Well, I hope we don't have a repeat of the situation."

"We won't." Louisa smiled. "If the brigadier has learned his lesson." She stepped from the deck onto the rocking, less sturdy stairway, holding the handrails for stability.

Behind her, the colonel chuckled and said, "When hens grow teeth."

When she reached the cobbled street at the end of the pier, she cleared the boat, and the other side of the river became visible. Farther up the shore, an unimpressive metal bridge connected the hills of Porto to the less built-out city on the other side. On the water between the river's banks, small barges, shaped like oversize gondolier boats, sat low from the weight of giant wine barrels on board. These barrel haulers glided up and down the river, but most originated from, or were destined for, the far side where long warehouses stood.

"Hey, stranger." Eugénie leaned down to give Louisa a quick hug.

Louisa hugged her back as Marie and Virginie huddled around her. She looked at her friends. "I'm starving. Does anyone have anything to eat?"

Virginie and Eugénie shook their heads, but Marie held up her hand, smiling. She put her suitcase down and dug into her handbag, then produced a handkerchief-covered bundle. She untied the cloth to expose a fist-size lump of yellow cheese. After breaking the chunk in two, Marie handed the more significant piece to Louisa.

Louisa took a quick bite and mumbled while chewing, "Merci. What did I miss?"

"Gabrielle is making Virginie's life hell. Nonstop Simon insults and slights." Eugénie stared over Louisa's head, her eyes throwing daggers.

Following their trajectory, Louisa found the blonde target. She frowned at Virginie and said, "It will only worsen."

"I'm steeling myself. Maybe I'll feign an illness, so I don't have to go tonight." Virginie took her spectacles off and rubbed her nose.

"Tonight?" Louisa turned to Eugénie. "It starts tonight?"

Eugénie nodded. "We are staying at a small convent next to Bolsa Palace. They are having a dance there tonight."

Louisa sighed. "Better to get it over with, I guess."

"I'm excited to speak to the nuns at the convent. Maybe I could join an order outside France."

Louisa's stomach turned at the mistake her friend was making, and she looked at her hunk of cheese with distaste. *We have got to do something about this.*

The colonel stepped next to the clan's huddle. "Mademoiselle Coffinières de Nordeck, did I hear you correctly?" His brows furrowed. "Do you want to become a nun?"

"She's a martyr," Louisa quipped.

Marie slapped Louisa's arm. "Be quiet, Daring." She gave the colonel a rueful smile. "Don't listen to her. I've made up my mind to become a novice after graduation."

Louisa elbowed Marie in the ribs and said, "She thinks she has to pay for the sins of her father."

"I apologize for my *former friend*'s bad manners, Colonel." Marie's face had gone red, and she scowled. "Please, excuse me." She snatched the cheese from Louisa's hand, picked up her suitcase, and stomped toward the nuns.

Forlorn, Louisa watched Marie go and thought, *Did she have to take the cheese?*

The colonel shook his head. "I served with her father at Metz. Does he know her intentions?"

Louisa shook her head. "I doubt it. She just told us."

"I see." The colonel stared for a long moment toward Marie, then turned to address the group. "Bring your luggage, and follow the lad there." He pointed at a boy of about ten wearing a wide-brimmed straw hat, leaning against a fountain. The piazza was the only open area near the docks. "He will lead us to where we are staying. It's not far."

As Louisa picked up her suitcase, her stomach roared more than grumbled.

Chapter 15
Thieving Flirtations

"**M**ademoiselle, may I have this dance?" The pimple-faced teenager spoke better French and had more pluck than any of the other young men standing around the edge of the ballroom.

"No. But merci for asking."

The boy looked as if he'd eaten something sour and turned to leave. Louisa touched his arm. "You speak excellent French. May I ask you a question?"

The young man's face lifted. "Of course."

Louisa nodded toward Gabrielle, "Do you see the pretty blonde in the gold dress?" While she and Marie looked like they were attending a funeral in their black uniforms, Louisa couldn't help but admire her enemy's dress. Her golden silk gown had a floral pattern, ribboned shoulders, and a small bustle, which seemed modest compared to the extravagance of the rest of her ensemble.

The young man's eyes moved around the two-story-tall main hall. Located in the middle of the massive rectangular palace, it also served as the city's stock exchange. Vast arched windows and pairs of glass doors surrounded the ground floor, allowing anyone to see into the enormous area from the palace hallways.

A fishbowl to watch the prisoners dance, Louisa had thought upon entry.

Countless olive oil–burning wall sconces lit the cavernous area with a romantic glow, highlighting the many coats of arms painted around the curved ceiling. From the first floor, small balconies looked down onto the dance floor, its chessboard pattern of fancy marbled tiles, and the incredible mosaic at the heart of the room.

"I don't see her." His head swiveled as he tried to locate Gabrielle among the crowd.

Young men in formal wear guided young women wearing silk gowns around the center of the room. They kept time to a small orchestra in one corner playing a waltz. Eugénie, Catherine, and the Jetons moved to the synchronized flow with their partners while Marie and Virginie tried to blend into the wall behind Louisa.

Louisa raised a finger to help the youth locate her target. His eyes followed her hand.

He gulped. "Her?"

Head tilted back, Gabrielle was laughing at something said by the very handsome young man with her. After further evaluation, Louisa decided that *gorgeous* was a better description. With high cheekbones, an olive complexion, and brown hair, he had a make-you-look-twice smile. Louisa admired his laugh when he joined the blonde.

"Yes. Have you spoken to her?"

"Not yet. No point." He shook his head. "She's with João Lopes Gomes. The man can have any woman he wants."

Interesting.

"He's Adonis reborn, and his family is wealthier than all the families in this room combined."

"It appears the Roman god has lost interest." The gorgeous man had just bowed and walked away from Gabrielle's table. "I would like you to speak with her."

"Well, I'm not sure."

"If you lose your tongue, ask her what she thinks of me and my friends." Louisa glanced at Marie and Virginie.

The young man's forehead wrinkled. "Why?"

"She is as deceptive as she is beautiful." Louisa clucked her tongue. "I believe she is telling everyone lies about me and my friends. I would like to know what she's saying."

"I don't think I should get involved." He held up both hands.

"Wise, but it gives you an excuse to speak with the most beautiful woman here."

"I already am."

Louisa chuckled. What the young man lacked in looks and stature, he certainly made up for in confidence. "I'll tell you what. You learn what she is saying, and I will dance with you."

He grinned.

She held up her thumb. "Once."

The song ended, and the musicians paused to give the dancers time to find new partners if necessary.

"Done." Mr. Confidence bowed and headed toward Gabrielle and her lackeys, who had returned from the dance floor.

Marie stepped next to Louisa. "Did you break another heart, Daring?"

"Hardly. That one's tougher than he looks."

"I wish Mère de la Nativité had let me stay back." Marie sipped her wine, eyes following one of the couples as the music began and the pair spun around the dance floor.

"What, and miss all of this excitement?"

"Mademoiselles." A skinny young man with curly hair and a cleft chin bowed. His eyes darted to Louisa but settled on Marie, and he grinned. "I am Paulo Ferreira da Fonseca. My French no good."

Louisa asked in English, "I know that many of the Portuguese speak English. Do you?"

The grin turned to a full smile, and he replied in perfect English, "Yes. Thank you for saving me." His eyes never left Marie as he continued, "I would very much like to ask this amazingly beautiful woman to dance."

More flowery talk. Is he serious? Louisa narrowed her eyes. "Why?"

He scrunched his face, puzzled. "Why what?"

"Why do you think she is amazingly beautiful?"

A dimple formed as his smile grew more expansive. Marie fidgeted under his stare. He answered Louisa without taking his eyes off her friend. "Even though she's dressed like a crow in a crowd of peacocks, her grace called out to me. Her eyes are weighed down with melancholy, but I can tell that they are usually full of joy." He turned to Louisa. "I want to see her smile. Will you help me?"

Interesting. God does work in mysterious ways.

"Marie, the gentlemen would like to dance with you. He is very insistent."

Marie shook her head.

Louisa grabbed her friend's hand. "He seemed sincere. He wants to help you smile."

For several seconds, a battle raged behind Marie's eyes. "I'm sorry. No. Tell him I'm going to become a nun."

Louisa erased her scowl and said to Paulo, "Not right now. Please come back in a few minutes."

"She said no?"

"Correct, but I want to see her smile as well. Let me speak to her."

His face drooped. "Very well. My heart prays for your success. *Muito obriga-do.*" He bowed to Marie and walked away.

Marie watched him until he disappeared behind the dancers, and she sighed.

"Joy, you need to listen to your heart. It might be God speaking to you."
Marie's complexion darkened, and Louisa decided to escape the coming storm.
"I'll be back in a moment."

I need the cavalry. Or, in this case, the retired infantry.

Louisa hurried away, weaving through the crowds along the wall to where the
tour chaperones sat. As she passed a group of young Portuguese debutantes, she
understood the pointing and snickering even if she didn't know the words.

Ugh. Gabrielle.

The music paused as she stepped to the chaperones' table.

"Colonel Theuvez, may I have this dance?"

Mère de la Nativité frowned, but the bored expression on the colonel's face
brightened. "Mademoiselle Sophia, it would be my pleasure."

Mère Sainte Adeline's eyes twinkled as she asked, "May I have a dance as well,
Colonel?"

The other sister targeted the cheerful nun with a deeper scowl.

Mère Sainte Adeline seemed unperturbed. "Let them praise His name with
dancing."

The colonel stood. "Quite right, Good Sister. I'm all yours when I return."

He took Louisa's hand, and they went to the outer edge of the dance ring.
They assumed the position, his hand on her back, and her hand clasped in his.
When she'd practiced with the other girls at school, the smaller Louisa always had
to follow, which ran counter to her instincts to lead, but she'd gotten used to it.
As "Il Bacio, a Kiss," by Arditi began to play, the colonel stepped to the tune, and
Louisa followed in the graceful sweeping arc of the Viennese waltz.

"Colonel, I require a father figure."

The man missed his step but hurried to find his rhythm again.

"Don't worry, Colonel. It's not for me. I need your assistance with Mademoiselle Coffinières de Nordeck."

"Oh. How can I help?"

"It's about Marie's decision to live a consecrated life."

They continued making their way one, two, three, one, two, three around the room as the colonel said, "That's a very personal decision."

"The press and gossip about her father have been constant since the new year. Until then, she'd spoken of nothing but raising a family."

"Hmm." The colonel took a deep gulp of air but soldiered on, taking the lengthy strides with gusto.

"You know her father. Do you think he would want his daughter to be another casualty of the war?"

His jaws tightened.

Stupid, Louisa. So stupid. The man lost his children in the war.

His voice choked up. "No. A father would not."

"Please speak with her as her father might."

He nodded, his face red. With the song in the middle of the third and final refrain, Louisa finished the dance, singing the words in Italian. Every head they passed strained to hear the sound of her voice.

I do not desire gems or pearls, nor do I seek others' affections.

Your look is my delight, your kiss is my treasure.

Ah! Come! Do not delay!

Ah! Come! Let us enjoy love's life-giving intoxication.

Ah!

The colonel finished with a bow and said, "You have a marvelous voice, Mademoiselle Sophia."

Louisa curtsied. "Merci, Colonel. When you catch your breath, please speak to Marie."

"Right away." He held her hand as they left the floor. When they reached the table with Marie, Louisa excused herself and went to find Paulo.

Not far away, he sat around a table with three other gentlemen. As she approached, the gorgeous man she'd seen earlier ensnared her with a glance. He followed her progress, his gaze wistful as if remembering something amusing, and the corner of his mouth quirked upward.

Wow. Louisa forced herself to stop chewing on her lower lip and focused on Paulo.

"Pardon me," she said in English.

All four men looked her way. "Paulo, may I speak with you?"

He glanced around the table as he stood. "*Com licença.*"

Two perfect eyebrows rose, and the gorgeous man's head tilted as if in reflection. Behind him, a tall menacing man whom Louisa had not noticed bent to whisper in the handsome man's ear.

Pay attention. How did you miss the servant? Louisa chided herself. A mistake like that could be her undoing. She couldn't let the man's looks turn her into a simpleton.

Away from the table, Louisa motioned Paulo to lean in. "Marie." She looked toward where her friend should be and could not find her. It didn't take Louisa long to locate Marie's Saint-Denis uniform in the mass of green, red, yellow, and cream-colored dresses.

The old soldier had caught his second wind.

The colonel's straight arm guided Marie through another turn as Louisa pointed at the couple. "When the colonel is finished speaking to Marie, you should approach her again."

"Are you going to translate?"

"Marie speaks Spanish, Italian, and Latin. Do you speak any of those?"

His cheek dimpled again as he smiled, showing a pair of off-kilter bottom front teeth. "*Con fluidez. Muchas gracias.*" His attention went to Marie, and he fell silent, his eyes drooping with puppy dog longing.

Louisa shook her head and started to turn, then bumped into something firm and white. She went to catch herself and felt rippling muscles underneath a starch-stiff shirt. The musky smell of peppered caramel made her mouth water as she looked up and stopped motionless. Her reflection shone back at her from two rich pools of bronzed brown. Louisa gulped, her mind blanking.

His olive-hued cheeks turned ruddy.

Is he embarrassed? He has to be used to this.

A shy smile flashed before he said in impeccable French, "I'm honored to meet you. João Lopes Gomes."

Louisa jerked her hand away from his stomach, and he stepped back and bobbed his head. Still speechless, she wanted to say something, but her mind expelled all thought. Instead, she thrust her hand out.

He chuckled, his hand engulfing hers. A jolt went up her arm as soon as his warm skin touched hers. When he moved his arm up and down, instinct kicked in. She clasped his hand as hard as she could, as she did with everyone.

His eyes widened, and he pressed harder. The pressure brought Louisa out of her trance, and she said in English, "Louisa Sophia, it is a pleasure to meet you."

With a slight British accent, he asked, "Are you in mourning?" Their hands still locked, his eyes moved down her dress and back up.

She shook her head and let go. "Trying to avoid attention."

His head tilted. "You didn't come to find a husband?"

"Hardly."

He leaned forward. Louisa's breath came in short rasps as he whispered, "You devastate me."

He moved away, and she inhaled deeply to capture more of that peppery, sweet musk. "Why?"

"I, too, did not come to find a spouse, but you are exactly how I picture the most beautiful woman in the world."

"So many flowery words. Are any of them sincere?"

His sly smile made him look as if he had secrets she wanted to know. He waved his hand around the room. "I challenge you to find a woman more beautiful than you."

"That one." Louisa pointed across the room, where Gabrielle glared at her. The blonde's pert nose curled up as if she had indigestion. When João turned around, Gabrielle blinked and smiled her prettiest smile. He gave her a nod and pivoted back to Louisa as smugness settled on Gabrielle's face.

"Nothing but pyrite."

Louisa laughed, and Gabrielle's sour expression returned. "There you go again, speaking such sweet words to me."

"She's just jealous," he said with sincerity.

"Her hatred goes much deeper than that."

João shook his head. "I can't let you change the subject until you prove me wrong. Are you not the most beautiful woman here?"

He's insistent.

"Should I swoon now?"

"I would be disappointed if you did. But since you have conceded my original point, what *would* make you swoon?"

Louisa put disdain into her voice. "Let me guess, you're about to tell me about your wealth or how you can make all my dreams come true."

Dummy. Louisa tried to wipe her frown away. *Get him to talk about his wealth.* She'd been so distracted that she hadn't thought about João as another rich mark. Disturbing. How could she have been so gullible? *Focus: it doesn't matter how handsome he is or that he smells like candy.*

"Hmm. The lady doth protest." He reached inside his collar, pulled out a gold chain with a key for a pendant, and held it up. "See this?

She nodded. "What is it?"

"When I find the love of my life, I will use it to make all her dreams come true."

"And if I'm your soulmate?"

"That's a little presumptuous of you." João chuckled and dropped the chain, the key landing on his bleached shirt. "We haven't even kissed."

"Who's being presumptuous now?"

"True, forgive me." His eyes sparkled but not with contrition.

"I forgive you." She reached for the key and picked it up with her thumb and finger. She rolled it around, measuring and weighing each groove, trying to visualize its locking mechanism mate. "What does this do?"

"It protects treasures worth a billion réis."

The gears in her mind whirred. *Twenty to twenty-five million francs.* To hide her excitement, she tilted her head. "Is that a lot?"

"Enough."

"For what?" Disappointed, she dropped the key. While the key appeared simple, it had more complexity than any she'd ever encountered. She didn't like her odds of picking the lock on her own.

I need that key.

"Anything you can think of." He tucked the chain back inside his collar.

"And you have all those réis here in Porto?" *Must keep the white whale hooked,* Louisa thought.

"Not in Oporto. Lisboa."

"Ah. Guess I'll never get to see my dreams come true."

A wall of lavender silk flashed in the corner of Louisa's eye.

"What dreams could a half-breed like you have?" Joséphine Maneval sneered down at Louisa. "João, I'm here to save you."

The broad-shouldered Jeton Deux filled out her starling-colored gown well, and Louisa might have thought her pretty except for the derision in her eyes.

"Joséphine, I love your dress. It makes me think: giant bilberry."

"At least, I don't look like an altar boy."

"Ladies, please." João put his arm between the two women who threatened to bump into each other. "Senhorita Maneval, you think too little of me. I do not need saving, nor do I need you butting into my conversations." He held out a hand to Louisa. "Shall we dance?"

Louisa wrinkled her nose at Jeton Deux, whose face glowed a rosy pink. Louisa put her hand in his and whipped her braided bun behind her as she let João lead her away.

The farther they went from the dance floor, the more puzzled Louisa became. They approached one of the long, food-covered tables against the wall. João plucked a fruit from a bowl as they breezed by the table.

"You made me hungry." He smiled and popped the large purple berry into his mouth before veering toward the dance floor.

Louisa watched him, her eyes locked on his mouth. *What must those lips taste like?*

She had been kissed before, and her heart had thumped in her chest when she held hands with someone, but those were mere boys. Not a João. "How old are you?"

"Twenty-two." He smiled, and she felt a strange flutter in her stomach.

Five years. That's not bad. Ten years would be the maximum. That doesn't matter. Concentrate on getting the key.

João's hand went to her shoulder blade, and the butterflies danced to the pounding drum of her heart. He was so much taller than the colonel that Louisa had to reach high to touch his back. Another waltz began, and the gorgeous candy of a man swept her along in his arms. Her thoughts of the key went poof.

Louisa saw nothing but his eyes, heard nothing but her pulse in her ears, and didn't recall moving her feet. His lips moved, and she grinned like a fool. Those lips moved again, and somewhere far away, a voice said, "Will you come see the magical room?"

She nodded as she thought, *Anywhere with you.*

The music echoed to a close, and a hundred conversations filled the silence. João tugged her toward the exit. His manservant appeared out of nowhere like a splash of freezing water, reminding Louisa of the chaperones. The danger of what she was about to do snapped her out of the fevered dream.

Focus, you fool.

The man with the physique and bearing of a soldier nodded and stepped back after João shooed him away with the flick of a few fingers.

"Just a moment. We can't get caught." She pulled João to one of the drink stations.

She sipped a tart white wine that tasted of fresh-crushed grapes and peered over her glass. Mère de la Nativité had her back to the room, fixing a plate, and Louisa spied the colonel with Mère Sainte Adeline, spinning around the dance floor.

As the tempo of the music quickened, she put her glass on the table and looked him in the eye. "Walk right behind me."

With practiced indifference, she strolled to the exit with João blocking her from the view of most people in the room. When they turned into the hallway, she placed him between her and the windows surrounding the ballroom.

Chapter 16
Promenade For Two

"How do we get there?" Louisa asked the gorgeous man whose arm she clung to.

"It's this way." João led her up a grand staircase.

Louisa put her hand on the railing as they ascended. "Tell me about your parents."

If she ever found her way to his family's residence, she needed to know who and what she would be dealing with to acquire part of the fortune he bragged about.

João frowned. "They're seldom around. We have multiple properties across Europe and in the Kingdom of Brazil. They've been absent most of my life."

That's awful. Are all rich parents like my father? Louisa thought before she asked, "Surely, you weren't raised by wolves."

He shook his head and chuckled. "Like Romulus and Remus's long-lost triplet? Do I seem so wolfish?" He flashed his perfect teeth.

Louisa's mouth ran dry, and she licked her lips trying to generate saliva. "No. I didn't mean to imply you were uncouth."

He smiled. "I know." They reached the top step, and João turned to face her, his expression melancholic. "My older sister raised me. Her absence has been hard on me, but meeting you has raised my low spirits."

Joy swelled inside Louisa. She liked making this man happy. Such a new experience for her. "How long has it been?"

João tilted his head. "How long has what been?"

She shook her head at her stumble and rushed her next words. "Your sister. How long has it been since you've seen her?"

"She married and left Lisboa just after I turned seventeen." A fierceness steeled his gaze. "Tiamat taught me how to turn agony into elation. To get the most out of life." His wolfish grin returned. "You remind me of her in so many ways."

Strange name, Louisa thought, but she didn't want to insult him. She tugged at his arm, and they walked side by side down the corridor. She craned her neck to see his face. He glanced down, his brown eyes finding hers.

Louisa's heart thumped faster. "You're lucky to have someone who cares so much about you."

"Don't you have anyone like that?"

"Just my friends. My mother died when I was twelve and my father . . ."

João frowned. "I'm sorry about your mother, and I get it. My father can be a real ass at times."

The grandeur of the hallway's marble flooring, dark wood paneling, and molded ceilings was muted in the glow of wall sconces spaced between the building's many offices and meeting rooms.

Louisa chuckled. "If only he were just an ass."

"Other than your classmates, you're alone. Like me."

Louisa nodded. "I guess so."

João's lips creased into a sympathetic grin, the emotion never touching his eyes.

She needed to change the subject back to him. It wasn't so much that she hated discussing her family circumstances; the topic was just too brief and pathetic. "Enough of that."

"Quite right." He patted the top of her hand that she had snuggled into the crook of his arm.

They turned the corner at the end of the floor, where at least one worker blazed the midnight oil, light spilling from the corner office at the far end.

"Am I right to assume you've been living a bachelor's life the last five years?" Some distant part of her deployed a warning flare. She had to remember that this was no innocent boy. Her lack of courting experience left her at a decided disadvantage in these matters, and she told herself to take the passion out of their interactions. To treat him like the mark that he was, but it was so hard. Those eyes. Those lips. And that enthralling sweet spicy scent left her pulse racing and her mind in disarray.

Stay on mission, Louisa admonished herself and sent a salvo to put him on his heels. "How do I know you're not some common rake?"

João's hand went over his heart, and his voice seemed distressed. "Madam, you wound me." A spark flared from deep within his brown eyes. In a heartbeat, unquenchable flames consumed his liquid gaze like Greek fire. "Fear not. I will honor you like my sister honored me."

Nice sentiment, I guess, Louisa thought.

They passed the lit doorway of the bright office. Louisa glanced inside. His back to them, a man with salt-and-pepper hair leaned over his desk, studying a blueprint. She and João turned the corner and faced another long passage.

Louisa tapped his arm. "I should get back soon. Where is this special room you wished to show me?"

João waved his hand forward. "We're almost there."

Chapter 17
Waltz of the Djinn

João guided Louisa down the hallway until they came to a set of double doors with beautiful stained-glass windows of white and gold beneath a Moorish-style arch. "Here we are. The room is only half finished, but it is already a masterpiece."

He untied the gold rope blocking the doors and swung them open. "Welcome home, Princess Badroulbadour." With a huge smile, he waved her inside.

As Louisa passed the threshold, her breath caught in her throat. Like a palace from *Arabian Nights*, the second half of the long oval room glittered with gold. Her steps on the marvelous inlaid wooden floor echoed in the empty chamber as the doors closed behind her.

Even this late at night, the space was filled with a glow as if sunshine peeked in from behind other stained-glass entranceways bordering the room. Thin columns lined a sitting area that supported an upper-floor balcony.

Near the halfway point, the unfinished work showed where partially painted moldings with complex designs and Arabic lettering were plastered to the walls. She passed these and entered another time and place. A gold diamond geometric pattern anchored the layout, while white, red, and pastel blue filled the other aspects—the intricate motif covered every available centimeter of the room from floor to ceiling.

Louisa walked to a column and ran her hand over the molding.

"And this is only part of the magic. I promise."

With a smile, Louisa turned and said, "This is spectacular. Thank you."

He came closer. She shuffled away until her back pressed against the column. She gulped as he leaned in. A wave of some alien emotion flowed through her. His berry-scented breath made her lick her lips and close her eyes. He caressed her cheek and neck. Their lips touched, and she melted into him. Her hands went to his face as his tongue grazed her lips.

This is very different, was all Louisa could think. She ran her fingers through his hair. Rough, swollen scars ran along the tops of both ears. *Weird.*

As their kiss deepened, her usual calculating self fought a perilous battle against a strange new person, desperate to let go of all rational thought. To give into these raging desires.

She pulled away from his kiss, gathered herself, and moved a hand to the back of his neck. He smiled, his eyes a reflection of her own smoldering fire. As she leaned into another kiss, she squirmed a finger inside his collar, seeking the clasp to the chain with the key.

Their tongues began a slow, languorous dance. From far away, her consciousness whispered, *Get the key.* That thought fled before her rising need to merge into him.

His hand moved to her waist, and he kissed her neck. He placed his other hand on the small of her back, then pulled her off the column and into his unyielding body. Passions Louisa had once scoffed at surged inside her, and all control teetered on the very edge.

The hand at her waist moved up and groped her chest through her uniform. Her eyes snapped open.

He bit her neck as his hand squeezed.

No!

Unspoken panic took hold, and she stayed mute, until his other hand grabbed her bottom and pulled her hard against him. Fear turned to determination.

She pushed against his shoulders. "Stop! This is not what I want."

"You'll come to enjoy it," he mumbled against her throat, and her breast exploded with pain as he squeezed harder.

"I said no!" Louisa pushed with all her might.

The pain stopped as he moved his hand to cover her mouth. In a rage, Louisa bit into his flesh.

"Ow!" he yelled and pulled his hand back. He raised his head, and a demon stared back at her from remorseless lakes of brown ice.

"You bitch!" João gripped her upper arms and slammed her against the column.

Louisa felt dizzy. With a shake of her head, she glared at him, trying to think. She needed to stall him while remembering everything her uncle had taught her about breaking free from a man. She snarled, "Let go of me, and I won't hurt you."

João laughed, and nothing could have been uglier to Louisa. When the laughter stopped, he shook her shoulders. "I'm going to enjoy our time together."

Her eyes darted around the room. No one would save her. "Were your words all lies?"

He shook his head and said, "You are beautiful." Then his eyes narrowed. "But you're just a lowly bastard and a troublemaker. Tonight, I will give you a taste of your future, then—" His eyes glowed with anticipation. "No one will care when you disappear."

Until that moment, Louisa had worried about how he would destroy her virtue, the last of her innocence, but his threat to end her life doused her anger in kerosene.

Tossing a lit match, Louisa slammed her knee into his groin as hard as she could. He bent over. She swung an elbow toward his high cheekbone, and a loud, satisfying crack followed.

Going completely limp, she dropped like a heavy sack out of his clutches to the ground. Free, she scrambled around the column, jumped to her feet, and ran toward the closest doorway.

After throwing it open, she stopped and stared at a small closet with a lit wall sconce.

His derisive snort made a chill run up her spine. Pain shot through her scalp as he yanked the hair of her coiled bun in the opposite direction. She fell back with a scream. The instant she slammed onto the hard wooden floor, his knee drove the wind from her lungs, and he straddled her.

With shallow gasps, Louisa fought for air.

Her uniform skirt flew up, and rough hands pulled at her knickers. The rage came back with her first small intake of breath. Her uncle's words pulsed inside her ringing head. "Do anything to stay alive. Use every weapon: teeth, forehead, your tools, anything."

As the fiend's laughing eyes locked with hers, her thoughts screamed, *Tools!*

A sucking gulp brought life back to her chest, and she moved both hands to her braids. He grabbed one of her wrists and pinned it to the floor. With a hand still free, she pulled a lock pick from the bundle of hair around the tie.

With a roar of fury, Louisa unleashed her arm. Her hand flashed upward, and she jabbed the point of the metal pick into the black center of his golden-brown iris.

João snapped his head away, and the horrific howl of an evil Djinn echoed around the chamber. His hands flew to his face, but he still had her pinned under him with his knees. Louisa snaked her arm between the two of them and grabbed him through his pants. With the strength of years of climbing, she crushed him.

The devil's hands dropped as if a puppet's strings had been cut. His eyes rolled to the back of his head, and he collapsed on the floor beside her.

She squirmed free, hopped to her feet, and sprinted to the door she had entered. A groan followed her into the hallway. She glanced over her shoulder to see him standing.

What the hell?

She raced toward the light spilling into the hallway from the office at the end. *God, let the man still be there.*

The devil's boots pounding on the parquet flooring urged her to run faster. Louisa skidded to a stop inside the office and slammed the door shut. A bearded man in his fifties turned from the desk in front of a large window.

"Help me," she whispered in French. "He's going to kill me."

The man rose and put down his pen. "Who?"

Louisa shook all over. It was freezing.

The man walked to the door and moved her aside with a gentle touch. He opened it and ducked his head into the hallway. "There's no one there."

He closed the door. "You're safe now."

Grasping her elbow, he guided her to his chair and sat her down.

She rubbed her arms. *So cold.*

From a drawer, the man produced a black bottle and a clear glass. He poured a light brown liquid and pushed the glass into her hand, then tilted it toward her lips. "Drink this."

Who are you? With a leery stare at the man, she pulled the glass away. Teeth chattering, she asked, "Why?"

The man took a step back with his hand raised, palm out. "I'm sorry. You look as if you might faint. I thought some brandy might help."

That the man spoke French came as a sudden realization to her. "You're French."

His eyes softened. "Yes."

Louisa brought the glass to her lips. Her hands trembled, and her teeth clattered against the cup as she took a big gulp of brandy. A fire ran down her throat, but it pushed away the horrific visions forming in her mind. She took another large swallow, and the shakes began to subside.

She tried to smile. "Merci."

"You're very welcome. Who did this?"

"João Lopes Gomes." Louisa stared at the glass, rotating it in her hands. "He said he wanted to show me a magical room, then he tried to—" Teardrops fell with each blink.

"That's not good."

With her arm, Louisa wiped away the tears. "Too rich. Too powerful."

The man's eyes filled with concern. "Yes. It won't go well if you try to have him arrested." He growled. "He won't try anything with me around. I assume you came from the party downstairs. If you think you can manage it, let me escort you back."

"Merci. I'm Louisa."

"Louisa, I'm Gustave. Gustave Eiffel." He held out his hand.

Louisa fought back a sob and stood. She reached for his hand but couldn't bring herself to touch him. The man nodded and led her toward the door.

Death, danger, she had always pushed her luck, but that bastard had broken something inside her. In the most fantastic room she'd ever seen, that devil had ripped what little trust she'd had in men from her heart.

Never again.

Chapter 18

A Legion of Sisters

Gustave escorted Louisa to the ballroom, but she stopped outside the open doors. "Monsieur Eiffel, merci. I can manage from here."

"If you decide to press charges, don't hesitate to use me as a witness."

With a slight head shake, she said, "It would be his word against mine about what really happened." She gritted her teeth. "To get away, I hurt him. Bad." She gave a rueful smile. "That will have to be my justice."

"Very well. Take care of yourself, Mademoiselle."

Reluctant to face the Good Sisters and her friends, Louisa stalled for a moment, asking, "Before you go, may I ask what a Frenchman is doing working here?"

"I'm designing a new railway bridge to span the Douro and connect Oporto to Vila Nova de Gaia."

"That's wonderful. Good luck with your endeavors."

"Safe travels, Louisa." He smiled and headed back to the staircase.

She peeked around the open doorway, looking for her attacker before locating the chaperones. They were scattered around the room and appeared to be searching for someone.

Me.

When the Good Sisters' attention was elsewhere, Louisa darted inside and strolled to the closest food table. Her chills threatened to return, and her plate shook while she piled it with pastries. She thought of eating to ease her mind, but the urge ran counter to the bitter lump in her stomach. With the plate close to overflowing, Louisa walked toward an unoccupied table. The dance would last another hour, and time could not go fast enough.

"Mademoiselle Sophia, where have you been?" Never before had Mère de la Nativité's accusing voice sounded so welcoming, so safe.

As Louisa turned, her mind raced to come up with an excuse for her absence from the ballroom. On seeing the harsh disciplinarian, Louisa had to stop herself from throwing her arms around the nun. She counted to three, trying to use one of the calming techniques she'd learned from her uncle to overcome stress on a job. "I went to the lavatory and—"

"You were not there just now."

"No. On the way back, I met a nice Frenchman who works here. An architect named Gustave Eiffel. He showed me this amazing room they have upstairs called the Arab room." After trying to paint contrition on her face, Louisa gave up. "I should have consulted with you or the colonel first. I'm sorry."

Heavy wrinkles formed over the nun's nose, the expression she always wore after one of Louisa's suspected lies. "Hmm. After the incident on the boat, you are walking a dangerous line."

You have no idea, Louisa thought but instead said, "I understand."

"Mademoiselle. I'm sorry I did not get your name the last time." The skinny, pimple-faced youth had not only pluck but impeccable timing. "I believe you promised me a dance."

Mère de la Nativité raised a single eyebrow at the young man.

Unable to form a smile, Louisa said, "I did, didn't I? Please excuse me, Ma Mère."

Louisa left her plate on the table and touched his proffered elbow. Skin crawling, she fought the urge to yank her hand away as they walked toward the center of the room.

Hold it together. You are stronger than this. Be strong.

With the current song approaching its end, the young man addressed Louisa. "I spoke to the girl with the golden dress as you requested." Louisa simply blinked at him, and he continued, "You were right. She does not like you or your friends."

"Was there anything especially egregious that she said?"

His eyes drifted away from hers. "She called you a Greek bastard born of an English noble. She said your low breeding made you into a troublemaker with no manners who would do nothing but destroy the reputation of any man stupid enough to court you."

If she had felt like herself, Louisa would have chuckled. *Stop being weak,* she told herself. "That's better than what I thought she'd say." Her uncle's gruff voice echoed his advice on lying. *The best lies are always filled with some truth. Gabrielle's more clever than I thought.*

Her heart barren of joy for the coming dance, she sighed as the last song stopped. "She didn't lie."

The young man pulled his head back. "At which part?"

Louisa shrugged. "Most of it. Shall we?" She assumed the pose.

She winced as he took her right hand in his left, and she shivered when he touched her shoulder blade. She closed her eyes, trying to find her equilibrium.

The music started, and she was a half-second slow. They shambled into the first turn. True to his persistent personality, the young man endured the worst dance of Louisa's life with aplomb. He tried to carry a conversation between makeup steps and told her what Gabrielle had said about the rest of the clan. Louisa half-listened because it matched what she'd expected from the vengeful bully.

The young man tried to hide his disappointment when they exited the floor, but still, a slight frown touched his lips. "Merci, Mademoiselle."

"Monsieur, I do apologize." Louisa patted him on the arm. "You deserved a better dance partner, but I am preoccupied. I wish you well."

As she walked away, she thought she saw João across the room. Her breath caught, and she stopped mid-step. When a different man turned around, Louisa choked back a cry. Her eyes darted around the room. For the first time, she noticed Marie laughing as Paulo swept her through the steps of the waltz. Eugénie and Virginie were sitting at a table with Catherine, and Louisa walked as fast as she could to them.

"Where have you been?" Eugénie asked.

Louisa sat next to Eugénie and grabbed her hand. She couldn't speak and closed her eyes to hold back the tears, but they came anyway.

"Louisa," Eugénie whispered and pulled her into an embrace.

Louisa buried her face on her friend's shoulder and sobbed. "Shh." Eugénie pulled her tighter and patted her back.

Another pair of arms enveloped her from behind, and Virginie's cheek rested on Louisa's back. "We're here. We've got you."

Louisa let go of the fear and hurt, crying more than she had in years.

The current song entered its final refrain, and Louisa fought to regain her composure. No one but her friends should know the anguish she'd endured. She choked back a few more sobs and sat up. The music stopped, and her friends each held a hand on her as they pulled their chairs close.

Catherine stared from across the table while Louisa wiped away her tears with a napkin. The shy girl had a look of concern and something else in her eyes. Louisa surveyed the dance floor. Marie gazed up at Paulo with the same awestruck expression that Louisa must have had with that *kólos*. Her first instinct was to scream at her friend to run, but, seeing Joy truly happy for the first time in a long while, Louisa shook her head.

"Don't tell Joy," Louisa pleaded to both of her friends. Eugénie scowled, but Louisa said, "We'll tell her. Just not right now."

"What happened?" Virginie was insistent.

In a whisper, Louisa related the story up to the kiss. Then she choked up. The music began, and tears flowed, but she refused to sob.

Refused to let that man win.

With one friend holding her hand and the other rubbing her back, Louisa used their love to feel whole. She let their security fuel her anger.

"He started." She shook her head. "When I told him no, he tried." She felt her face grow hot.

"That son of a whore!" Virginie said loud enough to turn heads nearby. She glared at anyone who didn't look away in an instant.

"He didn't?" Eugénie asked through gritted teeth.

Louisa shook her head once. "No. I stabbed him in the eye."

"What?" Virginie whispered. "Is he dead?"

"No." Louisa pulled her other lockpick tool from her hair. "It was with one of these."

Eugénie leaned in close and whispered to Louisa and Virginie. "Whew. At least, we don't have to get rid of a body." Then she gripped Louisa's leg to the point that it hurt. "I'm going to kill that bastard as soon as I see him."

"I might have damaged his ability to have children as well."

Virginie chuckled. "That's a better idea. Let's make him a gelding."

In the loudest voice she'd ever spoken in, Catherine said, "We should hand him over to Mère de la Nativité."

Louisa saw the fire in the shy woman's eyes and did what she thought she'd never do again. She laughed. "Good idea, if I wouldn't have to take a beating as well."

"I'm going to pull out every strand of that witch's gold hair. I saw her spewing her lies to that—" Eugénie clenched her jaws, and her pale face turned bright red. "Snake."

Eugénie tried to rise, but Louisa grabbed her wrist and pulled her back down. "Don't give her the satisfaction," Louisa hissed. "She might be spiteful, but I'm to blame."

"No, you are *not*. That man is pure evil." Eugénie's conviction stamped out Louisa's moment of self-recrimination. "He'll pay. You hurt our sister, you hurt us all because we are––"

Virginie and Louisa repeated the clan's motto, along with their leader, "A Legion of Sisters."

Chapter 19
River of Realizations

Sailors strained against ropes, hauling a square sail, similar to that on a Viking ship, up the mast. The river cargo boat shuddered before rushing forward as the canvas puffed with wind. The pace of the *rabelo*, as the colonel named it, picked up, and they glided through placid water on the winding Douro River. Louisa patted beads of sweat from her forehead with a handkerchief. As the morning and the journey wore on, the sunlight became more intense and the temperature rose.

Small hills near Porto gave way to rugged rocky terrain dominated by browns and golds. The land seemed inhospitable to all but the hardiest crops and people. Phylloxera-withered grapevines lined the occasional terrace-carved mountain with random sections of olive or almond trees. The sight of so much destruction made Louisa feel for the people she did not see working the fields. How many livelihoods had been destroyed throughout the continent as the tiny insects from the Americas devoured Europe's nonresistant old vines?

Her eyes narrowed at the back of the gray-headed walrus of a general. He stood near the bow like an admiral in charge of his fleet. She had not had to endure that particular fool's presence since leaving the steamship. As much as Virginie missed Simon, Louisa was relieved when the general disappeared with his manservant on business elsewhere in Porto.

Three days had passed since the ball and Louisa's traumatic encounter with João Lopes Gomes. The colonel had set those days aside for gentlemen suitors from the dance to call on the young ladies from Saint-Denis.

Paulo had been the only constant visitor among Louisa's friends. A young suitor showed up on the first day to tell Eugénie he could not call on her again, given her family's situation in Algeria. Virginie had to physically stop Eugénie from yanking Gabrielle's hair out but could not stop Eugénie's unladylike words. Caught in the middle of the altercation by Mère Sainte Adeline, the clan's leader received confinement to her room until the journey upriver.

Each day, in a small windowless cell, Louisa sat in silence alongside Eugénie. Louisa desired solitude without being alone. Born with a maternal nature, her friend obliged without words needing to be spoken.

In those long hours of contemplation, Louisa hardened her heart and prepared her mind for the next time a man dared to trespass on her soul. For that was what that fiend had done. He had sought to devour the core of her being by stealing what only she could gift.

Each night, she retired to her room, where Marie regaled her in detail about Paulo's every word, sigh, and glance during his lengthy chaperoned visits. In Marie's rosy complexion, sparkling green eyes, and sincere words, love and happiness always surrounded the girl nicknamed Joy.

Louisa basked in her friend's aura of warmth, exuberance, and fearlessness about the future, making it a mortar to patch the damaged façade of her heart. Like Paris following the Siege, it might take years or decades for her to be whole again.

High above the riverbank, several workers walked through a vineyard, pruning away the blight.

Rather than a mason, maybe I'm more like them. I will persist until my vines once again bear fruit.

"You should have told me." Marie's voice cracked with anguish as she sat beside Louisa on the bench made for rowers.

Louisa grabbed Marie's hand. "It's better that I didn't."

"I would have been there for you." Marie's expression soured. "I'm angry you didn't want me to be there for you."

"But you were." Louisa smiled. "Your happiness has been a healing balm. I'm not a blubbering mess right now, in part, because you and Paulo have given me hope."

"In what? You never wanted to be in love."

Louisa laughed. "Touché. No, you give me hope in humanity. Hope that there are more men like Paulo, out there."

"Are you sure you're better?"

Except for the blasted heat, she thought.

Louisa patted her forehead before pointing to a small section of sheer rock cliff near the bend they were rounding. "I want to be up there right now." She nodded. "I haven't thought about climbing for days, but right now, I want my fingers to be dug into that rock wall."

"That's the Daring I know." Marie squeezed Louisa's hand and smiled.

Louisa frowned. "How did you find out? I told them I would let you know when I was ready."

"Don't be angry. Virginie only told me because I was about to share my big news with you. She didn't want me to upset you accidentally."

"What news?"

"Paulo received a telegram from my father."

Louisa scrunched her face. "Why would he get a telegram from your father?"

Marie giggled. "He asked for my hand in marriage, and Father said yes."

Speechless, Louisa just stared into her friend's eyes for several moments. *It's only been four days.* "Really? That was fast."

Marie threw her arms around Louisa's neck and hugged her. "Merci," she whispered in Louisa's ear before kissing her on the cheek and pulling away.

"What did I do?"

Marie gave her a playful push. "You spoke to the colonel."

"Maybe." She'd only wanted her friend not to become a nun. She didn't expect Paulo to be the *one*.

"I didn't know it, but the colonel telegrammed my father the day after the dance." Her eyes drifted to her hands as she blushed. "And Paulo telegrammed him the day after that, asking for my hand."

"You didn't tell me any of this." *And you told me everything that was said and done during Paulo's visits. Thrice over.*

"Right before we boarded, Paulo showed me the telegram with my father's blessing. He asked me to marry him." Marie squealed with joy, her green eyes sparkling like two bright emeralds.

Louisa blinked a couple of times before remembering that she needed to be happy for her friend. She gave Marie another hug. "That's wonderful."

They pulled apart, and Marie said, "My father's telegram expressed how happy he and Mother were for me. He told me to get married and stay in Portugal for at least another year. Until the gossip from Bazaine's court martial subsides."

What? With a gulp, Louisa tried to compose herself. *This is ridiculous, Joy. Have you lost your mind? Be happy for her.* "Get married. Now?"

Nodding, Marie looked ready to explode. "In a few days, before you go back to Porto."

Without you? How can we return without you? Louisa thought as Marie continued. "Paulo will get off the boat at Régua in a few hours to make the arrangements. His family owns a vineyard close by. We'll stay at another vineyard called Quinto do Vesuvio for a few days with his mother's cousin's family. They are the most important wine family in Portugal." She giggled. "When we start back, we'll stop at Paulo's house and get married."

With part of her skirt clenched in her fist, Louisa tried to calm herself. "Will you ever come back to Paris?"

"Maybe in a few years. Paulo wants to travel to London and Paris to learn everything possible from botanists researching phylloxera. We'll use that time to visit with my family."

I'll be at Girton. With a sliver of hope that she might see her friend, Louisa said, "I'll be in college in England then. You must let me know when you are coming and visit me."

Marie put her hand on Louisa's. "I promise." Marie stood. "I need to speak with the colonel. My father said he asked the colonel to be his stand-in." Her eyes filled with tears. "I can't think of anyone better."

As Marie walked away, Louisa stared at the boat's scuffed and battered decking. She had been oblivious, deep in her own morass of thoughts, until hearing Marie's news. Now she faced something new. A deep ache threatened to make Louisa lose her composure. The idea of separating from her friend so soon had never occurred to her.

No one to blame but myself.

Confronted with the reality that she must soon part ways with the only people in the world who cared for her, Louisa sought out Eugénie and Virginie. Simon kept a respectable distance between himself and Virginie as they discussed all that had happened in their days apart. Eugénie looked up from her drawing and gave Louisa a knowing smile before focusing back on her pad.

The thought of being alone didn't frighten Louisa. She had spent most of her childhood inside books, climbing to hide from bullies, taking care of her mother, or thieving in the dark.

Alone.

Her mother loved her, but after Louisa's father left them, her mother became frail and sick. From age six until her mother's death, Louisa ran the household. And although her uncle sat somewhere in the shadows during her jobs, he'd been explicit that he'd abandon her if she were caught.

She wasn't scared of what was coming but had grown accustomed to having people to depend on. The pain of losing them would subside, but she didn't know if she could ever open herself up enough to make new friends.

As the kilometers passed by, the clan shared a lunch of sausage, cheese, and bread. While Virginie, Eugénie, and Marie held council, discussing wedding preparations nonstop, humanity's altering of God's nature became more prevalent outside the boat. Louisa added an occasional nod or a verbal affirmative while she watched the shore, half-listening.

Her heart filled with awe and wonder at the harmony painted within the valley of gold. Never had she been any place where man's work had not detracted from but instead enhanced what God had wrought. They passed multiple docks, each marking the entrance to a winemaking estate. Some had stuccoed buildings in various hues near the shore, while others commanded views from higher up the terraced mountains. The meal ended, and Louisa excused herself. She went to the stern to find shade, to think, and to marvel.

Everyone took a break ashore when they docked at the little town of Régua. Before reboarding, Louisa watched the engaged couple say goodbye, making do with a simple handshake for propriety. For the rest of the trip, Louisa perched on top of a pyramid of empty wine barrels near the back of the boat. Twice, she watched the sailors transition from wind power to ropes tied to oxen along the shore to traverse narrower and more treacherous sections of the river.

With half the valley in the shade and the other half still kissed by the sun's passing, a sailor's cry of, "Vesúvio!" brought Louisa to the deck as the crew lowered the sail. The prow pointed toward a dock that lay ten meters below a complex of white-plastered buildings parallel to the shore. The largest, a three-story U-shaped mansion, was the most impressive building Louisa had seen since leaving Porto.

Once the ship moored, the passengers were helped over the gunwale and onto the dock. The pompous walrus took the lead and bowed to a woman standing at the top of the small road leading to the main house. As the last in their small column, Louisa formed the end of a semi-circle created by the students, with the nuns and the colonel in the center.

A distinguished woman in her sixties, wearing a black work dress and a wide-brimmed straw hat, awaited them. To her left and a little behind her stood a bearded man with a bronzed, weathered face, wearing a dirt-smudged, white linen shirt with brown pants.

The woman's serious face lit up with a welcoming smile, and she opened her arms as she said in French, "Welcome to Quinto do Vesúvio. I am Dona Ferreira, but please call me Ferreirinha. Everyone does." She stepped forward. "Which of these beautiful young women is Marie?"

Marie curtsied. "I am, Madame Ferreirinha."

"Just Ferreirinha. Please." She moved to stand before Marie and put her hands on her shoulders before kissing both of Marie's cheeks. "We will soon be family. Paulo is my cousin's boy and is near to my heart. He and my eldest grandson, José, are best friends." She stepped back and addressed the rest of them. "Until the wedding, we are hosting a social gathering for the rest of you exceptional young women to meet some of the Douro's best and brightest young men."

Ferreirinha chuckled. "Who knows? Maybe there will be more than one wedding."

Louisa cringed.

Chapter 20

Ferreirinha

"Who wants to help us in the fields?" Mère Sainte Adeline bounced into the small dining room and greeted the girls with a cheery smile. The students stopped eating their humble breakfast of cheese, sausage, and bread.

"Must we?" Gabrielle frowned.

"Of course not. I just thought it might be good to show our appreciation to our hosts and get outside for a little activity." Expectant, the nun looked down the line.

"I'd love to help." Marie wiped her mouth with her napkin and raised an eyebrow to the clan. "What about you three?"

Eugénie and Catherine shook their heads.

"Will we get dirty? I don't have another clean uniform." Virginie stuffed an olive into her mouth.

Mère Sainte Adeline nodded. "Of course, but we'll be back in plenty of time to do some laundry."

"I'll go, then," Virginie took her spectacles off and wiped the lenses with her napkin. "What will we be doing?"

"Ferreirinha said they had some almond trees to plant."

Louisa shrugged. "I'm in. I can use the distraction."

"Non, merci." Gabrielle smiled at the nun and reached for the butter dish.

"I'll stay with Gabrielle," said Joséphine.

Julie narrowed her eyes at Louisa for several seconds before she said, "I'll come."

We almost dodged all the bullets, Louisa thought while she savored a sliver of the wild boar sausage.

"I'll meet you in the courtyard." Before hustling outside, the nun grabbed two slices of bread and built a cheese sandwich.

Louisa lifted her white sash over her head and handed it to Eugénie. "Can you put this in my room?"

"Sure."

Louisa followed Virginie and Marie to the little garden. Ferreirinha and Mère Sainte Adeline were laughing together. Julie stepped beside Louisa, elbowing her.

"Watch what you're doing." Louisa glared at Julie.

Gabrielle's number one lackey, Jeton Un, looked down her hawk nose at Louisa with disgust. "I didn't see you there." She lowered her voice to just above a whisper, "Whore."

Stunned, Louisa couldn't think for a few seconds. When she got hold of herself, she elbowed Jeton Un in her bony side and hissed, "Say that again, and I'll break that beak of yours."

The spindly, mean girl laughed. "What else should I call you? I saw you leave the ball with that man."

"Follow me, everyone." Ferreirinha waved and walked toward the small road that ran up the vineyard's terrace-carved mountain.

"Out of the way." Julie shouldered Louisa and marched ahead, leaving her flabbergasted.

"Let's go." Virginie pulled at Louisa's elbow. Louisa had seldom contemplated murder, but her run-in with João Lopes Gomes had caused the most shocking thoughts to bubble forth. She glowered at the back of Julie Paley as they marched, thinking about what she would do to the wicked girl if Julie continued to spread lies about Louisa and that demon.

The road ran parallel to the river and past a little chapel, a large barn, bunkhouses, and a few modest family cottages until they reached the last building in the estate village. Each girl was issued a pair of gloves, a canteen, and a shovel or a hoe to carry.

Louisa leaned the wooden shaft of her hoe against her shoulder and fantasized about striking Jeton Un in the back of the head with its sharp metal blade. The column of women turned onto a smaller path, passing rows of grapevines as they went higher. Flowering blue and purple lavender plants punctuated the end of each row, filling the air with soothing scents that helped calm Louisa's bloodthirsty resentment.

At a small intersection, the path formed a Y, and they took the prong that angled toward the summit. Louisa shielded her eyes as she looked toward the top. A single castle tower made of local rock guarded the vineyard and the river below.

Nice view, I bet. Louisa began to daydream the view into existence.

The incline increased, and no one spoke as they hiked. Though it was only morning, Louisa's dress stuck to her skin under the intense Douro Valley sun. Ferreirinha halted the procession in a terraced field just below the crown of the mountain. They stopped next to an ox-pulled cart filled with small saplings. For several minutes, the girls caught their breath as Ferreirinha spoke to one of the nearby workers.

Louisa took a sip of water from her canteen and looked toward the tower about a hundred feet higher up the rise. Disappointed that it was only three stories tall, she still wanted to climb up the stony face and squeeze between the merlons to look over the valley. On the way up the mountain, she'd kept her eyes forward, wishing to savor the view behind her once she reached the very top of the tower.

"I know what you're thinking." Marie leaned on the handle of her shovel. "During lunch, I'll keep Adeline occupied so you can go up there."

Louisa grinned. "You know me too well."

"I know you miss climbing like I'm going to miss good croissants." She shook her head. "From now on, my new favorite will be those yummy little custard pies they have everywhere here." She paused and tapped her chin for a moment. "*Pastel de nata*. That's what they're called."

"Those are great, but I'm already sick of that salted cod thing they go on about." Louisa wrinkled her nose.

"How can a Greek not like fish?"

"I love fish. Grilled, baked. Not salted or stewed."

"Well, when I start talking to Adeline, you make your move."

Louisa nodded. "Thanks."

"Everyone, gather round." The nun motioned them toward the cart.

Ferreirinha pointed to the worker next to her. "Leonor will demonstrate what you will be doing. Then, working in pairs, you will pick a row. We will break for lunch when we have finished six complete rows."

"Yes, Madame," Julie Paley said. She stepped beside Louisa. "Come on, Greek Girl. You're with me."

Louisa's eyes narrowed. "Not unless you want to eat this." She pushed the blade of her hoe toward the bully.

Virginie stepped between the two. "You'll work with me."

Jeton Un shook her hawkish nose. Lances shot from Virginie's eyes as the pair jousted with a look.

Julie curled her nose in disgust. "Whatever you say, Four-Eyes."

The worker, Leonor, couldn't speak French, so she demonstrated each step: digging a hole with her shovel, placing her hands twenty centimeters apart to show

how deep, planting a sapling, filling in the dirt around the little tree with a hoe, and taking seven long steps and simulating digging again.

With a grin that showed a missing front tooth, Leonor said, "*Compreender?*"

"*Sim, obrigada.*" Marie pointed Louisa toward one of the rows with a jut of her chin.

Louisa held up a finger. "You dig first. I'll bring the saplings and fill them in while you dig the next ones. We'll switch jobs every eight."

The work wasn't too difficult, but without a break from the constant sun, Louisa was drenched with sweat by the time they reached the end of their third row. She pulled back her shoulders and arched her back. Her muscles would be sore from the unusual bending, stretching, and pulling.

She looked over their little almond grove. They had planted twenty trees in each row, each two feet tall. One of the workers had come along behind them with a water bucket, soaking the ground around the plants. A feeling of accomplishment settled over Louisa, the type of satisfaction that she experienced only through physical labor well done.

Virginie and Julie were finishing their row as Mère Sainte Adeline yelled at them to come to the little cart. The nun handed each girl a small linen-wrapped bundle from a box in the back. Marie gave Louisa a nod as she asked the nun if she had ever worked on a farm or a vineyard. Virginie flashed Louisa a quizzical look as she trotted up the small hill with her bundle, heading toward the tower. Louisa trailed her hand over the rough stone as she traversed the round building and moved into the shade until everyone below disappeared. The masonry grooves between the irregular rocks would make this climb child's play.

Louisa put the linen knot between her teeth and pulled on the strings at her waist. Her dress rose up past her ankles and inner thighs. After tying the strings into a bow, she dug her fingers into the first hand hold. All thoughts and worries fled before the peace that settled over her as she reached for the next hand and toe hold.

The three stories took less than a minute to scale. A slight sense of disappointment broke her heightened concentration as she pulled herself through the gap between merlons. She wanted more.

"Don't like stairs?" From under her wide-brimmed hat, Ferreirinha chuckled, startling Louisa.

She had been so fixated on her next hand hold, she had not checked to see whether the tower was occupied. Louisa blushed and gave the older woman a sheepish smile. "I hope you don't mind if I join you." Louisa hopped down from the crenel to the tower landing.

"Not at all." Ferreirinha pointed at Louisa's pantaloons. "Interesting dress. Did you make that yourself?"

Louisa undid the bow, and her skirt billowed outward into its standard shape. "Yes, Madame. To climb better."

"Impressive." The older woman waved her over. "Come see the view." She turned her back on Louisa and looked out from the gap in the wall.

Louisa went to the next empty crenellation and took in the view that, until now, she'd denied herself. With the sun at its zenith, the etched mountains on both sides of the river valley glowed in brown, green, and gold hues. The water reflected a muted mirror of the glory before her. She sighed.

Ferreirinha pointed down to the cluster of white houses where they were staying. "I was twenty-four when my father-in-law first showed me Vesúvio from here. Even today, after seeing it a thousand times, I still have that same sense of wonder. Of his many *quintos*, this one was his pride and joy. Unfortunately, his son, my late husband, was a disappointment to us both. Still, in the short time I knew my father-in-law, he instilled in me a love of this land and the promise of its future."

Louisa untied the linen cloth as she shook her head. "You were lucky. It's rare."

"What's rare, dear?" Ferreirinha tilted her head.

Louisa laid the cloth on the stone before her, exposing more sausage, a handful of almonds, and a small apple. "To find any man who isn't disappointing."

Ferreirinha laughed. "True. I take it you've had your share of disappointments."

"You could say I've yet to find a man who wasn't." Louisa chewed on the most fantastic almond she'd ever eaten.

Ferreirinha said, "They do exist. Your friend is marrying one of them. Paulo has a good heart."

"For Marie's sake, I pray you're right." Louisa held up one of the almonds. "These are incredible."

"Aren't they?" Ferreirinha pointed down the hill toward the new little grove. "Almonds, olives, and herbs must carry us through until the blight ends."

Louisa scanned the hillside, finding more diseased grapevines than healthy ones. "It must be difficult."

"More for them than me." The older woman stared at the clump of workers sharing their meal. "My dreams are withering, but their hard lives are becoming even harder. I must keep fighting for both of them."

"Both?"

"If I help my workers live better lives, I believe that God will grant me my dreams." Ferreirinha took a bite from her apple.

"Ah." Louisa enjoyed her meal and took in the view while contemplating her own dreams and goals.

The attack had changed her. Deep down, she was different than she had been when this trip began, but when she thought of her future, nothing had changed.

Unlike Ferreirinha, she wasn't fighting for some grand dream or even to help others.

Louisa wished only to depend on and to serve herself. If she managed to do some good along the way, so be it, but to hope for more was unrealistic. She had never been anything but a realist. She looked at the older woman. "I admire you."

"Why would you admire an old woman like me?"

"You have complete control of your life. Few women can say the same. That's what I want more than anything."

"Demand respect. Accept nothing less, and you shall have it." Ferreirinha stepped closer.

"Is it really that simple?"

"Nothing worth having is ever simple." She patted Louisa's arm. "Merci for sharing a meal with me. What is your name?"

"Louisa Sophia, Madame."

"Well, Louisa Sophia, you're welcome to use the stairs this time."

Louisa grinned as she stuck the linen cloth in her pocket. Then she tugged on the strings at her waist, transforming her dress again into pantaloons. "Going down is harder and almost as much fun as going up." She curtsied and grabbed two merlons to pull herself up and into the gap at the top of the wall. With a spin, Louisa looked the matronly woman in the eye and grinned. "Merci, Ferreirinha. I shall—"

She squatted and dropped outside of the tower. She hung from the crenellation by her fingertips as Ferreirinha gasped.

Louisa yelled as she moved down the wall. "Demand respect!"

Chapter 21

A True Knight

"**D**on't get your hopes up. I doubt *he* will come," Gabrielle whispered in Louisa's ear. "I'm sure once is enough with a tramp like you."

An injection of fear paralyzed Louisa's pre-armed retort. The insinuation that the rapist might attend the social gathering sent goose flesh racing across Louisa's arms. Julie Paley spreading her disgusting lies to her master wasn't a surprise, but the terror Louisa felt at the mention of that man was concerning. She rubbed her arms as her nemesis brushed past—the bully's demure blue dress accentuating her blonde hair in the twilight.

Louisa glanced toward the entrance to the courtyard as if half-expecting that bastard to appear in a cloud of smoke. She had played out that very scenario a thousand times since the attack. Sometimes she killed him, sometimes she avoided him, but always she made sure he stayed away from her friends.

Because he'd received a serious injury, she doubted that he'd come tonight. If he weren't blind in that eye, it would take weeks, if not months, for his vision to heal from being poked by the equivalent of a big sewing needle. Remembering the pain she had inflicted on him added a sliver of resolve to her thoughts. *He has no hold on me.*

The dock workers' yells to the approaching boats signaled the arrival of the gentlemen callers. Louisa went to the shadiest corner of the courtyard and sat at one of the small wrought-iron tables. For this party, she had decided to fade into the background and interact with the visitors as little as possible.

Mère Sainte Adeline clapped her hands. "Mademoiselles, form a receiving line."

The other girls shuffled toward the nun, but Louisa shrank in her chair. She moved her arm across her sash to hide the white. The nun began to count out loud. "One, two . . ." When she reached seven, she spun around, inspecting the square. Her eyes squinted toward the darkened corner where Louisa sat. "There you are. Mademoiselle Sophia, please inform Madame Ferreirinha that the guests have arrived."

With a sigh, Louisa stood. "Yes, Ma Mère."

As she opened the door to the main house's foyer, Ferreirinha bumped into her.

The older woman stumbled and grabbed Louisa's shoulders to steady herself. "*Com licença*," she said before switching to French. "I didn't see you there, Mademoiselle Climber."

"Excuse me, Ferreirinha. The guests have arrived."

The older woman nodded. "I was just going to greet them, but it's much cooler tonight than I thought. Be a dear and fetch my shawl. It's on the chair in my office. Second door on the left." She pointed inside the house toward one of two halls leading from the entranceway.

As if given a momentary reprieve, Louisa smiled. "Yes, Madame." Ferreirinha went outside as Louisa turned toward the hallway.

She walked down the corridor, running her fingers over the grout lines and smooth surfaces of a blue-and-white-tiled mural. Louisa admired the unique artwork that told the story of the wine-making process. The first third of the painted tiles showed workers tending the vines. The second portion displayed the workers harvesting the fruit, and the tableau finished with the workers in a line, arms locked, stomping the grapes.

Every Portuguese person Louisa had met loved four things: their port wines, those little pastries, salted cod, and painted tiles. Decorative tiles covered the outside of many buildings, while various styles trimmed public rooms. Where others would hang paintings or tapestries, the Portuguese used tiled murals, giving their homes a colder yet more permanent feel.

The office door was open. Louisa located the dark blue, wool-and-silk shawl in the light from the desk lamp. Out the window, she glimpsed the first male caller bowing to Ferreirinha. The young man wore a black wool suit and held a top hat in his hand. When he stood, she found herself holding her breath.

It wasn't him.

No more. You are stronger than this, Louisa chided herself.

Jaws clenched in determination, she carried the shawl to Ferreirinha, who stood at the front of the line. As she helped the older woman wrap her shoulders, Louisa froze. Near the end of the queue of young men, the devil's piercing eyes stared at her, a sly smile on his face.

"How?" Louisa stammered out. *There's not even a scratch on his face. Did I imagine it? Did he block the strike with his hand?*

"Merci." Ferreirinha tugged the shawl closer. "I've got it."

On the woman's second tug, Louisa shook off the spell and let go of the cloth. "Sorry."

She spun and had to restrain herself from running as she fled toward the main house. Each breath and each step took immense effort as if a stone sat on her chest. She dared a glance over her shoulder. He stared back at her, his hungry eyes transfiguring his face into something less human. More animalistic.

Bile rose in her throat. She fought to keep from throwing up as she flung open the oak door and slammed it shut. Inside, she leaned against it. She went through her breathing exercises until she could hear more than her heartbeat booming in her ears.

I shall not be afraid. Louisa had never been one to call on God to get her out of a tight spot. Raised Greek Orthodox, then taught to be a thief before she had years of instruction by Catholic nuns had left Louisa conflicted. She believed in God. That was her only certainty, and she called on him now to help her face this evil. She crossed herself and whispered a quick Lord's prayer.

"Our Father who art in heaven, hallowed be thy name." Her breathing slowed.

"Thy kingdom come; thy will be done, on earth as it is in heaven." Her presto heartbeat softened to an allegro tempo.

"Give us this day our daily bread." The pounding of her pulse in her ears disappeared altogether.

"And forgive us our trespasses as we forgive those who trespass against us." As always, during this line, she pictured the last thing she'd stolen and the person she'd taken it from. The money and the pervert on the barge. But instead of giving her usual forgiveness to Gabrielle or one of the jetons, this time she imagined João and shuddered at his sinister eyes. Dismissing his visage, Louisa knew it would take a long time before her words would ring true in respect to him. She hoped God would be patient.

"And lead us not into temptation but deliver us from evil." A calm settled over her, and she could once again reason.

Her mind poured over the checklist she'd prepared as part of the plan for this event.

Weapon.

Louisa ran to the kitchen. The staff gave her a strange look as she lifted a meat cleaver off a hook on the wall and gave it a test swing. Satisfied with the weapon's balance and the sense of security it gave her, she inspected the other utensils. A smaller knife would be good, but she remembered her uncle's warning that a knife without a handle guard would slip when you stabbed someone. It was suitable only for slicing.

This will do. Louisa gripped the cleaver tight.

One of the staff raised a finger and opened her mouth, but Louisa stopped her with a quick "Merci" and darted out of the kitchen.

As she raced toward the stairs off the foyer, the front door opened, and she slid to a stop. Several Saint-Denis girls were coming inside. Behind them, João's head bobbed into view. Louisa turned and ran back to the kitchen.

A man was carrying a stack of wood through the back door, so Louisa altered her escape route.

"Excuse me." Louisa side-stepped a woman with a tray of bread and ran to the servant's stairwell.

She bounded up the steps two at a time. João Lopes Gomes's smooth Portuguese words chased her up the stairs.

Hide! she screamed inside.

Louisa grabbed the first doorknob. Locked.

The third door swung open, and she found a tiny room with a small bed, a desk, and a window. She closed the door, pushed the desk chair under the doorknob at an angle, and turned to the window.

"Keep your head, or you die." Her uncle's words bounced around her head, tempering her growing fear.

After unhooking the latch, she pushed the window and poked her head outside. Bereft of handholds, the smooth stucco walls made it impossible for her to climb up. Yes, she might be able to jump up and grab hold of the second floor window, but she didn't like the odds. Worse, she'd fall even farther if it was locked.

Louisa looked down. Now on the first floor, she would need to drop from this window and use the wooden support that stuck out a few centimeters from the outside wall to slow her fall.

That's a thin margin, she thought while pulling the strings at her waist and tying them into a knot. She dropped the cleaver to the ground a little to the side of her planned landing spot and turned around. She was halfway out of the window, with her feet leading the way, when the doorknob turned and rattled.

"I know you're in there," the demon hissed.

Hands clammy, Louisa wiped her palms on her bodice. *I control my outcome.* She kept repeating the mantra to herself as she squirmed to back out of the window.

Boom! A fist slammed into the door, jolting Louisa. The door shuddered under the blow, and the chair clattered to the floor. She squirmed out and hung from the ledge by her fingers. The door banged open, and Louisa let go. In a free fall, she relied on her instincts.

Now.

Her fingers slapped at the little ledge, and her nails dug into the wood for half a second before she lost her grip. The pause decelerated her fall enough, and she landed in a soft crouch.

The demon called from above, "Go ahead. Hide. I'll find you, my beautiful bastard."

Louisa grabbed the cleaver as she looked up. João's head extended from the window. He grinned, and her stomach churned. His head disappeared. She ran.

Even more than worrying about herself, Louisa needed to make sure her friends were safe. The estate's staff had either retired to their homes or were serving the party in the courtyard. She thought about going to the guard tower, but there was too much open ground. He would catch her well before she reached it. That left some of the work buildings, which would be empty.

Come get me. This time I won't miss. Louisa hefted the cleaver and snarled, hoping that her rage at this animal could push out her fear.

She ran along the dirt road next to the vineyard's small village. At the first break between buildings, Louisa turned into a small alley. The *quinta*'s layout flashed into her mind, and she took the next turn, racing between the small chapel and one of the dormitories. As she popped out of the shoulder-width space, a pair of large barn doors gaped open before her.

Pausing, she remembered that the building with the inviting doors had several exits. She sprinted inside and up a set of stone stairs to a level about two meters off the ground. She ran past large, plastered troughs. They were sunk into the floor on each side of the walkway that ran the length of the building. Each vat had a slight slope leading to a grate at the center, used to capture the stomped juice.

Louisa hopped into the stone tub two vats away from the back stairs and leaned into the wine-stained wall. Her breath came slow and shallow as she used her training to become a shadow.

Time stopped.

Like a lifeline, the cleaver's well-worn wooden handle kept her panic at bay. She tried to plan out her next three moves if he were to find her.

If her uncle hadn't corrected her instinct to flinch at the unexpected, she might have moved or gasped when she heard boots thumping on the first set of stairs. Still as a statue, she let her ears try to see for her. Heavy boots scraped against the stone stairs. The rhythm of her heart picked up despite her efforts to remain calm.

"I know you're in here. Your heart is as loud as a drum." The devil's voice held no emotion. The crunch of his footsteps bounced around the barn. "I'm not here to hurt you. I just want you to come with me. I'll take care of you."

Louisa fought the surge of fear that threatened to turn her into a mindless creature fleeing for its life.

"I will show you love like no other."

What is this? The monster wasn't making sense. Every nightmare scenario Louisa had dreamed of ended with him killing her in a horrible fashion. She'd come to think of him as one of those predators who must inflict pain and degradation on others to find pleasure.

"Sure, there will be pain like you've never thought possible, but with the suffering will come so much ecstasy." The madman's voice quickened with excitement.

There it is. Louisa stomach roiled along with her thoughts. The deranged man would torture and kill her for his sick amusement.

His voice cracked with emotion. "You'll come to love me, Louisa. The same way I love you."

Louisa wrinkled her forehead in consternation. *Kill me. Love me. This man has a serious mental illness.*

His next step was halfway to Louisa. She prepared to jump up and flee down the back stairs.

"Daring?" Virginie called out. "Are you in here?"

The crunch of running boots echoed from the opposite direction.

No!

Louisa popped her head out of the vat. João raced down the stairway out of sight.

"Virginie! Run!" Louisa shouted.

She climbed onto the walkway and ran toward her friend, with a new kind of fear driving her. At the landing, she stopped, putting the cleaver behind her back. João had his arm around Virginie's neck. Her eyes bulged as she struggled against him. The brute had knocked off her spectacles, which lay on the ground.

"Come with me now, or you can watch your friend die." He tightened his choke hold. "My man is waiting at the boat."

Virginie slapped and pulled at his arm, her face darkening.

"No!" With the meat cleaver pressed to her side, Louisa hopped down the steps three at a time. At the bottom, she slowed and spread her free arm wide, palm out. "Don't hurt her. Let her go. I'll go with you."

Virginie's struggles became weaker, but he loosened his grip a little. She wheezed in a ragged breath before giving Louisa a feeble shake of her head.

Louisa ignored her friend's plea and nodded. "That's right. I'll go with you." She squeezed the wooden handle as tears of frustration and fear streamed down her cheeks.

Should she rush him? *No, must get closer,* Louisa thought as she crept forward.

The madman's body relaxed. "Stop and turn around. Put your hands behind your back."

"João. I'll go with you. Don't you trust me?"

His arm tightened on Virginie, cutting off her next breath. "Do what I said."

Boots pounded on the hard-packed dirt outside the building.

João twisted his head around.

A blur flashed through the open doors. "You bastard!" Simon screamed as he punched João in the side of the head.

The crazy devil let go of Virginie and stumbled away. She fell to her knees, coughing and gasping for breath. Simon landed one giant swing after another while João held his arms up to shield his face.

Louisa ran and kneeled beside a dazed Virginie, who groped for her spectacles. A blow to João's cheek sent him sprawling. Simon ran to the side and grabbed a shovel from against the wall. He walked toward the downed man and raised the blade high over his head, his face contorted with rage.

"Don't!" Louisa and the colonel yelled at the same time.

Simon's swing stopped a few centimeters from João's head.

The colonel stood in the opening, moonlight casting a long shadow into the building. He marched over to Simon and tore the shovel from his hands. "Back up." He shoved Simon away.

Simon seemed to gather himself, his rage turning to concern. "Virginie?" he whispered.

Virginie croaked out a raspy, "I'm alright." She struggled to place one of the spectacle's wires behind her ear.

"Thank God, you arrived when you did, Colonel. This man attempted to murder me." A frightened-looking João pointed at Simon.

Gios pórnis. Louisa stood and started toward her tormentor. "Colonel, he's a lying son of a pig."

João glanced at Louisa. His pleading eyes locked with hers for a heartbeat before returning to faux fear.

Louisa thought, *I'm going to end you,* as she flashed him the meat cleaver. His eyes widened, and someone grabbed her arm.

"There will be no more violence." The colonel shook his head. "We are returning to the main house. Now." He jabbed a finger toward the open doors. "Lead the way, Monsieur Gomes."

João dusted himself off and stormed into the darkness. The colonel nodded to Louisa and her friends. Louisa put her arm around Virginie's waist and helped guide her out.

After a bit, Virginie said, "I'm alright." She gave Louisa a wincing smile as she rubbed her neck.

Louisa stepped in line with the colonel. "Simon was defending us. That man was hurting Virginie."

"That may be, but my intuition tells me you are at the heart of the matter." The colonel sighed. "You are all lucky that I got there when I did."

Louisa asked, "Why did you come?"

"As soon as the party began, all your friends left to find you. I went to find them and you." He gave her a hard stare. "Do you want to tell me what happened?"

"Colonel, have you ever met a man who is insanely evil?"

"I'm afraid I have."

"João Lopes Gomes is such a man. I rebuffed his advances at the ball, and he has wanted to hurt me ever since. He was choking Virginie to make me go with him when Simon saved us."

The colonel's eyes flashed to Simon, and he frowned.

The nuns, the brigadier, and Ferreirinha awaited them in the courtyard.

The colonel asked, "Where is Gomes?"

Ferreirinha shook her head. "He said the young man tried to kill him because he was kissing one of the girls. He left to bring back the Municipal Guard to have him arrested."

"That's not true." Virginie ran to Mère de la Nativité and grabbed her hand.

"I don't care to hear your excuses." The brigadier pointed at Simon. "You're dismissed. Never show yourself before me again."

The walrus made a perfect military turn and walked away, his cane tapping his displeasure.

"But Simon saved me," Virginie pleaded to the man's back. "He saved me!"

A forlorn Simon stared at Virginie, his hands clenching and unclenching. Louisa wished the young man could comfort her friend.

Since he couldn't, Louisa put her arms around Virginie's shoulders while addressing Ferreirinha. "Simon's innocent. Gomes wanted to hurt me, and he attacked Virginie to force me leave with him. He said he would make me suffer."

The older woman tilted her head toward Louisa. "Why would he want to hurt you?"

"I refused his advances. I don't know why he's obsessed with me." Twice now, Louisa had downplayed what that man had done, leaving a sour taste in her mouth. Still, she could not bring herself to say that he tried to rape her.

Mère de la Nativité interjected, "You should have told us that he was inappropriate."

"I had no idea he would be here," Louisa whispered.

"I'm sorry I invited him." Ferreirinha shook her head. "I've heard rumors that he has a . . . How do you say, *coração de pedra* in French?"

Mère de la Nativité answered, "A heart of stone."

"Yes, that's it." Ferreirinha looked at Simon. "You need to leave before he returns. Doesn't matter if your story is true. He can buy your imprisonment. One of my boats is leaving for Oporto at first light. You will be on it."

Virginie began to cry harder, and Louisa pulled her close.

Chapter 22
The First or the Last

Louisa grabbed Virginie's hand and shoved two hundred francs into her palm. It was all the money she, Eugénie, and Marie had brought on the tour. "Take it."

Her face troubled, Virginie nodded.

"I should have kept more of the cheater's money." Louisa choked up. "I'm sorry. None of this would have happened if I hadn't gone with him."

"You don't know that." Eugénie stepped next to Virginie. "If not you, he would have targeted someone else. That's what rabid dogs do." She tapped her lucky medal twice.

Marie completed the circle. "Gaiety's right. We're lucky. He picked on the most dangerous of us." She put a hand on both Louisa and Virginie. "What's happened to Simon is unjust, but it could have been much worse."

Virginie's bloodshot eyes started to water. "Maybe you're right, but I keep thinking how things could have been different."

Marie put her arm around Virginie's shoulder and pulled her close. "We need to pray that God will turn this tragedy into a blessing for you and Simon."

"Amen." Virginie flashed a half-hearted smile. "It was impressive how he saved me."

"Yes, it was. He seems like a good man," Louisa said.

A knock came at the door. "It's time," said Mère de la Nativité.

The clan's circle became a group hug.

After several seconds, Virginie pulled back. "We're coming, Ma Mère."

She broke the embrace and opened the door. They followed the nun out of the main house toward the docks. Just visible at the edge of daylight, a hazy gray mist drifted over the river below. Simon stood at the end of the pier next to the plank leading to the riverboat. One by one, the girls said their goodbyes as Mère de la Nativité watched over them.

When it was Louisa's turn, she hugged Simon and whispered into his ear, "*Merci beaucoup*. I can never repay you for saving Virginie's life, but I'll try."

As he hugged her back, his voice filled with anguish. "Take care of my girl."

The nun coughed, and Louisa took a long step back to stand beside Eugénie and Marie.

Virginie stepped forward and took Simon's hands in hers. "I'll see you in Paris. Take this." She handed him the money.

Simon's voice broke. "I'm not going back."

"What?" Virginie lost her balance, and Simon grabbed her arms to steady her.

"Tonight decided it for me. I'm going to America." He bent his head to be at her eye level. "I don't want to end up like my father."

"You won't." A tear dropped to Virginie's cheek.

He shook his head. "What happened last night, and how the general always looks down on me. It won't stop."

"The same things happen in America," Virginie pleaded.

"They do, but a man has a better chance of being judged by his work and his word alone."

One of the boatmen said, "*Hora de partir.*"

Mère de la Nativité said, "Time to board."

Simon nodded toward the nun and then looked at Virginie. He lifted her spectacles and wiped her tears with his thumb. With a sigh, he pulled a folded piece of paper from his coat pocket and handed it to her. "This is not *adieu*. I'll see you soon."

As he wrapped his arms around her, Virginie mumbled, "*Au revoir*." She buried her face in his shoulder and started weeping.

Simon kissed her forehead and pulled away, but Virginie wouldn't let go. Tears streamed from Simon's blue eyes as he grasped her arms to break her hold. He looked toward the other members of the clan, his face twisted with pain.

The three of them surrounded Virginie, holding her up. Simon grabbed his valise, bounded down the plank, and leaped into the boat. The fog scattered from the day's first rays as the rabelo pulled away from the dock. Simon stood at the stern, facing them. He lifted his arm as the boat reached a bend in the river, and the girls waved until he disappeared.

"Mademoiselles, let's go back." Mère de la Nativité strode toward the road.

Virginie blew her nose into a handkerchief before moving forward in a daze under Marie's and Louisa's guidance. Eugénie plucked the paper from Virginie's hand and unfolded it.

While they walked, Eugénie read the note. "*Parbleu*," she hissed, keeping her voice low. "He's going to Lisbon. He says there's a ship going to America. It leaves after we arrive, and he wants you to go with him."

Virginie did not react. She just kept shuffling forward.

"Did you hear what I said?"

When Virginie didn't reply, Louisa said, "Leave it for now. Worrying about what will happen in Lisbon can wait."

Louisa ignored her own advice and wondered how Simon planned to pay for the trip for himself, much less for two. She didn't want to see another friend go, but now she knew what she could do to start paying down her debts to Simon.

Chapter 23
Heavenly Advice

At the end of the line, Louisa trudged up the small road leading to Marie's fiancé's home. A few hours after Simon had left Quinta do Vesúvio, João came ashore with his henchman and two guardsmen. The girls stayed inside their rooms, guarded by the nuns, as Ferreirinha and the colonel dealt with them.

Ferreirinha told the guards that Simon ran into the hills. She told them she believed the young man was innocent and João was the culprit. When the devil protested, she gave him a tongue lashing and sent them all packing. An hour later, the girls bid Ferreirinha *au revoir* and boarded a boat destined for Paulo's family vineyard.

Louisa returned to the here and now as the procession turned a corner. A tall man and a short, plump woman––both in their fifties––waited to greet them.

Mère de la Nativité translated their host's Portuguese words into French. "Welcome to Quinta do Vallado. We are so excited to have you." With an infectious smile, the woman motioned them forward with both hands. "I'm Paulo's mother, Catarina Ferreira da Fonseca, but call me Catia. And this is my husband, Adão."

The tall, graying man with a cleft chin that matched Paulo's gave them a shy wave.

As the girls moved forward, Catia said, "I'm sorry that Paulo is not here. He is in Lamego making all the arrangements."

The girls greeted the pair, as Paulo's dad shook hands with each girl before passing her on to his wife. Catia hugged every tour participant before kissing each girl's cheeks.

When Marie stepped before her, the older woman said, "*Minha linda menina.*" She hugged Marie and kept speaking in Portuguese, her excitement evident even if the nun could not keep pace with her translations.

Catia's misty eyes ran counter to the joy in her wide smile as they released their hug. "Come."

Louisa shook Paulo's dad's hand and hurried to catch up with the rest of the girls. Catia led them inside the long, white-trimmed, two-story mansion plastered in a deep saffron color. They raced through the foyer, past the dining room and the kitchen, to a large, bright sewing room. The expansive windows revealed views of the Quinta's vineyard that stretched up and across the large hill behind the house. In the center of the room, two women stood beside a gorgeous, white-lace wedding dress hanging on a dress mannequin.

After all the girls had shuffled in, Paulo's mother tilted her head to Mère de la Nativité, and the nun nodded.

"Marie, I'm sorry that we don't have time to create a dress of your own. This was my wedding dress, and now it is yours." Catia clasped Marie's hand. "My beautiful daughter, tomorrow, everything I have will be yours."

Marie started to tear up.

Catia sniffled, and one of the ladies handed her a handkerchief. "Please take care of him. He is my heart."

Marie brushed the tears off her cheeks. "I promise to cherish him as you would." She paused a beat. "It's my honor to become your daughter and to call you Mother." They hugged again.

Behind Louisa, Gabrielle snickered in a low voice, "Pathetic."

"The whole thing is nauseating," Jeton Un hissed.

Louisa stepped backward and dug her heel into the toe of Gabrielle's shoe.

"Ow!" the blonde yelped.

She tried to pull her foot away, but Louisa added more weight.

The boot popped free, and Gabrielle leaned close to Louisa's ear. "You better watch yourself, Greek Bastard."

Louisa glanced over her shoulder and hissed, "Or what? Are you going to say more mean words?"

Gabrielle curled her lip in disgust, her face bright pink.

Catia said, "I will leave you with our town's two best seamstresses. They will prepare the dress by tomorrow."

Gabrielle pulled back. "Ma Mère, may we be excused?"

Louisa turned around to find Mère de la Nativité glaring at her and Gabrielle. The nun held a finger toward them as she said something to Catia in Portuguese.

"*De nada.*" Catia patted Marie's arm and left the room.

Mère de la Nativité waited until she had disappeared and scowled at Louisa and Gabrielle. "Enough. This backbiting will stop, or I will come up with consequences that will make you regret ever knowing me."

Louisa chuckled inside. *That would be different, how?*

The nun poked a finger at one, then the other. "Am I clear?"

"Yes, Ma Mère," the two echoed.

"Mademoiselle Chanzy, I believe it best that you and your friends find your rooms." She turned to Marie. "Your friends should stay and help you prepare." She marched out with Gabrielle and the Jetons in tow.

Eugénie slapped her hip. "Thank God. I was about to kill them."

Virginie fingered the lace on the dress. "It's beautiful, Joy." She gave Marie a rueful smile.

Catherine chirped, "You are going to be gorgeous."

"I hope so." Marie grinned, looking at the dress.

The seamstresses motioned Marie forward and had her stretch her arms out wide. They used long, thin paper strips with spaced-out black marks to take her measure.

"Joy, there's still time to run." Louisa raised her eyebrows at her friend.

Marie tsked and said, "The only running I'll be doing is down the aisle."

"And to the bed chamber afterward." Eugénie giggled.

"Eww." Virginie wrinkled her nose.

Louisa's skin crawled at the thought of a man touching her. "Are you scared?"

Marie looked at her with concern. "No." Certainty buoyed her next words. "I trust Paulo."

"Is he a virgin?" Eugénie's face was red, but her eyes sparkled.

"He said he is."

Virginie asked, "Is that good or bad? Having a man who knows what to do might not be bad."

"Is there something you want to tell us, Pleasure?" Louisa gave Virginie a sideways glance, and her friend blanched.

"They can learn together," Catherine said with more excitement than Louisa had expected.

Eugénie shook her head. "Of course, it's best if they're both virgins. That's what God expects of us."

Louisa wanted to shake her friend and tell her to be careful. Instead, she said, "Make sure he listens to you and respects you."

Marie nodded. "I will. Mère de la Nativité already spoke with me."

Eugénie wrinkled her forehead. "What does she know?"

"She was married before she became a nun," Louisa said.

The heads of the other girls, except Marie, swiveled toward Louisa.

"And just how do you know this?" Virginie crossed her arms. "And why didn't you tell us before?"

Louisa shrugged. "I thought I had. Sister Adeline messed up and said something about it during the dinner with the captain. I didn't get to finish the meal and didn't see any of you for three days. By then, it slipped my mind."

"She told me what to expect and what I should do to be a good wife." Marie laughed, her freckles framing jade eyes full of mirth. "It was very instructive advice and nothing I thought I'd ever hear from a nun."

Catherine leaned closer, her eyes wide. "Tell us what she said."

Eugénie nodded and cleared her throat. "Word for word."

Chapter 24

Stairway's End

Marie stepped into the open carriage and adjusted the bustle of her wedding dress. With a loud sigh, she plopped onto the seat next to Louisa. "The whole town of Régua must be here."

The day had just begun, and the bride-to-be looked exhausted.

"I'd wager that most of the Douro Valley is here," said Virginie, wearing a brave face, from the seat opposite them.

So long as that demon doesn't show up, Louisa thought as the carriage began to move. She yawned—the result of waking up hours before sunrise. She had dressed for the wedding by lantern light. When she'd descended the stairs to eat breakfast, she found a giant party in progress. Well-wishers from as far away as Porto were eating, and many were already drinking as a rooster announced sunrise in the valley.

Poor Marie.

At least a hundred strangers lined up to hug and kiss the bride as soon as she appeared in the kitchen. After a short boat ride across the river, Catia hustled the tour group to the first few carriages in a long line of horse-drawn conveyances. Marie's future in-laws had hired every wagon and carriage in the area to transport the wedding guests to the mountain town of Lamego.

Louisa looked over her shoulder and shook her head. A large dust cloud obscured the end of the caravan. *Thank God, I'm with the bride.*

"In a few hours, you will be Marie Ferreira da Fonseca. Are you excited?" Eugénie's voice rose with anticipation.

"The Portuguese don't do that." Marie leaned forward.

Virginie shifted the large bag in her lap and tilted her head. "Do what?"

Marie smiled. "Women don't take their husband's surname. Legally or in common usage."

"That's good. It's not like it's much shorter than your name now." Louisa pushed down the skirt of her blue silk tea gown.

"Three. Ferreira da Fonseca is three letters shorter than Coffinières de Nordeck." Marie chuckled. "Our poor children."

"What is your father doing for your dowry?" Virginie asked.

"Paulo didn't ask for one," Marie replied, "but my father insisted. He is wiring Paulo's father twenty thousand francs."

The four young women spent the next three hours discussing Marie's future, from her children's names to her role in the vineyard business. Everyone avoided any mention of the recent troubles or the final goodbyes that would happen later that night. Near noon, they turned onto another small dirt road and wound their way up toward a church on yet another small mountain.

The carriage lurched to a stop in a cobblestone courtyard beside the church. With a red-tiled roof and white-plastered walls, the two-steepled chapel appeared small for such a large wedding. Louisa hopped to the ground first and helped Marie down the carriage steps.

"Welcome to Santuário de Nossa Senhora dos Remédios."

Louisa turned to find Ferreirinha, her husband, and a young man waiting.

Louisa curtsied. "Madame Ferreira, so nice to see you again."

"Just Ferreirinha, Mademoiselle Climber." She bowed her head to the bride. "All of you have met my husband, but my son, José, insisted on meeting the woman who captured his best friend's heart."

A young man with big ears poking out from his long black hair stepped forward and hugged Marie. He moved back and said in slow, deliberate French, "Marie, you are every bit as lovely as Paulo said you were. He is inside, pacing a hole in the floor." He held out his elbow to Marie. "Please, let me take you to where you may rest until the ceremony begins."

José led her toward the front of the church with the clan following. As they rounded the corner, a spectacular view unfolded. In front of the church's baroque-style façade, stairs led below to a garden with a fountain. In the center, a tall column jutted into the sky. Yet, it was what lay farther down the mountain that stopped Louisa in her tracks.

Framed by woods to either side, more stairs led down to more gardens, the process repeating all the way to the village in the valley below. To Louisa, the tiered gardens looked as if a giant had carved a colossus-size staircase into the side of the mountain.

"Impressive, isn't it?" José waved across the view. "Paulo wanted this to be your first wedding gift."

"It's stunning," Marie whispered.

"Please, follow me." He led the group through the church's tall, narrow double doors to a room off the narthex.

"Make yourselves comfortable. The ceremony will begin as soon as the rest of the guests arrive. We will have plenty of time to get to know each other better in the coming days."

Marie smiled. "I look forward to it."

José bowed and left them alone.

Marie sat in an oversize, padded, high-back chair. Louisa and Virginie positioned three simple wooden chairs in a semi-circle in front of the bride while Eugénie poured everyone a glass of watered-down wine.

As they sat, Mère Sainte Adeline poked her head into the room. "Mademoiselle Coffinières de Nordeck, you make a gorgeous bride. Do you need anything?"

Marie shook her head. "Ma Mère, were you able to arrange the *carre*?"

The nun grinned, her face radiating excitement. "We have it. Mère de la Nativité and I will hold it over you two lovebirds. I'll have the best view in the church."

"Wonderful, *merci*."

The nun nodded and ducked out, shutting the door. Marie leaned her head back, closed her eyes, and sucked in a deep breath.

"You all right, Joy?" Eugénie asked.

"If you have any doubts, it's not too late to call it off." Louisa tapped Marie's shoe with her toe. "Say the word, and I'll have four horses ready to go in ten minutes."

Marie's eyelids drooped, and in moments, her breath became slow and steady.

Virginie slapped Louisa's hand. "Stop it, Daring. Don't screw this up for her, too." She began to say something but turned away.

Louisa ignored her. Guilt wasn't part of her normal emotional makeup. It was useless. Feeling guilty never changed what had happened and never made things better. All she could do now was put her energy into paying back the debt she owed Virginie and Simon, even if it meant she would have to say goodbye to Virginie as well.

While Marie snoozed, Eugénie clasped hands with Louisa and Virginie as she prayed blessings over Marie and Paulo's marriage. Eugénie must have run out of ideas because she started repeating her litany of prayers when a knock came at the door, and Catherine walked in.

"They're ready. The colonel is waiting." Catherine put her hand to her mouth when she saw Marie.

The bride was snoring, and a line of drool ran from the corner of her mouth.

Eugénie smiled. "Give us five minutes."

Catherine bobbed her head and closed the door.

Virginie shook Marie's shoulder. "Joy, wake up. It's time to get married."

"Huh." Marie half-coughed and started to wipe her arm across her mouth before Virginie grabbed her wrist.

"I've got this." Virginie pulled a wedding veil out of her oversize bag. She handed it to Louisa and dug back into the bag until she found a handkerchief. After dipping the cloth into her watery wine, Virginie cleaned Marie's entire face before finishing with the drool.

Marie softly slapped her cheeks a few times. "How long?"

"Long enough to have bad breath." Virginie laughed and handed Marie a dried clove. "Suck on that until we go outside."

As she moved behind the bride, Virginie held her hand out. Louisa relinquished the veil, glad to see her friend shed her melancholy. While Virginie adjusted the veil, Eugénie tightened the braid of Marie's chignon.

"I'll get the bouquet." Louisa stepped outside and almost ran into the colonel.

He took a quick step back. "Pardon, Mademoiselle Sophia."

"Quite all right, Colonel. Have you seen the two bridal bouquets?"

He pointed to a table with two bunches of wild reddish-pink gladiolus mixed with yellow marigolds.

"Interesting choice." Louisa shrugged and picked up the bouquets.

"I thought so as well. Catia said it was something to do with their coat of arms." He stuck his thumb over his shoulder. "They are getting restless."

A small mob waited in the narthex. Catia patted a nervous Paulo's arm as they stood in front of the sanctuary doors. Behind them, several women tried to rein in three little girls wearing blue lace-and-silk dresses. The children swung their baskets full of flower petals as they chased one another around the crowded space. One woman shook her head and stooped to pick up the trail of spilled petals the girls left in their wake.

"Should just be one more minute." Louisa went back inside and closed the door.

Marie smiled at her, and Louisa's heart soared. The pure jubilation and certainty in Marie's eyes eased Louisa's worry. This was Marie's destiny. Louisa might never find the same joy, love, or certainty in a man, and that was fine. Part of her knew her thoughts were irrational. A reaction to the damage done to her. Maybe when her recent wounds scarred over, she might see a path forward. Might imagine a relationship with a man who was neither disastrous nor perfect but normal.

"Come here." Marie's voice broke, and her eyes watered.

The Clan of the Dissipated hugged.

"I love you all." Marie's face was flush. "You will be my sisters forever."

Louisa mumbled, "I love you, too." Her eyes misted as Virginie and Eugenie expressed their love.

Marie squeezed a little harder and then let go. "Let's do this." She took one of the bouquets, and Virginie helped her bring the veil over her face.

Louisa shoved the second bouquet into Eugénie's hands and opened the door. From the doorway, Louisa nodded to the colonel, who waved to José. The doors swung inward, and the cacophony of a hundred conversations burst into the narthex but died almost as fast.

Inside the nave, attendees were squeezed shoulder to shoulder into the pews, with the overflow crowd standing two deep against the wall. The church organ began to play a piece by Bach, and Catia escorted her son, Paulo, down the center aisle. A rococo-decorated ceiling brightened the white limestone sanctuary. The church radiated a simple beauty and elegance.

Just like Marie.

When Paulo and his mother were no longer visible, Louisa moved out of the doorway into the chapel's foyer, followed by Virginie, Eugénie, and the bride. The colonel took his position with Marie on his right as the rest of the clan followed after Paulo. Louisa thought about how much Marie must miss her parents.

For a brief second, Louisa imagined her own mother and blinked away a tear that threatened to fall. She marched toward the altar and the golden, floor-to-ceiling reredos behind it with slow, steady strides. Blue-and-white-tiled murals covered all the other walls around the altar.

A youthful priest waited on the sanctuary platform with the nuns from Saint-Denis on either side. Each nun held a tall pole with a purple silk canopy stretched between them. Wearing a nervous smile, Paulo stood at the bottom of the steps.

He nodded to Louisa. She smiled back before she moved down the first pew and waited. When Virginie and Eugénie joined her, the organ sounded the first notes of "Air" from Handel's *Water Music*.

The congregation turned toward the entrance, eager to glimpse the bride, but Louisa kept watching Paulo. In an instant, his eyes lit up, and the worry drained away from his face to be replaced by a huge grin. Louisa let go of the last bit of tension in her body. No one could know what the future held for Marie and Paulo, but Louisa was confident that the love-addled fool waiting for her friend at the altar would cherish her for the gift that she was.

Louisa followed his gaze to Marie. The red-and-yellow flowers embellished the lacy angel gliding forward on the colonel's arm. The bride's bright smile was apparent even through the gauzy veil. Marie had never been so beautiful. The clan's Joy had never looked so serene as when the colonel passed her hand to Paulo's.

Louisa sniffled and resisted the urge to wipe away her happy yet sorrowful tears. The Mass and the couple's vows went by in a blur of emotion. Louisa choked back a sob when the groom lifted the veil and gave his bride a long, tender kiss. The fear of never finding the same kind of love became a growing void in Louisa's gut.

I've never wanted that anyway, she thought, trying to console herself.

The couple turned around to face them. As the priest pronounced them husband and wife, the dread inside her disappeared. Elation for her friend filled Louisa's heart near to bursting. She jumped to her feet, joining the applause and celebratory shouts that drowned out the organ playing inside the church. Marie smiled at each of her friends and mouthed, "*Je t'aime.*" Then she latched onto Paulo's arm. They made their way up the aisle together, shaking hands with the closest well-wishers.

With all the attendees in the crowded church following the couple out, it took a while for Louisa and her friends to reach the church's main doors. Louisa went with the flow until she reached the first balcony overlooking the garden with the fountain. A roar came from below. Unable to get a good view, she pushed through the milling crowd and climbed onto the stone railing.

"Be careful!" Eugénie yelled.

In front of the columned fountain on the terrace below, Paulo dipped Marie, and the two kissed with passion. Musicians with guitars, fiddles, and some type of bagpipes stood nearby. They struck up a fast folk song while the wedding party that ringed the couple clapped to the beat and sang along in Portuguese. When Paulo and Marie came up for air, he escorted her to the next set of stairs, and the pair started down.

Louisa shouted over her shoulder, "See you at the bottom!"

Balanced on the balustrade, she spread her arms wide and tightrope-walked to the stairs. With a warning cry of "Tally ho!" she danced down the banister, hopping and skipping over anyone's random hand using the stone for support.

Louisa reached the end and leaped down. Someone shoved a wooden mug of wine into her hand as soon as her feet touched the ground. She sipped her wine and took in the splendor of the blue-and-white-tiled mural below the balcony, which hadn't been visible from above. The image showed Jesus's mother, Mary, receiving a crown.

When her mug was empty, Louisa followed the crowd. The party continued this way for the next hour. Music, dancing, and songs accompanied the newly-weds down the hill. Shouts and hoots marked each time the couple christened the new level with a kiss. The procession continued until the celebrations spilled into a giant piazza at the bottom. Tables with food and drink awaited there.

Long shadows stretched from the trees along the boulevard from the piazza into the village. Louisa's stomach rumbled at the sight of food. She, Virginie, Eugénie, and Catherine sat at a four-person table. The rest of the tour participants sat at a larger one nearby.

Famished after having had no lunch, Louisa tore a leg from one of the two roasted chickens on the table.

Gabrielle snorted from the next table. "The Greek girl has the manners of a monkey."

Jeton Deux——Joséphine—said, "The difference is you can train monkeys to use a fork and a knife."

Gabrielle and the other lackey, Julie, started snickering.

Louisa tugged the drumstick free. She waved it toward her hecklers. "Good luck finding utensils." She bit off a chunk of meat and grinned at them with her mouth full.

Gabrielle's expression soured as she searched her table, only to confirm what Louisa already knew. There were no forks or knives, just a single serving spoon for the bowl of roasted root vegetables.

Turning back to the table, Louisa found Eugénie holding a drumstick with two fingers on one end while another finger balanced it with as little contact as possible. She took a dainty bite.

Louisa swallowed and shook her head. "You, too?" Lowering her voice, she hissed at Eugénie, "I once saw you gnaw on a dog's thigh bone for an hour."

Eugénie frowned at Louisa. "I was twelve, and that was during the Siege. Remember what Buttons said. We must always conduct ourselves with dignity."

Louisa rolled her eyes and was happy to see that at least Catherine had given up her inhibitions. With grease glistening on her lips, the shy girl popped a roasted carrot into her mouth while holding a roll in her other hand. Virginie found a middle ground between high and no manners. She split a roll in two and created a chicken sandwich.

All around them, the guests sang, danced, and drank, only stopping for short respites to eat and refill their mugs. Chicken fat dripped from Louisa's fingers. Without a napkin in sight, she sucked the juice off each digit. Her hunger satiated, she dropped a cleaned bone onto her wooden plate.

Mère de la Nativité stopped beside their table. "We will be leaving the party in two hours. We have a long day of travel tomorrow."

"Where are we going, Ma Mère?" Catherine piped up loud enough to be heard over the noise, her speech slurring a little.

"We are staying at the cathedral down the street tonight and taking carriages to the University of Coimbra tomorrow. They are holding a social for you and the students."

"That should be fun." Eugénie put her hand over her mouth to stifle a yawn.

Virginie said, "I'm ready to go home."

Catherine's green eyes were so dilated that they looked black. "I'm not," she said. "I'm ready to sing." She stood and stepped over the bench, grabbing the table as her foot caught.

As Catherine stumbled toward the small band, Mère de la Nativité appeared worried.

Eugénie giggled and scooted off her end of the bench. "I'll watch over her." She turned to address Virginie and Louisa. "We might want to think of a nickname for our new friend."

Louisa's anger flared. "What the hell, Gaiety? We haven't even said goodbye, and you're already trying to replace Joy."

Rocking back at the rebuke, Eugénie said, "I'm not trying to replace anyone, Daring. I just think Catherine needs a place to belong." She jabbed a finger at Louisa. "I remember the angry little waif who showed up one day and couldn't even speak two words of French. She didn't know it, but what she needed more than a language lesson was a friend."

The retort on Louisa's tongue went poof, and she dropped her gaze. "I remember." She looked up. "What about Tipsy?"

Virginie chuckled. "Not bad. Let's think about it as the trip unfolds. Maybe she'll show us something better."

Eugénie nodded.

"Ahem." Mère de la Nativité nodded toward the retreating Catherine. "Mademoiselle Savant, she is your responsibility until we leave."

"Yes, Ma Mère." Eugenie hurried after her charge.

Catherine huddled with the musicians, waving her hands in an attempt to overcome the translation barrier with exaggerated sign language.

Eugénie stepped into the conversation, and soon everyone was nodding. The guitar and fiddle players helped Catherine ascend to the top of the closest table.

She swayed for a moment before spreading her feet to brace herself. After cupping her hands to her mouth, she shouted above the din, "Quiet!"

"Woah. Didn't think she could be that loud." Virginie nudged Louisa with her elbow. "What are the chances she falls off?"

Behind Catherine's silhouette, the moon had risen over the town, and the sinking sun turned the sky above the church a marbled pink, yellow, and orange. As the noise dropped to a whisper, Catherine yelled toward the table where Marie sat with Paulo. "This is for my friend Marie! May God bless your union!" She nodded to the musicians at her feet. The first few notes of the guitar and the fiddle were soft but unmistakable to everyone as a hush fell over the piazza.

Catherine's French version of Schubert's "Ave Maria" sent chills down Louisa's spine. By the end, Louisa had to admit that maybe Catherine was the best voice at Saint-Denis. The partygoers erupted with applause as the last notes drifted into the darkening sky.

Virginie leaned to touch shoulders with Louisa, saying, "That was heavenly."

"What about Aria?" Louisa offered.

Virginie laughed. "Not bad, but I still like Tipsy better."

Louisa nodded, but her eyes began to mist as Marie released her hug of Catherine. She marched toward them, arms locked with Eugénie. Tears streamed down Marie's cheeks, and her eyes were hard with forlorn resignation at seeing her clan sisters leave.

Chapter 25

American Style

The handkerchief in front of Louisa's mouth and nose kept the worst of the dust out of her airways, but her eyes stung from the small floating particles. With no bride to give them the prime spot, the remaining clan members and the new initiate, Catherine, scrunched low in the last of the tour's three open-air carriages.

This trip is every bit as horrible as I predicted. Louisa's thoughts turned to the tearful goodbye with Marie and then to the current journey. They had at least three more hours of eating dust. That was still better than being in the second carriage with the buffoon.

When it had been time to depart that morning, everyone stood waiting because the brigadier had disappeared. An hour later, his bellicose voice announced his return. From his faltering steps, unkempt hair, and bloodshot eyes, Louisa deduced the old fool had stayed at the wedding reception the entire night, drinking. As he fell into the second carriage, smelling like a distillery, she thanked God she didn't have to sit near him for the whole trip.

"Poor Gabrielle," she snickered to herself, giving thanks for small blessings.

The other carriages had disappeared around a curve in the road when shouts came from ahead, disrupting her reverie. As they rounded the turn, their driver yelled and sawed left and right with the reins to slow the horses. He leaned back, straining to pull the reins to his chest. The carriage screeched to a halt, and Louisa flew forward. She clung to the rail at her side, or she would have landed in Catherine's lap.

To get a better view, Louisa stood. Halfway around the curve, she could see only the second carriage. The carriage horses neighed and stomped their feet. A gunshot rang out ahead, and she ducked. Another bang came from behind, and Louisa spun around, poking her head up enough to see above the seat. Two men, one dressed as a field worker, while the other wore a long, expensive coat, had dark bandanas masking their faces. There was something familiar about the well-dressed robber, but Louisa couldn't make the connection. He held a rifle, while the more disheveled man had a revolver.

The man with the pistol made eye contact with her. He motioned his head and gun toward the ground.

Louisa looked at her three companions, who had shrunk in their seats, their eyes wide. "They want us to get down," Louisa said.

A girl's scream and the faint commanding voice of the colonel couldn't take Louisa's eyes from the two nearby gunmen. She'd been at gunpoint a few times in her life and never found the experience enjoyable. Their driver hopped to the ground and raised his arms.

"I'll be damned if I allow you to harm these demoiselles!" The brigadier's shout came out as a slur. Louisa turned her head in time to see a third gunman use the butt of his rifle to whack the general in the back of the head. The older man collapsed to the ground with a grunt. He lay still.

He's not a coward. He didn't exaggerate that.

The rifleman closest to her yelled in perfect English, "Get down. Now."

Louisa twisted her head back and nodded. She patted Eugénie's shoulder. "Let's go."

Virginie shook her head from the other bench, tears pooling behind her lenses.

"Stay calm and do what they say for now. It's probably just one of those American-style holdups." She smiled at her frightened friend. "I'll go first."

With care, she stepped around her friends' legs and reached outside to open the carriage door. It swung out, and she jumped to the ground.

The one with the pistol said, "*Ela é a única.*"

Her jaw went slack as she thought, *It's that demon again.*

Before she could digest this realization, the bandit with the revolver pointed it straight at Louisa's chest.

Cold terror shot through her body, leaving her fingers and toes tingling. Her torso shook, her breathing was erratic. Louisa bit the back of her lip hard. Her eyes stayed locked on the gun barrel, but she focused on the pain, forcing herself to savor the metallic taste of her blood. The pain brought her back to the here and now, just as her uncle had said it would.

She raised her hands slowly and stepped out of the way as the other girls descended to the ground. The man with the rifle leaned it against the carriage while his friend kept the pistol trained on them. He stepped before Louisa, and his rough hands spun her around.

Catherine started whimpering, and Louisa caught a whiff of urine. The man with the pistol yelled something in Portuguese, his voice full of disgust. Catherine bit back another cry.

"Stand strong," Eugénie admonished them. "Remember who you are."

The sound of a slap carried to Louisa, and Eugénie grunted but didn't cry out.

With a harsh grip, the man at Louisa's back jerked her hands behind her. She spread her fingers wide to make her wrists as big as possible and stayed flexed while the man tied her wrists together with long leather straps. When he finished, a black cloth sack went over her head, and he cinched it closed around her neck. The overwhelming smell of shallots made her eyes water. She saw only reddish-black shadows through the cloth, so she shut her eyes, her ears becoming her sight.

The other girls were tied up as well.

Louisa found the courage to say, "You don't need them. I'm the one you want."

"Shut up." The man's English accent was laced with danger.

Louisa went quiet and filtered out her friends' fearful sobs to find the sounds that mattered. In a few minutes, at least two men ran toward her from the direction of the other carriages. The clip-clop of several horses mixed with their footsteps. Then there were sounds of horse tackle being unfastened as their carriages horses were unharnessed.

Big hands hoisted her up, and her stomach slammed into the broad bare back of a horse. A rope encircled her feet and tightened. The cord came under the horse and wrapped around her arms. The line pulled tighter, jerking her feet down. It burned her armpits as a knot completed the loop. Louisa wiggled her body, but she was well strapped to the horse. They had made one big mistake. The ties around her wrists wouldn't be easy, but she'd freed herself from more difficult restraints.

But never strapped to a moving animal. Louisa winced at the thought of how much pain it would take, but she visualized the face of João Lopes Gomes. Her hatred fed her resolve.

The horse jerked its neck, and they moved in what Louisa assumed was the direction they had come. At each fourth hoofbeat, she increased her road-walking tally. The counting would allow her to estimate how far they had come in each direction.

When the cadence changed to a trot, she started a different type of counting. Her breathing came in short gasps because of the constant bouncing. Her shoulders rolled with each movement of the animal's broad, muscled haunches.

After she counted several thousand trots over at least an hour, they veered off the road to the left, and the horse scrambled uphill. They had been a little more than an hour past the last village at the time of the ambush. That meant that the bandits had probably turned before reaching the town.

After topping a rise, they walked up a twisting path for several hours. For the most part, it was difficult for Louisa to make out the other girls' soft sobs or sniffles. The kidnappers stayed silent except to call out an obstacle to avoid or to hush one of the hostages. From those few louder interjections, Louisa estimated that the bandits were traveling in a single file, and each gunman pulled a prisoner-laden packhorse. Three men were ahead of her, with at least one behind.

Louisa kept opening her eyes and checking how much light there was before shutting them and resuming her count. On her last check, the darkness had increased to the point that she thought the sun had begun to set.

She changed the position of her hands, from fingers spread wide to fists, and she shifted her wrists. She felt a small gap in the bindings, allowing her to twist and wriggle, trying to stretch them. She repeated the process a hundred times with the straps rubbing her wrists raw. Sweat from her exertions added salt to her wounds.

Gritting her teeth at the pain, she used the devil's face for motivation as she worked. Soon, her wrists were slick with blood. As the leather became saturated, it became more pliable. The tiny gap grew a millimeter at a time. When it was big enough for her to twist her hand, she untied the knot holding her wrists.

To suppress a yell of triumph, Louisa buried her face in her mount's side and let out a short, muffled shout. In a small way, the catharsis helped numb her pain.

A few centimeters at a time, she moved one arm from behind her back and over the hump of the horse's neck. Tiny pinpricks signaled her muscles reawakening, adding to her discomfort. As she moved, she prayed a "Hail Mary," asking for divine intervention. If the rider behind her had seen the movement, all her efforts would have been wasted. When the blood flow returned to her fingers, she found the tie to the sack on her head and undid it.

As Louisa lifted the veil, she gulped in the cool, crisp mountain air, as much to taste something other than shallots as to fill her lungs. She stopped raising the hood when she saw the ground and the knot that kept her tied to the horse. It would take her only a few moments of work, and she would be able to slip off.

The darkness of night was almost complete, but dusk left enough of a glow for her to barely see the outline of a man atop a horse on the path behind her. On the trail to either side of the rider, clumps of small bushes appeared and disappeared like apparitions. She glanced in the other direction but couldn't even see the horse in front of her, though she could still hear its faint hoofbeats.

If Louisa waited for total darkness, the brigands might light lanterns or torches, and she would lose her opportunity.

Last chance.

She lifted the sack off her face and stuffed it inside a pocket. Slow and steady, she moved her other hand forward with the same discomfort as the limb came alive. She untied the primary knot using both hands and pulled the rope from around her arms.

Still not free. Louisa's thoughts raced with her escape plan.

While she waited for the numbness in her arm and hand to return to normal, she tracked the outline of the rider behind her. The next step had a lot of risks. She could roll off the horse going feet- or head-first. Each direction had issues. The horse might startle, she might fall off a cliff, or the long rope might get tangled in the animal's legs.

The torso of the man's shadow twisted, and Louisa threw the long end of the rope under the horse and slid off feet-first, turning so that she landed facing away from the horse. As her toes touched the ground, knives shot up her abused limbs. Arms waving, she tottered on her tied ankles but stayed upright. Her horse's haunch bumped into her back as it moved forward, prompting her to action.

Ignoring the pain in her feet and legs, she dove behind a small bush on the edge of the trail.

No!

She dug her fingers into the dirt, desperate to stop herself from toppling over the slope that dipped almost right behind the bush. As soon as her slide stopped, she shifted to her side and pulled her legs behind the leaves. She grabbed the rope tied to her ankles and hauled it off the trail. With a quick jerk, she pulled her white sash off and stuffed it into the pocket with the black sack.

All of that had taken precious seconds. The sounds of the horse and the bandit behind her came closer. With her eyes closed, Louisa turned away from the trail and lowered her breathing. Seconds before the other rider reached her hideout, she was nothing but the bush's shadow. The hoofbeats drew alongside her bush. The man coughed, hacking for a moment before he spat, striking her hiding spot. Drops of spittle ricocheted onto her cheek and neck.

Disgusting.

Not a muscle moved. Louisa's uncle had done much worse to make her react.

When the sounds of her kidnappers receded to a whisper, Louisa raced to untie her feet. She rubbed them for a few seconds, trying to restore blood flow. The effort brought forth more aching twinges. Desperate to stay close to her friends, she hurried to sling the coil of rope over her shoulder and transform her skirt into pantaloons. Sticking to the slope side of the hill, she moved down the trail, following the kidnappers.

I'm coming.

Chapter 26

Away in a Manger

"*Onde ela está?*" one of the kidnappers shouted.

Louisa didn't wait to hear the entire conversation and ducked behind the small farmhouse. The shouting match that echoed to the back of the small cottage didn't need translation. At the far corner, she peeked at the scene in the clearing next to a substantial two-story stone barn. Two men held lanterns, casting a glow over the four men and eight horses milling around. The kidnappers had removed their masks, but in the low light, Louisa couldn't make out any of their faces.

One of the farmhand kidnappers had dismounted and said in broken English, "When Gomes get here?"

The leader, a man wearing an expensive long wool coat and boots whose spit shine reflected in the lantern light, replied in a pure British accent, "Enough. I told you, no names." He dismounted and pointed at the two fieldhand-dressed gang members still on their horses. "Since those two idiots lost her, they can find her. Tell them. She will be heading back to the road. Get there before she does and catch her."

The Portuguese bandit who first spoke in English asked, "And if they can't? Do we kill her?"

"No, he wants her alive." The British man jabbed his finger at them. "God help you if she gets away."

Fils du diable. There will be a reckoning for that scoundrel. Louisa clenched her jaws.

The man nodded and spoke in Portuguese to the other riders. They started back down the trail, struggling with the horses. The animals shook their heads and whinnied their displeasure at having to go back to work.

"Help me get the girls into the barn." The Englishman began to untie Eugénie.

The Portuguese kidnapper approached Catherine's horse and started working on her restraints. "When he get here?"

"Tomorrow. He's visiting with the local constabulary." The man's mustache quavered as he laughed.

João, you rotten fiend, Louisa considered how the man's influence could cause real problems in the future, but she had more immediate concerns and put it from her mind.

The Portuguese bandit nodded. "And if they not catch her. How much these worth?" He waved toward the girls.

"It's up to him, but you'll be lucky if you get half." The British man threw Eugénie over his shoulder, picked up a lantern, and carried her into the barn.

The Portuguese man lifted Catherine onto a shoulder. "Ugh. This one wet self."

Be careful, you lout, Louisa snarled at her friend's poor treatment.

They carried all three hostages inside and began putting the animals into the barn.

"Make sure the horses are out of sight. Last thing we need is someone wandering by and seeing animals where they shouldn't be. Give them some fresh feed, too."

While the kidnappers were inside the stable, Louisa raced across the thirty meters of open space to the side of the barn. She peered through the crack of a shuttered window. An odor of stale manure and rotting hay wafted through the hole.

With a hood still on her head, Virginie said, "Lavatory? Outhouse?"

The British kidnapper covered his nose with his bandana and pointed at the other man. "We'll let them use that stall. One at a time."

After pulling his mask up, the Portuguese man untied Virginie's ankles and yanked off the sack. He dragged her to her feet, and she wobbled. Pointing to a big empty stall, he said, "Do it in there. You have five minutes."

"Revolting." Virginie scrunched up her face as she stepped into the stall and shut the gate.

"Me, too," Catherine said.

The girls took care of their needs, and then the kidnappers tied each of them to a support post. The men showed a small mercy. They sat the girls on the ground, and with each girl's bound hands in her lap, the bandits put the sacks back over the girls' heads. With the last one secure, the bandits removed their masks.

For the first time, Louisa had a direct view of their faces.

The well-dressed kidnapper looked familiar; then she remembered him from the dance in Porto. *He's João's manservant,* she thought, swallowing the hiss that threatened to escape her mouth.

At the dance she'd marked him as a soldier. She took the current opportunity to memorize every wrinkle and imperfection of the valet-turned-bandit-leader. He would never be considered handsome, but his manicured, curled mustache and clean-shaven cheeks added an air of regality to his weathered face. The set of his shoulders and his hard, piercing brown eyes reminded Louisa of the colonel.

She turned her attention to the second man.

Just as ugly as I expected, she thought. With sallowish brown eyes, a scruffy half-grown beard, and a never-healed broken nose set over a bloodied fat lip, the Portuguese kidnapper was a stark contrast to the British man. The former soldier acting as the devil's right hand made a formidable opponent. When it came time to make her move, her odds were better against the Portuguese kidnapper.

Standing next to the open door, the Englishman gave instructions to the other kidnapper. "We'll take turns guarding them. I've got the first watch. Take my place at midnight."

"Yes, sir." The other kidnapper marched into the darkness.

After shutting the door, the leader sat on a milk pail. He took a small book from his jacket and leaned against the wall. A lantern hung on a post above Virginie's head, and another sat beside the reading man on a second milk pail.

"Are you alright?" Eugénie whispered to Catherine.

"Be quiet, or I'll gag you," hissed the kidnapper.

The barn went silent except for the horses munching hay or slurping water. The kidnapper went back to his reading.

If you hurt them, I swear— Louisa left the thought unfinished and began inspecting the outside of the building in more detail. Five meters off the ground, on the far side, were two large shutter-like doors that opened outward. Quiet as a lizard, she climbed the wall. Using the door frame as a launch point, she hoisted herself onto the tiled roof, her feet scuffing against the wood.

She lay still for a full minute to make sure she hadn't been heard. To avoid making more noise, Louisa bear-crawled upward in slow motion to the roofline. Once there, she stood and took in the heavens. It was so much brighter there than back at Saint-Denis. An infinite number of stars sprinkled the sky while the north star flared and throbbed like the beacon it was.

Lord, give me the strength to do whatever it takes.

With a shake of her head, she set her shoulders. She'd prayed enough. God would do what he willed, and she would do what she needed. Right now, that was determining their escape route.

A decent-size glow signaled something more significant than another vineyard a little to the right of the trail. It had to be the last village the carriages had passed on the road. The trail was out of the question. Louisa didn't like their chances of crossing so many kilometers of rugged terrain at night while avoiding the bandits.

It had been about six hours since the holdup. The remaining tour participants should have found help by now. By morning, news of the kidnappings would spread to every town within riding distance. The search would begin, but how long would it take before anyone looked in this direction?

Louisa turned in a circle. Where the stars were blocked, she made out the contour of several lower ridges at the far end of the valley. The farm bookended the slight depression, and she assumed the farm's fields stretched to the low-lying ridge line at the other end. Beyond that hill, far in the distance, was another glow.

A village or a big estate?

With half the kidnappers on the trail, Louisa and her friends would go through the fields. Having decided on their initial route, Louisa backed down the roof. Reattaching herself to the wall took more effort, but soon she spidered along the stone to position herself next to the suspended doors. She poked a slender finger through the gap in the doors and lifted the latch. The latch fell, scraping against the wooden door. She stopped and listened.

After a minute of nothing unusual, she stood under the door frame and opened it enough to peer inside. In dark shadows, several hay bales lay scattered over a wooden floor that spanned half the length of the building. When she heard nothing else, she opened the door and squeezed through. Like navigating one of her uncle's obstacle courses, she moved so slowly that someone listening would attribute each floorboard creak to a barn mouse. Inside, she closed the door and put the latch back in place.

What now?

She searched the loft, looking for anything that might inspire a plan. The handle of a pitchfork standing straight up from a pile of loose hay provided the spark. After making her way to the edge of the overhang above Eugénie, she peered between two hay bales.

Nothing to do but wait.

Time passed at an excruciating pace while she watched the man read. Her wrists throbbed where the skin was raw, and her muscles ached. Louisa used the discomfort to keep herself alert. At long last, the British kidnapper checked his pocket watch, and his eyebrows furrowed. He stood up, stretched his arms wide, and said to his captives, "Don't do anything stupid."

The man left the barn door open as he headed for the farmhouse. Louisa waited until he was out of sight. She leaned around a hay bale and poked her head out past the overhang. "Psst. Gaiety. Nod your head if you're awake?"

Virginie gasped out a low surprised, *"Sapristi."*

"Shh," Eugénie hissed and bobbed her covered head twice.

"Good. I've got a plan. About an hour after the next guard comes, you need to get him to come close to you. Understand?"

Eugénie nodded.

"See you soon."

Louisa retrieved the pitchfork and ducked back into her hiding place just as she heard the crunching of the next guard's footsteps. After closing the door, the new guard yawned and slapped his cheeks. With a revolver tucked into his belt, he marched in a big circle, muttering for several minutes. Finally, he picked up a broken board and sat on the pail by the door. He took out a pocketknife and started carving.

As Louisa's eyelids drooped, Eugénie cleared her throat, and the guard looked up from the wood. "I need to go again. Lavatory."

The man frowned but stood, placing his knife and partially finished carving on the pail. A jolt of excitement rushed into Louisa's veins, and she had to calm her breathing. The plan didn't call for her to kill anyone, but she steeled herself to do just that if she had to. She squeezed hard on the pitchfork handle while the man headed toward Eugénie. As he pulled his bandana over his misshapen nose, he crossed Louisa's point of no return.

She gripped the handle with both hands and jumped to her feet. With the pitchfork above her head, she used one leg to launch herself off a hay bale toward the kidnapper. His eyes darted up and went wide as she swung. The flat side of the pitchfork struck the top of his head with a sickening crack. His eyes rolled back into his head as Louisa flew by.

Several gasps came from the hostages.

When her feet touched the ground, Louisa tumbled over her shoulder. She refused to let go of her weapon and landed wrong. Pain shot down her back.

With sheer determination, she came to her feet and spun, pitchfork extended, ready to stab the bandit. The man lay in a heap, blood oozing from his scalp.

Virginie hissed, "What happened?"

Wincing, Louisa bent next to the body and felt for a pulse. Relieved to find one, she left the pitchfork next to him and raced to the pail to grab the knife. After setting all three girls free, she pocketed the knife and retrieved the revolver from the man's belt.

Catherine pulled the sack off her head and pointed. "Is he dead?"

Louisa squatted and tied the man's hands and feet with her rope. "No. Pretty sure he'll live." When she finished, she used the kidnapper's bandana to gag him.

Catherine, her uniform stained, stood and threw her bindings aside.

After hopping to her feet, Eugénie hugged Louisa. "Merci."

"Thank me later." Louisa flashed Eugénie a rueful smile and handed her the gun. "We have a long way to go."

Catherine's cocoa face reddened and twisted with rage. She took two quick steps and kicked the unconscious man in the side. Louisa grabbed her waist and pulled her back so that the second booted toe flew over the man's chest.

"We should kill them all," Catherine seethed.

After putting herself between the kidnapper and the ordinarily reserved girl, Louisa shook Catherine's shoulders and said in a low voice, "Stop. We need to get away."

Fists clenched at her sides, Catherine flexed her jaws several times before her body relaxed, and she nodded.

Louisa smiled and looked at Virginie. "What about the name Passion?"

"Not bad. That's two possibilities." Virginie rubbed her wrists. "What now?"

"We ride two of the horses that way and free the rest." Louisa pointed toward the valley. "Help me put on the reins."

Virginie grabbed two bridles from pegs on the wall while Louisa found the two most docile animals. The last thing they needed was to get a high-spirited mount that would be unmanageable. When they were ready, Virginie led the two horses to the barn door with a tug of their reins.

Louisa said, "For this part, we want as little light as possible."

She took the lantern down from the post and worked to cover both lanterns with horse blankets, leaving just enough light to see inside the barn. One by one, they turned the other four horses out.

"If we have to run, follow me." Louisa waved everyone forward.

On Louisa's heels, Virginie pulled the two horses outside.

Louisa spun at the sound of broken glass. She raced back into the barn. Catherine held the downed kidnapper's revolver at her side. Louisa's jaw went slack as she stared at the rising flames in the hayloft. Eugénie held the unconscious man's feet and was dragging him toward the door.

"What happened?" Louisa could make no sense of what she was seeing.

Eugénie glared over her shoulder. "Don't just stand there. Help me get him out."

Louisa shoved Catherine toward the door and ran to take an ankle. The two of them jogged outside, dragging the man and leaving a trail in the dirt.

Eugénie tapped her father's medal and said in a low voice, "People will see the fire."

Not a bad idea, Louisa thought but couldn't bring herself to praise her. Instead, she chided her. "You should have told me. João's man is sure to wake up now. We must go."

Her friend shrugged and redoubled her efforts. Ten meters beyond the door, Eugénie let go of the unconscious man and took hold of Louisa's arm. "Which way?"

Smoke rose to the rafters and started to billow outside. The closest horse whinnied and stomped its foot. Louisa dropped the man's leg and ran toward the agitated animal. She slapped its flank hard, and the horse reared up and galloped toward the mountain trail. The other untethered horses ran after it.

Louisa snatched Eugénie's hand and then Catherine's, half-dragging them to where Virginie waited. The others mounted while Louisa used her foot to scrape away their footprints. Taking Catherine's proffered hand, she got on the horse in front and took hold of the reins. Louisa looked around Catherine, who sat behind her. A light flickered in the house, spurring her on. She clucked, nudging the horse with both heels. They moved down a row of grapevines with Virginie and Eugénie behind them.

Chapter 27
Running Blind

As soon as they were halfway across the valley, Louisa hopped down and took her horse by the reins. Without moonlight, traversing the fields became an almost unnavigable maze of grapevines and small orchards. Maybe bringing the horses was a mistake. No. With no footprints near the barn, until sunrise the two pursuers would have trouble determining which way the girls ran. If they found the hoofprints, the girls would have to split up. Did she choose the wrong direction?

Second-guessing would not get them farther away from the kidnappers, so Louisa stared at the shadowed ground before her. If she twisted an ankle, that could spell doom as much as her other decisions. The goal was to get as far away as possible before daylight. They had three, maybe four hours of darkness left. She checked the way they had come. Smoke from the barn wafted into a glowing sky, proving that the fire still burned.

Louisa topped the rise and came to a stop. "What?"

The glow from the town that was their destination had disappeared. It made sense. People didn't usually keep lanterns lit in the middle of the night.

"What's wrong?" Eugénie asked from the back of the second horse.

"From the roof of the barn, I saw lights from a large farm or village." She shook her head. "The lights are gone."

"Do you know the general direction?"

"Yes, but with all these hills, it will be easy to get turned around."

The almost imperceptible reflection of a star sparked off Virginie's spectacles. "Look at the next hill. Pick some distinguishing features near where we need to go. Keep your eye on that. When we get there, pick the next destination."

"Good idea." Louisa selected her focal point on a rise, about a kilometer away. The slight slope leading in that direction disappeared into blackness. It did not look inviting.

The sharp pop, pop, pop of gunfire reached them, and everyone turned toward the distant glow.

Not good.

"Maybe it's the police," Virginie offered, her voice full of hope.

"Too soon. They couldn't have gotten there that fast," Eugénie replied.

Worried, Catherine said, "What if it was some nearby farmers?"

Eugénie put her hand in front of her mouth. "*Mon dieu, non.*"

Louisa shook her head. "It's not a farmer, Gaiety. It's João's man covering his tracks. We have to hurry."

Louisa turned back to the downward slope and its nightmarish depths.

Just like Dante.

The mare resisted until she rubbed the horse's nose. "It's all right, girl. We need your help."

After another hard tug, the horse followed. The temperature dropped during the descent. The chill air reminded Louisa that despite her goosebumps, she should be grateful for such nice weather. Rain would have made this slope a slippery slide. With each step, the darkness became more oppressive until she could see no more than a meter in front of her.

As the incline leveled out, the gurgle of a stream grew. Louisa checked her destination on the hill and shivered. At least, the barn had been warm. A yawn snuck up on her, and she felt a terrible weariness that sunk past her aching muscles to her bones. Sleep called out to her.

Instead, Louisa put one heavy step in front of the other. Her foot snagged on a root, and she stumbled. She put her free hand out to catch herself and scraped her palm on the bark of an inky black trunk.

Louisa stood up. "Everyone, come down."

She turned around, unable to see beyond the faint outline of Catherine atop her mare, but she heard her friends' feet as they hit the ground.

Virginie's voice floated toward her. "It's too dark. We need to stop."

Louisa would have agreed if not for the clock ticking in her head. They were running out of time. The ex-soldier would be methodical in his search.

From the blackness came Eugénie's stern words: "You heard the gunfire. We keep going. We are the daughters of not just French soldiers but heroes. We must be courageous."

Without seeing it, Louisa knew that Eugénie double-tapped the medal on her chest.

Louisa sought Catherine's hand and passed her the reins. "Stay close enough to see the person or horse in front of you. If you can't, speak up, and we'll reconnect."

With both hands stretched out in front, Louisa snaked around the tree and groped her way forward. Lush plants with fern-like-leaves blocked the path ahead, and Louisa had to backtrack several times. At one point, Virginie squealed as an animal scurried through the underbrush nearby. Another time, Catherine yelped when a low branch struck her in the face.

It took an hour of detours and regroupings to reach the stream. By then, Louisa was using a long branch to prod the way forward. At the stream, she pushed the stick into the creek bottom and was grateful. The water was only ankle-deep.

"Be careful with the rocks. Secure each step before taking the next." Louisa reached back. "Catherine, take my hand. Gaiety, hold the horse's tail."

Chained together, they forded the stream and continued out of the woods on the other side. When they reached the slope to the ridge, it was much steeper than the way down. Louisa zigzagged up the hill to give the horses better footing. While going back and forth, she questioned again whether they should have left the animals.

At the top, she found some hope. Stretched out in front of them was a gradual slope that turned into flatlands. Few features were visible from so high, but they might be able to ride again.

We're exhausted. Time to rest, but not up here. They needed to get to the bottom of the hill. Silhouettes stood out even against a dark sky—one of the first lessons a thief learned.

Looking behind her, against the backdrop of stars, Louisa discerned the outline of the ridge. With no glow, the barn was now just a bad memory. She was determined to make it stay that way. "Let's get to the bottom and take a rest."

Unlike the harsh climb up, they strolled down the easy incline. When the girls reached level ground, rocky dirt transitioned into a field of high grass. Visibility once again stretched to ten meters.

Louisa found the current patch of grass to be as good as any. "Let's rest for twenty minutes."

Virginie sank to the ground and lay down. "Yes."

Everyone else sat without comment. To find a little warmth, Louisa pulled her knees into her chest, too tired to speak. Gentle snores came from Virginie's direction. Louisa envied her, but she was too afraid to close her eyes, or she might sleep for hours.

When Louisa's agitation at not moving became unbearable, she roused her friends. With a few groans and sighs, the girls climbed on the horses. Worried that the grass might hide small holes or rocks, Louisa kept the mare to a slow walk. At least, they were conserving their energy.

Catherine sniffed twice. "Do you smell that?"

Louisa took a deep breath through her nose. The fresh, fruity, sour scent of strawberries on the vine made her mouth water.

"It smells delicious. I'm so hungry," Virginie whined.

It didn't take long before they came to a low stone fence that marked the beginning of a field. Louisa's heart soared. Fields meant people. They walked the wall for a while before finding a partly tumbled section. As the girls dismounted, the night lightened, and the stars faded into the predawn gray. By the time they coaxed the horses over the broken wall, the sun had stacked the stratosphere into a layer of orange yellows under a spectrum of blues.

Mounded rows topped by strawberry plants filled the field. Ripened fruit hung off the sides of the mounds.

Louisa plucked a handful of the walnut-size fruits as she walked down a row. The first bite sent a ripple of pleasure through her weary body. With desperate urgency, she stuffed two at a time into her mouth, closing her eyes to savor the taste. She didn't even pause to wipe the juice that ran down her chin.

Between chews, she heard, "Mmm," "So good," and "I'm in heaven" from her friends.

When Louisa opened her eyes, she saw several messy, blissful faces with cheeks stuffed to bursting. Regretfully, she swallowed one last bite and tossed the hull of the strawberry away.

"That's the best part." Eugénie scowled at her.

Louisa frowned at her food-obsessed friend. "I'll be sure to save mine for you." She grabbed the mare's mane and jumped, swinging her leg over its back. She stared at her friend. "We need to go."

This time, she didn't slow down. With ever better visibility, they trotted down the green rows spotted with red. When they reached the end of the long field, Louisa could see a small dirt road stretching away. The path led toward smoke trails rising from behind a copse of trees.

They walked the fence line and headed toward the exit closest to the road.

A stone only centimeters in front of Louisa's horse exploded. The bang reached her as the mare stepped sideways, braying in fear. Catherine screamed and clamped onto Louisa's stomach while Louisa kept a death grip on a fistful of mane. She fought to keep Catherine and herself on the animal.

Another bullet whistled by.

Louisa yanked the bridle, twisting the horse's head toward the exit. Catherine moved closer, shoving Louisa forward, almost on the mare's neck.

Louisa bowed her back to find room and yelled, "Yah!"

She slammed her heels into the horse's side, grateful she'd spent one summer break riding every day with Eugénie at her aunt's estate outside Paris. Her friend hadn't even gotten a kiss out of the handsome stable boy, but at least Louisa had learned how to handle herself on a horse. The mare took off at a gallop, and Louisa leaned low. More hoofbeats told her that Eugénie was following. They raced toward the exit in the corner of the field. Another shot rang out.

Catherine yelled into her ear, "It's the kidnapper! He's on foot!"

That didn't matter to Louisa. The exit was to the left, and they were going too fast to turn. She kicked the horse again. The mare snorted and picked up her pace.

"You're not going to—" Catherine's worried voice trailed away as she hugged Louisa's waist tighter.

Fly, horse.

The mare's pace stuttered at the last moment as she hurdled the meter-high wall.

Another bullet zipped through the air. Louisa focused on the landing. She jerked the reins hard to the left, and the mare galloped onto the road. Only then did Louisa peek around Catherine to see Eugénie and Virginie's horse jump. She watched until she was sure they were following and urged her poor brave mount to go faster.

They dashed around a curve in the road, putting the stand of trees between them and the strawberry field. A few kilometers ahead sat a cluster of white-plastered buildings with red-tiled roofs.

Elation replaced the fear fueling Louisa's flight.

A chapel bell tolled, calling its parish to morning Mass and the Clan of the Dissipated to salvation.

Chapter 28

Austerlitz

Propped up in his bed, the colonel rubbed the elbow of his injured arm while he appraised the four students with one good eye. Swollen shut, the other eye had the color and shape of an overripe plum. "Tell me everything."

Eugénie curtsied. "Colonel, it was that Lopes Gomes man, again. He sent the kidnappers after us."

"Are you sure?" Mère de la Nativité tilted her head from where she stood on the opposite side of the colonel's narrow bed.

The colonel held up his hand. "Did you see him?"

Eugénie lowered her head while touching the medal on her chest.

"We heard them say Gomes." Catherine's soft voice filled the sullen silence that had descended on them.

The colonel chuckled. "Is that all?" He glanced at each of them.

Several girls nodded, and he shook his head. "Do you know how many men in Portugal have the name Gomes?"

"There were four kidnappers, and the leader was a British man. A soldier. He was at the dance in Porto with Gomes." Louisa scanned the colonel's face for his reaction.

Inscrutable, the colonel said, "You're probably correct, but there is not much we can do. Word came from the Municipal Guard around noon. Their men arrived at a farm where the barn had been set ablaze. They found three men dead. I assume they were some of the kidnappers. There was no sign of a fourth."

Catherine hissed, "They deserved it."

Louisa shook her head and thought *Fury* could be the shy girl's nickname. Of course, thoughts of revenge, no matter how sweet they might be, couldn't shake Louisa's feeling of impending doom.

She had kicked a den of vipers.

Virginie grabbed Eugénie's arm, leaned in, and whispered, "Good job with the barn."

Eugénie pulled her shoulders back and had the same smug look she wore after every academic battle she'd won.

Louisa chewed on the inside of her lower lip. *João's a crazy devil, and his man is a cold-blooded killer. Neither will hesitate to hurt my friends. We need to leave.*

Hope seeped into Louisa's voice. "Are we going home?"

"Brigadier Gerard insists that we continue. He has business in Coimbra and Lisbon."

I can't believe General Buffoon can even think straight after that blow to the head, Louisa thought before saying, "He won't stop."

The colonel cut her off. "Also, we are in the middle of nowhere. It would take us days to reach Lisbon, and our ship doesn't leave for ten days. Since we are stuck here, and the social events are already scheduled, I've decided, along with Ana, to continue the tour." He smiled at the nun, who frowned at him, wiping away the colonel's grin. The man turned back to them with a perplexed look.

Louisa ignored the colonel's gaff at the familiar use of the nun's first name. "That means whoever is behind the kidnappers will know where we're going. We'll be in danger the entire time."

The colonel nodded. "I share your concerns. That's why I'm hiring three armed guards tomorrow. Also, Ana—" Understanding flashed in his eyes. "I mean, Mère de la Nativité has called for help from some friends in the church." He smiled. "I'm just happy you are safe. I'm amazed at your resourcefulness, but you are fortunate to be here."

Virginie shook her head. "It wasn't luck. Dar–– I mean, Louisa saved us."

"We *were* lucky. They underestimated us." Louisa sighed. "They won't do it again."

The colonel locked eyes with Louisa. "Now that I know my enemy's purpose, I won't underestimate the threat again either." He grimaced.

Mère de la Nativité touched the colonel's good shoulder. "The colonel needs to rest. There will be a social event tomorrow night, but I do not expect any of you to attend unless you wish to. I'm sure you are all exhausted." She shooed them out of the room with a wave and turned back to the colonel. "I'll gather your laundry and take it with me."

Bone-weary, Louisa couldn't wait to fall into bed. The nun's voice trailed off as she shuffled after her friends into the hallway.

After the girls had found sanctuary in the small mountain village of Tourigo, they spent five torturous hours in the back of a kind farmer's wagon before reaching the university. The rest of the tour had arrived in Coimbra the previous day.

Louisa had started to follow Virginie when she felt a tap on her shoulder. She turned to find Gabrielle standing with her hands on her hips.

Beautiful, long golden curls flowed over the mean girl's shoulders, making a strange contrast to the ugly expression she gave Louisa. "Hello, Greek Bastard. You're back." She sniffed. "I was so *not* worried about you and your pack of peasants. I kept praying, but somehow, you still made it back."

Louisa couldn't even roll her eyes. "I'm too tired for this right now. Why don't you insult me tomorrow?"

Gabrielle's eyebrow shot up. "We aren't leaving?"

"No. The tour continues."

"Good, I told Julie and Joséphine that the robbery was just bad luck. I'm glad the colonel agrees."

"It was João. He sent men after us."

Gabrielle laughed. "I doubt that." Sarcasm oozed from her voice. "Did he want revenge after that ruffian, Simon, tried to kill him? Or was he angry because you gave him a disease?"

A small reserve of energy sprang up with Louisa's rage. She glanced behind her and then past Gabrielle. They were alone in the hallway. She needed to be fast because what she was about to do was certain to be heard in the colonel's room.

Louisa thrust her right hand past Gabrielle's head and grasped a fistful of golden locks. Gabrielle yelped as Louisa yanked her head down to eye level and hissed, "Listen, witch, that bastard tried to rape me." Gabrielle's eyes went wide. "To stop him, I had to hurt him. Badly. Ever since, he's been trying to capture me to do God knows what."

Gabrielle pulled her head back, but Louisa gripped tighter, pulling the blonde forward until their noses touched. "I don't like you or the lackeys with you, but since we're sisters of the Lègion, I owe you this: Gomes is pure evil. He won't hesitate to hurt you or anyone who gets in his way. Understand?"

Gabrielle gulped and nodded.

"Good." Louisa smiled. "One last thing, if you or any of your bootlickers call me a whore one more time, I don't care if I get kicked out. I'll hurt you so bad you'll never forget it."

Gabrielle's eyes radiated fear.

The colonel's doorknob creaked. Louisa threw Gabrielle's head backward and let go. She spun and marched toward her room with Gabrielle sputtering behind her. When she entered, the other girls were waiting. Louisa closed the door, leaned back, and sighed. "You won't believe what just happened."

"Tell us later. We've come to a decision." With her mischievous grin on full display, Virginie glanced at Eugénie, who nodded.

"We're tired of letting the enemy dictate the terms of battle." Eugenie clasped her hands behind her back, assuming her battlefield commander pose.

Her curiosity piqued, Louisa leaned forward. "What do you have in mind?"

"Do you remember how Napoleon won at Austerlitz?"

Louisa grinned. "A trap."

General Eugénie nodded. "It's time for the clan to go hunting."

Chapter 29

The Making of a Blueprint

Louisa woke to the sound of whispering voices. Every instinct she had told to keep her eyes shut and return to her dreams. As the mumbling continued in the background, she recalled last night.

Before the battle planning had commenced, the girls had agreed to rest. They took turns on watch while the others slept. Until there were armed guards, the group decided it would be safer to stay together in a room made for two rather than split up.

Catherine, who had shared the small bed with Louisa, had cuddled too close, so Louisa found herself on her side with her back against the wall.

The whispers became clearer.

"Your idea relies too much on Daring." Virginie's voice was quiet but insistent.

"Can't be helped. Before we initiate the plan, we must locate all possible opponents."

Louisa blinked a few times and pushed her aching body upright. "Just tell me what I need to do."

"How do you feel?" Catherine handed her a glass of water and a plate with two pieces of toast slathered with an unknown type of marmalade.

Louisa took two big gulps of water. "I feel like I was tied up and strapped to a horse for a whole day." Her nose wrinkled at the sour, quince-flavored marmalade as she bit into the toast. Sweetness soothed away that first burst of bitterness, and her stomach grumbled. The girls giggled.

With her body craving sustenance, she took another big bite. "Mmm-mmm."

"Do you think you are up to some climbing tonight?" Eugénie asked.

Still chewing, Louisa mumbled, "Am I still alive? Does rain make you wet?"

Eugénie smirked at Virginie. "I told you, Palisse would have said the same."

After Louisa finished eating, Catherine handed her a small glass jar. A whiff of cedar and rosemary wafted up to Louisa as she scooped up a glob of a thick, white substance with her finger. She rubbed the poultice into her angry-red, raw wrists. The stinging eased to a manageable burn. The parish priest in Tourigo had given her the jar of salve. He promised that if she used it daily for the next week, any scarring would be minimal.

Still hungry, Louisa wanted to hear the scheme but desired lunch more. No. *Food can wait for a few minutes.* She swung her legs over the side of the bed. "Let's hear it, Gaiety."

Eugénie placed her drawing pad in her lap as Virginie and Catherine closed the circle. The drawing had outlines of the university's campus drawn to scale. The university's extensive commons lay in the middle of the rectangle of buildings.

"Someone's been busy," Louisa quipped.

Catherine nodded. "I kept watch while Virginie and Eugénie scouted the campus."

"Right." Eugénie poked at a small X on the map. "Our room is here." She slid her finger from their room to a square drawn in the corner of the plaza. "The tower has the best view of the square, and we know that the university's chancellor assured the colonel that they would monitor the guests coming to the dance. The only entrance that will be open tonight is here." She tapped what appeared to be a door drawn between buildings. "The Iron Gate. And everyone will need to enter the ball through the main stairs. They are holding the dance in an old throne room."

"But aren't there other entrances into the campus?" Louisa waved around the drawing. "João or his English bulldog will probably come well before the dance."

"We're counting on it. The real risk we're taking is assuming the enemy will hold off their attack until the dance starts. They have the same problem we do. They don't know where we are."

"I think I understand. We throw out bait to discover where the scouts are watching us from. And I'm the bait." Louisa's stomach rumbled again. "I want to know every detail, but tell me the rest over lunch."

Chapter 30
Light Reading for Bait

Louisa stepped into the college commons, leaving the safety of their quarters. She hated being so exposed, but for their plan to work, she needed João or his man to see her and slip up. From experience, Louisa knew how hard it was to watch someone on the move and to stay still. It was up to her or Virginie from her lookout post to catch the spotter when he flinched.

"I'm glad you demoiselles are feeling better. You wouldn't want to miss this," Mère de la Nativité said over her shoulder. Eugénie, Catherine, and Louisa trailed behind her as they crossed the open plaza. The nun led them toward a building styled like a Greek temple. The arched entrance had a pair of massive wooden doors sitting between four columns. A giant, gray, artificial stone molding of a crown and the Portuguese coat of arms sat atop the arch.

The vista at the end of the plaza encompassed the hill on which the school stood. The small city of Coimbra spread to the winding river below. The view on this sunny morning stretched for miles beyond. Louisa found it quite enchanting until a tingle of danger ran down her spine.

She stood exposed in the open, and the hairs on her neck stood on end. Someone was watching. Without being too obvious, she scanned the nearby windows. When they had first walked outside, she'd admonished the other two girls to look straight ahead. Untrained in stealthy observation, they would have given away their purpose with their furtive glances and shifty eyes.

She or Virginie would root out the enemy scouts. Armed with a small pair of opera glasses, Virginie kept watch from the bell tower.

In her peripheral vision, Louisa observed each young man hustling from class to class. No female scholars were allowed in the school. The world was changing too slowly for the free-spirited Louisa, but she returned to inspecting the closest student. If she hadn't spent years training, she could not have memorized the young men's faces or picked up the minor differences in each student's uniform with such ease.

Like the black dress and the white sash that marked her as a student of Saint-Denis, these Portuguese university students wore their version of a school uniform. A three-piece black suit and a long black cloak flowing behind each scholar gave him an air of grandeur.

Louisa approved of the fashion style for studying, but she thought the cloaks were too impractical for the other kind of work she liked.

Bless you. Louisa thanked whoever first chose a simple colored sash as the mark of distinction for the Saint-Denis uniform.

As they took the short stairs, an older gentleman wearing a similar scholar's cloak opened a smaller door cut into one of the giant double doors. He waved them through with Mère de la Nativité in the lead. Before Louisa stepped through the portal, she glanced at the tower and made out a white sash flapping from a tower window. Virginie had located one of the spies.

Excitement that the plan had worked sent Louisa's mind racing. *Wonder if it's insane João or his attack dog?*

Inside, Louisa took a moment for her eyes to adjust. Another elderly gentle-man spoke with the nun in Portuguese. He guarded another massive set of oaken doors decorated by egg-size studs of brass knots. The man's cloak had a coat of arms embroidered over the breast. She hadn't noticed it on the first man, probably because of how the cloak fell.

The nun laughed at whatever the man had said. Still chuckling, he turned and walked to a stairwell to the side.

Mère de la Nativité followed him and said over her shoulder, "Originally, the library was the academic prison. Our guide, Mateus, wants us to see the lower levels of the library that still has jail cells."

Academic prison? Louisa wanted to ask, but the guide disappeared down the steps. They exited the stairs at the second landing. The man "shushed" them as he opened a wide door. They crossed the threshold from the stone landing onto cherry-red wood floors that stretched the length of a long, broad room with a vaulted brick ceiling. The air in the library was warm and dry.

Good for the books, I guess.

Shelves of books lined the walls, while several narrow tables occupied the center of the room. Crowded around the tables, cloaked students and older gentlemen researchers bent over opened volumes, scribbled on note pads, or whispered with colleagues in hushed tones.

The guide led them around the room, allowing the girls to browse.

Most of the titles Louisa noticed were published in the nineteenth century, but she found a few older works from the eighteenth century. The majority were in Portuguese, but there were plenty in Latin. Louisa even found a French copy of mathematician Pierre-Simon Laplace's five-volume work, *Traité de Mécanique Céleste.*

Eugénie whispered, "You do math now?"

Grinning, Louisa whispered, "You know me better than that. I mainly count francs, pounds, and réis. Sometimes, I even do fractions."

She replaced Volume One on the shelf and turned to find the guide waving them back to the door. The group followed him down the stairwell, which narrowed at the next landing and began to corkscrew down. Lanterns lit their descent in alternating patches of yellow and gray.

Louisa chuckled to herself as she imagined Mère de la Nativité pointing toward the darkened stairway and shrieking, *To the dungeon with you!*

The air grew colder and damper the lower they went. Drops of condensation had caused sections of the white-washed walls to peel, leaving behind layers of gray. At the bottom, the group crowded into a square room with the same vaulted ceilings as before, but sizable red bricks instead of warm wood covered the floor.

The guide spoke, and the nun translated. "Many of the university's buildings date from the Islamic era, and the Royal Palace building served as the first capital of Portugal when Afonso forged a separate kingdom. The academic prison was built when the university transferred from Lisbon to Coimbra in the fifteen hundreds while the library, which we will see right after this, was built in the early seventeen hundreds."

Catherine raised a hand. "Ma Mère, what is an academic prison?"

"Great question, Catherine. Many early universities policed themselves and even had their own courts. Students accused or convicted of crimes by the academic court were imprisoned here. That way, the scholars were not imprisoned with common criminals." The nun turned to the guide and had a quick discussion.

"Mateus says that they abolished academic courts and prisons in 1834."

Catherine nodded to the guide and smiled. "Very interesting. Merci."

A large door took up the middle of the closest wall, and two hallways branched away on the other side of the room. The guide gestured toward the one on the right. The low doorway would have made the colonel duck, but Louisa breezed under it into an even narrower walkway lined with three cells, their menacing doors constructed of hatched wrought iron.

Inside a tiny cell, a raised stone platform had probably served as both a seat and a bed. Louisa stepped into the cramped space and shuddered. She spread her arms wide, fingers touching the walls. She hugged herself, trying to warm up while she dispelled thoughts that had once been the scariest nightmare she could imagine.

Never, ever get caught.

The last room she peeked into made her nose wrinkle. It had two small holes cut into another seat of raised concrete. The ancient prison's toilet was cold and unappealing. Her creeping, oppressive feeling grew until Louisa hurried to the larger room.

Thankfully, the guide led them through the big door on the other side. They exited the prison into an outdoor space with a series of staircases shaped like a sunken amphitheater. The steps of the fifth level were broad at the top and narrowed toward the bottom. Near the top, two standard staircases ascended to the plaza level.

Eugénie grabbed Louisa's and Catherine's arms, pulling them close. "This is it. We confront him here."

Louisa gazed around. It was private, and during the dance, it should be empty. "I agree."

"Demoiselles?" Mère de la Nativité, her head tilted, called from the next level up.

The three of them took the steps two at a time to catch up. They walked back to the plaza and then reentered the building through the columned entrance. The first gentlemen nodded as the group passed back into the foyer.

Across the entrance hall, their guide leaned his shoulder into the small door that was inset in a massive one. The door creaked, and glints of gold flashed against black lacquered wood. The man stepped over the threshold and welcomed them to follow with an outstretched arm.

As Louisa stepped inside, the smell of old books and something foreign washed over her. She moved beside the others and took in the most impressive library she'd ever seen.

"This library is considered the best in Europe. They have more than fifty thousand volumes, most dating back to the fifteenth and sixteenth centuries," Mère de la Nativité translated for the older man.

Through high windows, the sun cast angled columns of light onto the marble floor. Three bookshelf-lined alcoves stood before them. Granite arches, each topped by a golden coat of arms, separated the rooms. At the end, a giant portrait of a man in seventeenth-century garb marked the end of the library.

To the left and right of Louisa, thousands of books packed the gold-in-laid black shelves that stretched from floor to ceiling. A walkway with a black-and-gold banister traversed around the first floor to give access to the higher shelves. Tapered columns stretched down, holding up the balcony.

A narrow ladder led upward, enabling people to reach the top two shelves. A fancy carved design topped the bookshelves underneath the ceiling frescoed with an artist's vision of heaven.

The guide walked backward, gesturing as he spoke.

"Built by King John V in the early eighteenth century, the library has been a destination for serious scholars for centuries." Mère de la Nativité continued sharing details.

The bookshelves of the second and third chambers were brown and inlaid with golden designs. In the library's last section, a massive table sat to one side, surrounded by upholstered chairs.

The nun asked the man a question, and he gave a lengthy reply while pointing to some shelves on the second floor. "I had heard that the library had an original copy of Cristine de Pizan's *The Book of the City of Ladies*. He said they had one of the early vellum versions and two of the first-ever printings of the book from later in the fifteenth century."

"That's incredible. The Mazarine only has two copies. And I'm sure the printed one isn't a first edition," Catherine twittered in her low voice.

Louisa thought, *That doesn't seem right*, as her brows knitted together in dismay.

For centuries, French women had admired the author's feminist writings defending the more exceptional sex. Louisa found it odd that the national library in Paris would have fewer copies than some library in the middle of Portugal. She also knew that Virginie was an ardent admirer of the author. Louisa needed to bring her friend back to see Cristine de Pizan's works. "Ma Mère, can you ask him if we can see one of those books?"

The nun and their guide had a quick exchange. "I'm afraid not. He says anyone who wishes to read any of these books must write to the head librarian with the reasons and obtain approval."

We'll see about that. Louisa shook her head, reminding herself to focus on the more significant issue. *All right, after we deal with that other matter.*

The tour ended soon after that. Louisa shaded her eyes as they stepped back into the plaza. She surreptitiously scanned the windows lining the campus commons for the spy. Unsuccessful, Louisa whispered in Eugénie's ear, "You see the marker?"

Eugénie nodded, and Louisa said, "I don't know where the watcher is. Go talk to Virginie."

Together, they hurried after Mère de la Nativité and Catherine, who were halfway to the building housing their living quarters.

As the nun reached the entrance, Eugénie asked, "Ma Mère, Catherine and I would like to see the view from the bell tower. Is that all right?"

The nun looked to Louisa. "What about you, Mademoiselle Sophia?"

"All those stairs don't appeal to me. I think I'll take a nap."

"Understandable. Mademoiselle Savant, stay together." Mère de la Nativité turned and entered the building.

Louisa followed the nun as her friends went to do their part in the next act of this play. At the second-floor landing, Louisa excused herself, went to their room, and headed straight to the window.

She threw open the curtains and stood looking into the plaza. She stayed that way for a full minute. More than enough time to make sure the enemy scout could locate her. As she moved her hand to the drape, another curtain fluttered in a first-floor window across the square.

"Got you." She closed the drape.

Chapter 31

Wellington Well Cooked

Louisa's thoughts were a cauldron of emotions. She sat cross-legged on her narrow bed with her eyes closed and her back against the wall. By habit, she had her hands in her lap, fidgeting and going through her lock-picking sequences by rote. She clenched her fists, stilling her fingers, and opened her eyes.

Controlling fear was a skill that few people innately possessed. Louisa's uncle destroyed her fight-or-flight reflex and molded a level of fearlessness into her, one scare at a time, until the unexpected became expected. Before most of Louisa's capers, she had to calm her excitement, but today was very different.

As what she hoped would be the final confrontation with João came closer, she felt only trepidation. The thought of him caused a slight tremble to seize her leg, reminding her of the damage that devil had wrought to her once un-shakable–– What should she call it exactly? Courage? Tenacity? Confidence? Whatever it was, she needed it now. She closed her eyes and meditated on the hurt and humiliation he'd caused. Slowly, the pain forged the dread in her gut into a white-hot flame of pure hate-fueled rage.

"It's time." General Eugénie clapped her hands.

Louisa's eyes popped open. She was ready to fight. Everyone stood, and Louisa took the measure of her comrades.

Shoulders squared, Eugénie wore an expression of confident resolve.

Catherine's beautiful chestnut skin had taken on a milky pallor.

Virginie quirked a smile, but her shaky voice betrayed her apprehension. "Before we start, we have some clan business to attend to." Virginie held a hand to either side and, when the four girls clasped hands, she said, "Catherine, the three of us would like to officially invite you to join the Clan of the Dissipated. What say you?"

The songbird's voice cracked. "Really?"

Louisa squeezed her hand. "If you'll have us."

Tears dropped to Catherine's cheeks. "I would be honored. Yes." She giggle-cried. "What now?"

"We bestow on you a clan name," Virginie said.

"After much debate, we have come to a consensus." Eugénie laughed. "From now on, you shall be known as Rapture."

"Rapture?" Catherine asked in a reverent voice.

Louisa replied, "It's what we felt when you sang."

Catherine smiled, the color returning to her face.

"Right. A battle approaches. Let us pray." Eugénie bowed her head, and everyone did the same. "Almighty and benevolent Father, bless us in this righteous endeavor, '*And in Your loving kindness, cut off our enemies, and destroy all those who afflict our souls, for we are Your servants.*' Amen."

"Amen," the others repeated.

The circle broke, and Catherine took turns hugging each of them.

Eugénie got them organized. "Attention. Status report."

The girls moved into a line before the general, and Virginie stepped forward. "Wellington"––the label Eugénie applied to the ex-British soldier who had kidnapped them––"is still in his location. No sign of the hunting dog's master."

"The barricade and prop?"

"In place and prepared to be deployed." Virginie beamed a mischievous smile and grabbed a wine bottle lying on the bed. She held it up, along with a corkscrew. "Prop ready."

Eugénie focused on Catherine. "Rapture, status report on our allies."

When the newly hired armed guards arrived a few hours before sunset, the Clan of the Dissipated devised slight alterations to the order of battle, giving Catherine more responsibilities.

Virginie returned to the line, and Catherine stepped forward. "One of the guards will be at the dance with the colonel. The other two are posted in the hall outside. I know what to do."

"And the brigadier?" General Eugénie inquired.

"Wouldn't call him an ally," Louisa grumbled, drawing a frown from her general.

"In the city, having dinner with business associates," Catherine tweeted.

Eugénie nodded and turned even more severe. "Weapon inspection."

The girls scrambled around the small room and soon returned to the line, holding their weapon of choice in front of them. Louisa placed the meat cleaver she had sneaked from Ferreirinha's vineyard at parade rest on her shoulder. Catherine and Virginie showed a matching pair of long brass candlesticks. Eugénie gave a satisfied nod and turned to the armoire. She dug in the back for several seconds and brought forth a long, thin rapier.

Virginie exclaimed, "Gaiety! Where did you get that?"

Catherine's eyes went wide. "Do you know how to use it?"

Eugénie swung the sword back and forth over an empty bed before she lunged. The point of the blade gouged loose a chunk of wood from the round finial atop the bedpost. The shrapnel hit the wall with a thud.

"Whoa." Catherine sounded impressed.

Eugénie saluted her mortally wounded opponent with a swish of her sword. "There are some antique pieces on display near the dining room. It wasn't hard for one to walk away and . . ." She turned to Catherine with a grin. "My father began teaching me to fence as soon as I could walk. Joy was almost as good as me. We practiced weekly to keep sharp together."

Now wasn't the time to contradict Eugénie, but from Louisa's recollection of her friends' many skirmishes fought with wooden swords, Marie had gotten the better of Eugénie more than half the time.

Joy, I wish you were here.

"Time to expose our flank. Godspeed, I love you all." General Eugénie dismissed the troops.

Now came the great deception. Both Louisa and Virginie wore their school uniforms and had styled their hair into identical buns. To hide her face, Virginie would wear a hood and keep her spectacles off until she reached the ambush point.

Eugénie donned her long formal cloak to cover her ball gown. Virginie did the same, and both young women hid their weapons while Virginie also tucked the bottle of wine under the folds of her cloak.

Eugénie reached toward her chest but found the silk empty. She frowned and her eyebrows went up. "Ah," she said and reached into the pocket of her cloak. She pulled out the red-white-and-blue ribbon, then pressed her father's medal to her lips. "Okay, Daring, bait the hook."

Louisa moved to the window and drew aside the curtains. She opened the windowpanes and sat on the windowsill, pretending to take in the night air. For three minutes she made herself seen, nervous as she weighed their plan's risks.

"I think that's enough. Daring and Rapture, we'll see you at the rally point." Eugénie motioned them into the hallway.

Everyone stepped into the hall and hugged again. Virginie and Eugénie raised their hoods and descended the stairs while Catherine went to the bedroom next to Louisa's. The newest clan member's first task was to announce the enemy's movements. Louisa nodded to the guard as she closed the door. She moved to stand in front of the draped window, counting aimlessly to occupy her mind. The enemy scout would see only her silhouette.

The next part of the plan scared Louisa the most, not because of the danger to herself but to her friends. So much could go wrong, and the timing had to be perfect. What if he didn't show up? If he didn't, she hoped their plan would at least take Wellington, João's queen, off the chess board.

Virginie and Eugénie were walking across the darkened plaza toward the building where the dance was held. Louisa shut down the urge to peek around the curtain at the British man's hiding spot to confirm that he was watching them. She had to trust that he was now uncertain of her exact location.

Distant voices, raised with excitement, identified small groups of partygoers trickling into the plaza from the Iron Gate. Her friends would join the growing throng that entered the party.

When Louisa reached three hundred, she moved away from the window and started another count. She wrapped the cleaver with cloth and placed it in the small haversack strapped across her chest. After patting her pocket to ensure the room key remained there, she tied her uniform into pantaloons and tucked her white collar under the black neckline to hide it.

After counting to fifty, she used pillows to form a human-like figure lying on the bed under the duvet. At one hundred, she twisted the key-shaped knob of the burner on the kerosine lantern. The room went dark. She moved to the side of the window and lowered a long board to the wooden floor in front of the window. Anyone trying to open the window was in for a surprise.

Fifty long nails, some of them rusty, were hammered through wood. The sharp ends now pointed to the ceiling. Eugenie had painted the wood and iron black, making the trap blend into the flooring despite a bit of moonlight filtering through the window.

Hope it hurts like hell, Louisa thought before going still.

A thief's life, if the thief wanted it to be a long life, required patience. Louisa had spent hundreds of hours as a shadow, waiting. To become an indistinct blot in the night required a person to empty herself of everything except a single-minded focus on the possible triggers—the small number of events that could morph a person from an ethereal inky mist back into flesh and blood.

Louisa gave up trying to reach that state of meditative nothingness while she waited. She feared she'd be overcome by paralyzing terror if she let go of her rage as the process required. For her friends' sake, she could not take that risk. While flattened against the wall, she allowed her hatred to seethe, unbridled. Her visions of what she would do to her tormentor became more dark and frightening as time crept on. Ten minutes, twenty minutes. Her count continued. It was time.

Five knocks. Virginie and Eugénie were approaching.

Eugénie's loud exclamation carried through the window. "Where did you get that?"

Louisa resisted the temptation to peek beyond the curtain. She had seen the two young women rehearse the play inside the room at least twenty times. They had repeated the performance until Louisa and Catherine judged it to appear natural. Marie could have gotten it right in two, maybe three tries. The absence of the clan's best actress and most cheerful, optimistic personality again tugged at Louisa as she imagined Virginie holding up the bottle of wine and the corkscrew in one hand.

"Keep it down," Virginie hissed much louder than someone who should be trying to be quiet. "I snuck into the kitchen while you were dancing with the clumsy fellow." She'd be waving the bottle around to make sure her uniformed arms were visible.

Louisa wondered what the spy must be thinking as he tried to guess her true location in their shell game. Was she out there on the square with the wine or in her room sleeping?

"Don't remind me, my foot is still sore." Eugénie's voice took on a conspiratorial tone. "We can't take that to our rooms. The Good Sisters will kill us."

"I know, but there is a place where we can enjoy it." Now Virginie would be hiding the bottle back under her cloak. "Follow me."

Giggles drifted through the window. The two would be locking arms and walking toward the end of the plaza with the panoramic view. Their destination was the enormous open-air staircase beside the library that descended to the now-defunct academic prison. Louisa prayed the girls would get to use the academic prison and its entrance on the third landing.

Six quick knocks, and Louisa shook her head. Something was wrong. She had to know. She lifted the curtain to see through a small crack. From the side of the window, her constricted view was a sliver. For a quick second, a woman in a silky violet dress walked through her slice of the cobblestone plaza in front of her window—golden curls bounced on the woman's shoulders. Gabrielle moved in the same direction as her friends.

Gabrielle, you idiot. Your tattle-telling may get you killed.

Catherine's three knocks came through the wall, and Louisa's heart pounded. Wellington was coming. The timing of this next part was crucial.

Four knocks.

It's him. Louisa unleashed the hatred in her heart, crushing the fear that sprang up at the thought of confronting João before it could strangle her. The plan pivoted on these next few seconds and what path the enemy chose. Would the despicable devil and his demon henchman split up, or would they both come for her? Louisa risked widening her view out the window.

A tall, broad-shouldered man in a long black coat had stopped halfway across the plaza. Another man in a student's cloak came into view and paused next to the first. The two leaned their heads together. If Louisa had had a gun, she would have pulled the trigger right then.

Never having fired a gun, she knew she'd have had little chance of hitting anything from this distance. The thought of firearms did spark her to rethink the plan. They presumed Wellington would be armed, but she now prayed that João hadn't brought a gun. If he had, her friends would be in over their heads. *Why didn't we think of that?*

The two men broke apart, and the evil djinn of Louisa's nightmares disguised as a mere college student hurried after her friends. Louisa forced herself not to dash back to the door and call for the guards. They had all known this was a possibility. The plan had encouraged their enemy to split their forces, and her friends would be ready for the predator.

Unless the crazy devil has a gun.

A knock was followed a second later by another. Wellington had reached the building. Louisa counted to five and opened the window. In the hallway, Catherine's door opened. Frantic, she said, "I saw a man with a gun. He's coming up the back stairs. This way, hurry."

As Catherine led the guards away from her room, Louisa assessed the plaza below. Fifty meters away, a few partygoers were coming or going between the Iron Gate and the Royal Palace building. In front of her window, the square remained empty.

The British man would probably be inside by now. She pushed the shutter-like windowpanes out and, avoiding the spiky board, stepped onto the windowsill. With a turn, she leaned outside and looked up to the molding a half meter above. A crouch and a jump later, her strong hands latched onto the ledge that was too thin to climb onto. Using her feet, she toed the glass panes shut.

Darn stucco, Louisa lamented. With no hand or toe holds on the wall, she had to swing-jump from this molding to its twin above the next window.

Must go faster, she thought while hand-walking to the end of the ledge. She locked onto her landing point and swung her body back and forth, building momentum.

On the fifth swing, her legs angled toward her target, and when her feet neared her shoulders, she let go. Monkey-like, she arched up and over the two meters of open space. She stabbed out, snagging the molding as she fell past it. Viselike, her strong fingers glued themselves to the stone as she fought to slow her pendulum swing.

When Louisa's momentum lessened, she kicked her legs forward and let go. She flew through the open window to land on the floor of the bedroom where Catherine had watched Wellington. She dashed to the door, cracked it open, and peered around the door jamb into the hallway.

The clan had placed a sturdy bookcase in the corridor between the two living quarters. They also propped up one side of the bookshelves with a small wooden wedge and tied a long rope to the top of the bookcase. The hemp rope hung down the side of the shelves where Louisa could grab it.

A dark-clad form suddenly blocked the view through the gap between the hallway wall and the shelves. Louisa held her breath, hearing jingles and clinks, the unmistakable sounds of an amateur attempting to pick a lock. After many long seconds came an audible click, and the intruder pushed the door open. He disappeared, closing it behind him.

Louisa plucked her key from her pocket as she stepped into the hall. She grabbed the rope with her other hand and pulled it around the case. She padded to the door and locked it.

As the mechanism snapped into place, heavy footsteps rushed back toward the door. Louisa grabbed the rope with both hands and pulled it with all her might. She leaned her slender frame away from the bookcase, straining with every bit of strength in her legs and arms. The doorknob jiggled, followed by a fierce boot strike that shook the door in its frame. The lock looked ready to give way. Fear rising, she channeled it into one last surge, and the bookshelf teetered on its edge.

Too late, kópanos.

Louisa fell, her posterior slamming into the stone floor when the tension in the rope was released. They hadn't practiced that part. A second later, the giant shelves slammed to the ground, blocking all but a meter at the top of the doorway. She jumped up, rubbing her bruised backside, and screamed, "There's a man in my room! Help!"

Catherine turned the far corner and raced down the hall, the two guards lumbering after her.

The door behind the barricade opened, and Wellington's head appeared in the space. Louisa smirked and waved, wiggling her fingers at him. The man wore a look of surprise, which changed in an instant to fury. He leaned against the shelf, and it moved a couple of centimeters into the hall.

"No," Louisa whispered, her smirk wiped away.

"*Pare!*" The closest guard yelled, and the case stopped moving.

Catherine and the first guard ran to Louisa's side of the blocked doorway. The other guard stopped on the opposite side, each man pointing a revolver toward Wellington. The door slammed closed but did not latch, leaving a small gap.

Louisa grabbed Catherine's arm. "Keep him here. I have to go."

She spun toward the guard beside her and, using both hands, snatched the gun from his grip with a quick twist. She saw the man's shocked expression as she raced to the stairwell and yelled over her shoulder, "*Desculpe!* Emergency!"

"Be careful!" Catherine yelled after her.

Louisa bounded down the stairs two at a time. At the bottom, she threw open the door. As she ran outside, a blood-curdling scream erupted out of the window above and behind her. She astonished herself by how much the man's pain pleased her.

Chapter 32

Waterloo

With a satisfied grin, Louisa sprinted toward the open end of the plaza. The gun was heavier than she'd imagined. She questioned whether it had been wise to bring it. If she pulled the trigger, she'd be as likely to shoot one of her friends as to hit her target. Nearing the giant stairway, she slowed and peered over the railing. *Could it be any worse?*

Within the glow of outdoor gas lamps, João stood on the third landing with his back to Louisa. He had an arm around Gabrielle's neck, restraining her. On the next platform below, Virginie and Eugénie stared up at the monster, horrified. Louisa crept down the steps to the next level.

João's head started to turn, and Louisa froze.

He hissed in French, "What was that?"

His head whipped back to Eugénie as she snarled, "That was your man, falling into our trap."

Louisa sneaked a bit closer. Eugénie glanced her way for half a second, and Louisa moved her free hand in a rolling motion, conveying that her friend should keep the vile man talking.

General Eugénie laughed. "That's right, you've walked into a trap."

"What?" João stammered, then shook his head. "Your false bravado won't work. That was probably one of the guards. I'm sure he has her already." His head twisted to Gabrielle. "I'm sorry, Mademoiselle Chanzy. I found you to be a woman of sophistication and fine breeding."

"Please," Gabrielle squeaked.

Passing the first landing, Louisa moved down the next shorter set of stairs.

"I can't leave any witnesses." The devil kissed Gabrielle's cheek. "Goodbye." He pulled away, and a knife appeared in his free hand, glinting in the lamplight.

Eugénie yelled, "Stop!"

Louisa panicked and with shaking hands tried to line the gun barrel up with the man's back.

The demon held the blade above his head, his shoulders shaking with laughter.

Moving again, Louisa slipped down the stairs, one at a time. On reaching the second platform, she risked a glance away from the target and suppressed a giggle.

Eugénie, dressed in her green silk ballgown, presented a fierce dichotomy with her knees bent and her rapier held in front of her in the on-guard position. Virginie, grasping a candlestick in one hand and a wine bottle in the other, did not seem so out of place. Louisa could imagine many an angry wife dressed in a work frock who might have used similar everyday items to threaten a wayward husband.

"It would seem you have brought a knife." João chuckled. "A really long knife." He squinted. "And a bottle of wine." He lowered his knife and, underhanded, tossed it at Eugénie's feet.

She hopped back as João's blade clattered down the stairs. He pulled a revolver from under his scholar's cloak.

"While I came prepared for a gun fight." He pointed the pistol at Eugénie.

Louisa stopped moving, braced her feet shoulder-width apart, and trained her gun on the middle of the man's back. She coated the following words with venom. "Not all of us. Drop the gun!"

An almost uncontrollable urge willed her to pull the trigger, but she wasn't sure she was ready for what would come afterward. Still, she half-wished for him to try something.

The miscreant's head twisted slowly, his grip around Gabrielle's neck never wavering. His eyes bulged, and his handsome face contorted into a warped mask vacillating between hatred and longing.

Louisa growled, "That's right. It's the bastard. That scream was from your man, Wellington."

João appeared confused.

With a shrug, Louisa said, "We had to call him something while we planned this ambush." Without moving the barrel, she motioned with her eyes to the ground. "Now. Drop it."

Surprise washed over his face, soon replaced by a death glare.

"One." Louisa pulled the revolver's hammer back with both thumbs until it clicked.

João opened his hand, and the revolver fell with a clatter. He spun Gabrielle around, using her as a shield. Louisa almost pulled the trigger but knew she would risk killing the wrong nemesis.

His eyes wild, the crazy devil spoke. "Back up, or I'll break her neck."

"Don't do it." Louisa pointed the barrel toward the ground and looked at Gabrielle. Tears streamed down the blonde's face, and she looked ready to faint. "Do you believe me now?" As much as the mean girl had made Louisa's life hell, she'd only wished the girl dead on a few occasions. Louisa softened her gaze. She'd be damned if anyone, especially this disgusting trash of a man, would be the one to get rid of Gabrielle.

Louisa flashed a look to Eugénie, who gave her a wink.

"Shut up, and put the gun on the ground." João placed his other hand on the top of Gabrielle's head. "Then move back."

Louisa nodded yes while watching Eugénie, then began to bend her knees.

A sneer stretched across João's face.

As silky quick as a mongoose, Eugénie rushed forward and lunged up the last few steps. She buried the point of her sword several centimeters deep into the man's fleshy rear.

João howled and stumbled forward, dragging Gabrielle to the ground as he went to one knee.

Before he could recover, Eugénie leaped up the last few steps like a pirate going over a gunwale. She placed the tip of her sword on the animal's neck. With a cold, lifeless voice, Eugénie said, "Let her go, or I will rip out your throat."

Blood glistened on the blade from where the steel had met flesh. João, trying to see who wielded the blade, let go, and Gabrielle scurried away, coughing.

Louisa rejoiced inside. *All hail the new Saint-Denis fencing champion. There is no way our sweet Joy could match that level of killer instinct.*

Gabrielle, her golden hair now a pile of windblown hay, wiped her runny nose as she ran down the steps. She stayed behind Eugénie, who stood like a vengeful Joan of Arc, facing her tormentor.

João grimaced as he raised his hands. Repugnance like Louisa had never known filled her body and soul. She raised the revolver. This disgusting rat didn't deserve to live. Just squeeze the trigger, and the nightmare would stop. It would be so simple. Louisa clenched her jaws.

João's chin quivered, his head shaking.

Virginie placed her hand on top of Louisa's gun. With a gentle push, she moved the barrel toward the ground and, in a soothing voice, said, "Daring. Give me the revolver."

João's fearful eyes locked with Louisa's and in that instant changed, oozing a desperate craving. The weird yearning sickened her but chased away her animalistic need to pull the trigger. *God protect me from this madness,* she thought.

The weight of the revolver disappeared as Virginie lifted the gun out of Louisa's hand.

The desire to watch him die had evaporated, but Louisa hated how dirty he made her feel. Her anger returned, along with the need to hurt him. She marched down the steps and stood before the kneeling man.

Her stare never wavered from his repugnant gaze. Revulsed as if a roach had crawled across her face, she had to get him away from her.

Leave me alone! Louisa screamed inside. *Why won't you leave me alone?*

She tugged on his shoulders until he stood on his one good leg. With her hands still on his shoulders, Louisa used them for leverage as she whipped her knee upward to slam into his groin. He doubled over with a moan and dropped back to his knees. His head drooped, and the gold chain around his neck glinted.

The key, she thought and glanced back at Virginie's solemn, spectacled face. Louisa remembered her tears when Simon had to flee––Virginie was always the Clan of the Dissipated's emotional bulwark. Even when Virginie's well ran dry, she always found a way to fill the other girls' cups.

It's my turn to support you now, Virginie, Louisa thought, her eyes narrowing on João.

She gave him a ferocious slap across the face. Pulling her stinging hand away, she yanked the necklace free and pocketed it. She dismissed him with a snort and jogged down to the broad door that guarded the entrance to the academic prison.

"Get up, scum," General Eugénie commanded.

The lockpicks whirred in Louisa's fingers, and she pushed the door open moments later. She turned and waved. "Gabrielle. Light the lantern next to the door."

As the still-shaken blonde walked past, Louisa pushed two matches into Gabrielle's palm.

The wounded man, a blade to his front and a gun to his back, shuffled toward the door. A wheezing groan escaped his lips with each shift of his weight. Louisa bit back a chuckle at the sight of the small, blood-stained hole torn in the rear of the man's pants.

Inside the threshold, an olive oil lamp blazed to life. Its glow shone out the door behind Louisa. The light reduced her vision so much that she almost missed the dark figure creeping along the banister across the plaza above.

Her instincts honed from hard-won experience, Louisa felt her hackles rise in alarm. The unfocused blob solidified into Wellington. He swung his arm over the railing and pointed a revolver toward them.

"Duck!" Louisa yelled, as she threw herself past the prisoner. Her shoulder drove Virginie to the ground. Her friend cried out as they slammed into the stone and rolled. From above, fire and black powder exploded. Chunks of cobblestone spewed into the air where Virginie had just stood.

Lying on top of Virginie's midsection, Louisa raised her head.

João screamed, "Save me, Stapleton! Kill them, all except for Louisa!" He turned and, with a herky-jerky limp, shambled down the stairs toward an iron gate at the bottom. It exited onto a street.

"Argh!" Eugénie lunged with a desperate outstretched arm. She twisted her wrist and plunged her blade into the man's other buttock. Another bullet whizzed overhead.

Louisa knew it had been meant for Eugénie.

Screaming, João rolled down to the final landing.

Her spectacles askew, Virginie shoved Louisa off her and rose to sit. She pointed the pistol upward and pulled the trigger. Flames shot from the barrel, and it jumped, jerking her arm up. Virginie brought her second hand to the grip as she fought to line up the wobbling barrel again.

The thief part of Louisa's brain screamed for her to escape. The friend inside Louisa, the desperate one terrified she'd lose one of her sisters, stole the thief's plan and bellowed, "Get inside!"

She scrambled to her feet and yanked Virginie's arm, dragging her toward the open door. More stone shards exploded. Virginie sank to all fours, and Louisa shoved her through the prison doorway. Eugénie loped inside, and Louisa dove into the lamplight, pulling her feet up as she landed. The door flew past the heel of her boot to slam shut. Gabrielle gave her a sheepish smile.

On her knees, Louisa turned and completed the desperate pilgrimage to the door. Her fingers found the lockpicks and moved through the memorized patterns. The mechanism clicked after a few heartbeats. She turned and collapsed, her back sliding down the thick oak door. A pistol shot rang out, the bullet clanging off metal.

Outside, the colonel's voice echoed down the sunken staircase.

Virginie peeked through a barred window that overlooked the open-air stairway. "They're getting away." Her voice cracked with resignation.

Louisa hugged her scraped knees to her chest and buried her face. The prison's damp chill leached into her bones in seconds as her thoughts turned black. Shivers set her teeth to chattering. Was she spiraling because of the shock of another near death experience or the utter despair that came with their failure?

We lost him. How? Worse, I almost lost them. Louisa cycled between Eugénie's and Virginie's faces as tears of fearful frustration fell.

Eugénie's robust, unwavering voice coaxed Louisa out of her daze. "Get up. We need to get moving." With forceful hands as unyielding as her voice, Eugénie lifted Louisa to her feet.

Chapter 33

The Hangover Job

Mère Sainte Adeline appeared regretful as she shut their door and then turned the key.

Eugénie spat out, "*C'est de la merde.*"

Louisa sat on her bed and stared at her feet. "I'm sorry."

"For what?" Eugénie turned to her.

"I should have just killed him," Louisa whispered.

"You followed the plan." Eugénie pursed her lips. "I'm just glad you brought that gun, or we'd all be dead." She kicked the wounded bedpost. "I can't believe I didn't account for that rat bringing one."

Eugénie crossed the room and bent down to hug Louisa. When she stood, she said, "At least, the colonel ended the tour. He seemed impressed enough by our plan that he didn't punish us directly."

"You can thank Gabrielle for that."

Eugénie chuckled. "Getting saved from certain death can change a person's outlook. Either way, you should be happy. No more dances, and we'll be well-guarded until we return to France."

Louisa hardened her heart as she glanced at the large bloodstain under the window. Its presence was a reminder of how close they'd come to success. It didn't make her feel better. They had underestimated the ex-soldier's perseverance—another failure.

Defeated, she said, "He won't stop."

"I doubt he'll come to France."

Louisa, too short for her foot to reach the floor, kicked anyway, her boot swooshing centimeters above the wooden planks. "Did you see how he looks at me? He'll just send more kidnappers. We need to end this before we get on that ship."

Through a yawn, Eugénie said, "Let's discuss it tomorrow after a good night's sleep. We'll have plenty of time since we're on house arrest."

Minutes after the light turned off, Eugénie's soft snores echoed at regular intervals.

Sleep would not come for Louisa. Her mind raced, thoughts vacillating among anger, depression, and trying to plan how to end this ongoing nightmare. After several hours of frustration, she stood. With her energy returning, she paced the room in her socks .

Maybe some fresh air will help.

She opened the shutters and stuck her head outside. The university plaza was silent and still. When she sucked in a deep breath, she fought back a cough and wrinkled her nose. Below and to the right, one of the guards leaned against the building entrance, smoking a pipe.

Louisa glanced to the left, past the two darkened windows on the same floor, her eyes stopping at the tower. That familiar itch, the one promising adventure, and the tease of the addictive rush to come made her lick her lips.

She conducted a quick risk/reward analysis, pausing on the pitfalls. How much trouble could she incur? If confronting two killers hadn't brought the biblical wrath of the Good Sisters down on her, this possible transgression should be a minor offense.

Her thoughts returned to the library at the opposite end of this very building. There was a particular book she had not been allowed to touch. Louisa loved the forbidden, and besides, Virginie liked the author, and she wanted to cheer her friend up.

Louisa grinned as the plan formed, and she added the variable of this being more than a joy climb to the risks. To be caught stealing from the library would result in her time at Saint-Denis ending, regardless of her father's influence.

Would that really be a problem?

Without a proper reference, she might not be able to get into Girton. She dismissed that thought. It would be easy enough to forge letters from Buttons and her teachers. Worst case, Portuguese prison. That didn't sit well, but she'd accepted those risks long ago.

With her mind made up, Louisa needed a distraction to help her put tonight's disaster behind her. She prepared the necessary items for her adventure, dropping a long rope into the haversack, along with three candles, matches, and a palm-size candlestick with a curved, polished reflector on one side.

A hand mirror allowed her to stay out of sight while watching the guard. He'd have to relieve himself at some point. While waiting, she ran through the actual burglary to come. Similar to her earlier maneuver, she'd cross from one windowsill to the next until she was beside the tower. Then she'd scale the tower to gain access to the roof. From there, it was a quick jog and a short climb down to the top-floor windows of the library. That was where the unknown came into play.

An hour later, the man tapped his pipe against the wall, emptying the spent tobacco on the ground. When he disappeared inside, Louisa opened the shutter and hopped to the windowsill. Outside, she turned to face the interior but looked upward.

The rush she'd sought came with that first jump to grab the molding above the window. A jolt of energy shot through her, and she grinned. Once again, she used the molded ledge to throw herself across the space between her window and the bedroom window where Virginie and Catherine slept. After moving hand over hand to the other end, she began pendulum swinging. This next step was the most tenuous part of tonight's job.

Be asleep. Be asleep.

Feet at the correct angle, Louisa let go, arching upward. As her stomach dropped, she grabbed the molding on the other side. While she brought her swaying legs to a standstill, she stared through the glass into the nuns' room.

For several thundering heartbeats, she looked and listened, her breath fogging the window. There was no movement, but the glass vibrated from one nun's loud snoring.

Louisa shook her head, thinking, *Who sleeps through that?*

One hand came free, and Louisa smirked as she drew a heart in the mist with her finger. She resisted the impulse to write an LS in the middle. The morning dew might expose her doodle, but what thief would be stupid enough to leave a calling card?

A few more hand-steps, and she hung from the corner molding where the tower wall met the living quarters. With her right hand, Louisa could almost touch the first of the bell tower's three small rectangular windows. She placed a foot into the stone corner, then glanced at the doorway. No guard. How much longer would she have?

Louisa's constant companion during any climb was the desire to go faster, to make the rush grow. Her uncle's incessant warnings against unnecessary haste bounced around her head––"Think, then move"; "Go too fast, and you die"; "Plan every step first"; "Go faster than you think, and you die."

Uncle's advice had almost always been about the craft, but Louisa found the advice just as wise for climbing. After identifying and imagining her next three moves, she bunched her leg and arm. Like a spring uncoiling, her kick propelled her over the short distance to the tower's closest windowsill. Strong fingers clamped onto the stone, and she hung from the first window. The window frame was deeper than the small ledge of the moldings, and she pulled herself up to stand.

The window above wasn't much higher than her bedroom's molding, and she leaped to snag the sill. The stone ledge crumbled under her fingers, and her hand plunged, with all her weight pulling at her other arm.

Sapristi!

Louisa put every bit of strength into that arm and jerked her body up and over. After hopping across the broken plaster, she reached up to grab the un-damaged part of the ledge. It held. She blew out a long breath and waited until her heartbeat calmed. It was a good six-meter drop, so she might have survived, but broken bones were a certainty.

Near misses came with the job, but one day even all of her preparation and training might not be enough. She didn't dwell on this reality because she'd rather die doing what she loved than live an adventure-less life. Her internal clock chimed, warning her she needed to hurry before the guard or someone else came outside.

After locating the most solid part of the molding, Louisa repeated the process and hung from the top window. Her feet dangled at the same height as the false crenels that ran along the building's roofline. Louisa swung again before flying left. She twisted her body to face forward as her feet passed over the closest crenellation. Hands and feet landed on the slanted roof's clay tiles. She lowered to her stomach and lay still.

When no sounds came from below, she crawled to the ridgeline and stood. A sliver of moonlight shimmered off the broad river snaking through the valley. The night's anemic crescent moon provided a little natural illumination as she padded across the roof of the building.

At the end of that church, the roofline changed into a transitional section connecting the chapel to the library. With two quick hops, she reached the library's roof and eased herself down the incline. Behind a more modern decorative roofline, Louisa peered down at the scene of their defeat.

She saw the bloody streaks on the steps marking the path of João's man, Stapleton. *The brute's tough. I'll give him that.*

That side of the building had six oversize arched windows along the length of the top floor. Louisa moved to stand above the entry point closest to her target.

She secured her rope around one of the roof's decorative finials and tossed the other end over the side. Not long enough to reach the ground, the rope hung down the brick wall between windows. If she couldn't open one of the six windows, the job would end like her last plan.

None of that.

Louisa focused herself and leaned back to rappel down the brick. At the target windowsill, she walked sideways until she could stand on the window's ledge. A long white curtain covered the window, and the glass reverberated with strange chittering sounds. Louisa's stomach clenched. It sounded like a nest of rats.

She shivered to remember once coming across a small horde of the long-tailed rodents in the attic of Saint-Denis. It had been miraculous that she'd escaped without any bites. Once again, her training had saved her. Ever since thief school had begun, her uncle had impressed on her the danger of the creatures and how best to avoid them.

Is it worth the risk?

Louisa would swing away if she opened the window and found any immediate danger. Besides, she'd come this far. With a big breath to brace herself, she
wrapped the rope around one arm and retrieved a thin metal file with her free
hand. The sharp point went into the crack between the two wood panes. For a
full minute, she levered up and down, trying to lift the hook out of its latch.

Grunting, Louisa gave up and took hold of the rope with both hands. Three
quick sidesteps brought her to the next closest window. Another white curtain
and chittering welcomed her. She frowned.

The file came out, and this time the pop of the latch sent a jolt of excitement
through her. Muscles tensed, Louisa cracked open windowpanes by pushing
them inward. With the file leading the way, she poked at the curtain. It lifted a
little, and then something slammed against the other side of the canvas, chittering.

Louisa jerked her head and almost flung herself away with the rope but
paused. The animal on the other side didn't break through, and she calmed down.
Another push with the file moved the material farther into the room. It wasn't a
curtain at all. A massive tarp hung from above and covered all the bookshelves.

Goose pimples spread across Louisa's body as the low-pitched squeaking
increased. For the first time, the flapping of wings filtered through the giant veil.
If her suspicions were accurate, the creatures on the other side would keep any
guards out of the room.

That's a positive, I guess.

Louisa eased inside the open window, using the file to push the tarp away.
She needed to keep those things as far from her as possible. Feet planted on the
carpeted floor, she found herself on the small balcony that held the upper shelves
of the library. The tarp hung in front of the short railing, then went up and over.
She contorted this way and that to get her haversack off her shoulders with one
arm.

She placed the candlestick, the candle, and the match at her feet. She struck the match along the stone windowsill, and a small flame sputtered to life. The noise from the other side picked up. After lighting the candle, she blew the match out and dropped the smoking stick out of the window.

The candle's bad enough. She pictured a painting she'd seen of the burning of the Library of Alexandria. *They'll hang me if that happens. So don't mess up.*

Louisa picked up the lit candle and used the file to push the cloth away. As she stood,

she yanked back and bit off a yelp. Through the canvas, the light showed the distinctive wavy form of a bat's wings, extending a good twenty centimeters to either side of an apple-sized blob.

Creepers. Why do they do this?

Before the tour left Coimbra, she would ask some pointed questions about what happens at night in the library. Louisa took a deep breath to find some inner peace. The bats and the covering made what she thought would be a simple process more complicated.

She moved along the narrow balcony to the target window, enlarging her small bubble as she walked, aggravating many a bat. The tour guide's finger-pointing had given her only an approximate location to start the search. At the bookcase closest to the window, she went to work, inspecting the spines of books on each shelf. The effort of keeping the tarp pushed back made her pause in frustration when she needed to search the higher shelves.

There had been ladders on the balcony during the tour. She didn't know where the closest one stood, but something about the angle of the ladder sparked an idea now.

Thankful for necessity's inspiration, she unshelved one of the more enormous tomes and walked toward the railing she knew to be a meter away. When the tarp material flattened against the wooden handrail, she pushed the book against the cloth at an angle.

Stepping back, she blew out another long breath. The tarp stayed angled away from the first six shelves. Still holding the candle, she moved as quickly as she dared, using more books to extend the tent along the balcony.

Dieu merci.

The search began again, with her climbing the shelves. When she lit her second candle, her ears started itching. The book had to be nearby. When she lit her last candle, her frustration mounted, but the sense that she'd find the book also grew. She did, three bookcases over, and a meter off the floor.

Yes!

With a gentle, reverent tug, Louisa pulled out the vellum copy of *The Book of the City of Ladies* and climbed back to the floor. After placing it on the ground, she flipped open the book and stared in awe at the medieval hand-drawn image of a woman at a desk. The elegant calligraphy of the text made Louisa want to steal this original copy.

Word of the missing book would spread far and wide. She made a point to never steal something you couldn't sell or, in this case, give away. Besides, the haversack wasn't big enough. After admiring two more pages, Louisa put the book back in its place and inspected the two smaller printed editions. The one in the best condition went into her sack. It took her another five minutes to replace all the books she'd used to brace the tarp.

Louisa kept the cloth extended as she spat on the charred wick of her last candle, dousing the flame. She rubbed the candle against her dress to dry it before placing the candlestick in the haversack with the book. After securing the sack over her shoulders, she stepped onto the windowsill and let the canvas tarp fall.

This robbery had proved to be a real challenge. Weary of mind and muscle, Louisa told herself to focus. She could rest soon, but until then, she needed to be at her best. Getting down the tower was more difficult than going up; one misstep could spell death. The very idea sent that familiar rush. She pulled the window closed and tugged on the rope to test it.

Louisa smiled, imagining Virginie's surprise on receiving a note of thanks from the Mazarine Library for her generous donation of a first printing of *The Book of the City of Ladies*. Louisa turned serious and climbed.

Chapter 34

The Friars Francisco

Revitalized by the morning's breeze, Louisa pulled ahead of her friends and picked up her pace. With a suitcase in one hand, she skipped across the large campus plaza, absorbing boundless energy from the bustling university's young scholars. With each stressed, happy, or determined face she passed, her fatigue from the previous night's emotional trauma and physical exertion faded.

Like the enigma of the egg and the chicken, she pondered how success bred attitude, which in turn bred more success. Or was it the other way around? The triumph of the previous night's theft had bolstered her outlook on life and blunted the creeping thoughts of doom and gloom. As she shifted the suitcase to her other hand, she fed her attitude more pleasant thoughts.

Despite the dangerous violence and unexpected twists encountered during the confrontation with João, she and her friends were still alive. They may not have beaten him, but they had bested him. Like all these cloaked students, the clan had come to the University of Coimbra with high hopes. And like the school's graduates, after some hard lessons learned, they were leaving better prepared for the next chapter. Eventually, the clan would devise a way to prevail over that evil man.

Besides, the skies were clear and the bright sun, warm. This was the kind of day to move mountains.

Louisa smiled. *Next time, we "will" clinch the prize.*

Through the shadows cast by the arched Iron Gate, she noted an extra buggy in the line of waiting carriages. In front of the first conveyance, the colonel and the brigadier watched two guards struggle to lift a large trunk to the rack on top. The big box slipped, and Brigadier Buffoon blustered, his face red as he yelled, "Careful, blast you! It's full of wine!"

With a grunt, the bigger of the two men caught the trunk against his shoulder, halting the slide. Disaster averted, the two men heaved as one and shoved the luggage over the iron rung. As they walked away, one of the men gave the old man a pointed stare.

"Well. Good. Merci," the brigadier mumbled and climbed into the cabin.

The colonel snapped to attention on Louisa's approach, acknowledging her with a frown and a playful salute of his one good hand. The man's sentiment made perfect sense. The previous night, the retired military man had scolded them for not coming to him with their plans. While admiring their pluck, he begrudgingly admitted that he could not have allowed them to use themselves as bait, so the clan had been correct in not seeking his cooperation.

Louisa slowed to a stop and said, "A beautiful day, Colonel, don't you think?"

With a furrowed brow, the colonel pursed his lips. "I'll decide once I lay my head on my pillow tonight and there have been no new issues." He took a breath and let out an exasperated sigh. "Do you think we can accomplish that, Mademoiselle Sophia?"

Louisa grinned. "Most assuredly, Colonel. I foresee nothing but blue skies and safe travels."

"Good. God knows we need a break from the trouble that seems to follow you."

"As they say, Colonel, *God gives the greatest tests to his strongest warriors.*"

The corner of his mouth quirked up, and he shook his head.

Louisa smiled and walked toward the rear carriages to catch up to her friends, who had retaken the lead.

Not a single barb or jibe came as she passed by Gabrielle and the Jetons loading into the second carriage. The blonde's exhausted eyes met Louisa's, and her nemesis––or was that former nemesis?––gave her a blink of acknowledgment. In the best mood she'd been in for days or maybe even weeks, Louisa nodded back.

As Louisa passed the third carriage, Mère Sainte Adeline's jovial laugh bounced out of the open window.

Next to the steps to the fourth carriage, Mère de la Nativité waited with her hands in front of her. Louisa stepped in line with her friends. A tall man with a full mop of brown hair streaked with white and a short, solid, balding man emerged from behind the carriage. In their late twenties or early thirties, both men wore brown friar habits covered by the distinctive white cloaks of the Carmelite order. They walked over to the nun, their faces inscrutable and backs stiff in the manner of soldiers.

"Demoiselles, let me introduce Brother Francisco Rodrigues da Cruz." Mère de la Nativité held her hand toward the tall man closest to her before motioning to the shorter man. "And this is Brother Francisco de São Luís. They will be helping to ensure our safety."

Louisa noticed the un-Carmelite red ribbon positioned above the men's hearts and pinned to their white cloaks. Curiosity piqued, she inspected the religious men's habits more closely. At noticing hidden bulges under the brown robes, she thought, *Strangest friars I've ever seen. The habit obviously doesn't make the monk.*

The shorter man bowed his head, and the taller man said in passable French, "Mademoiselles, it is a pleasure to meet you. The brother and I will do our best to make sure you're safe without being overbearing for the rest of your stay in Portugal." The man's smile did not reach his eyes. Unlike João's evil henchman,

Stapleton, whose eyes were cold and unfeeling, this former soldier's brown eyes seemed weighted down with regret.

Mère de la Nativité patted the man's forearm. "Merci, Brother Cruz." She turned a serious face to the girls. "Brother Cruz, the colonel, and I discussed the situation. Given that young man's vendetta against the four of you, we will change our traveling arrangements. From now on, one of the brothers, along with either Mère Sainte Adeline or myself, will ride with you. And you will sit in the seats facing the rear so that the friars may watch for dangers ahead."

The nun jutted her chin toward the third carriage. "Please divide yourselves and load your luggage on these two carriages. We still have two long days of travel before we reach Lisbon. We will be stopping in Tomar tonight." She clapped her hands. "Let's go."

Virginie and Eugénie hurried over to the third carriage. Eugénie called over her shoulder, "We'll rotate at each stop."

Louisa's mood soured a bit. *Great, stuck with Mère de la Nativité.* She shook her head, refusing to give in to the negativity, and attempted to douse the spark of morose thoughts. *No. This is going to be a wonderful day.*

The balding friar followed them, and Louisa perked up because she wanted to learn more about the French-speaking brother.

Catherine gave her a shy smile as she climbed into the carriage, and Louisa grinned back. She skipped up the steps and took her seat. She squirmed against the bench's worn cushion, attempting to get comfortable while the nun entered, and the friar took his seat across from her.

The cabin lurched forward, hoofbeats clopping as the wheels bumped over the cobblestones. For the first hour, the world raced by outside the small window. Periodically, Louisa would check on her traveling companions.

It surprised her that Mère de la Nativité was reading anything but the Bible, and she tried to read the title, but it was in Portuguese. Catherine hummed while working on a needlework design with a pair of orange-hooded, black-and-white swallows. Friar Francisco's eyes roved over the landscape ahead.

When the groves of shorn cork trees no longer interested Louisa, she turned her attention to the friar, whose eyes darted to hers for a heartbeat before returning to his task of searching out threats.

Louisa raised an eyebrow. "Brother Cruz, may I ask, how did you learn to speak French?"

Mère de la Nativité spared Louisa a look before returning to her book.

With his eyes focused outside, the friar said, "I was in the French Foreign Legion for many years."

"Interesting. Where were you posted?" Louisa asked. Her instincts pushed her to discover everything possible about this soldier masquerading as a friar. She had never seen a gun-toting monk, and now she'd seen two.

Sad eyes locked with hers for a long moment before returning to their duty. "Mexico for a while, then Algeria. A little in France. I left the Legion after the war."

Catherine looked up from her needlepoint for a moment. She leaned closer and tilted her ear toward the conversation as she returned to work.

"Mexico?" Louisa had missed the man's age by a few years if he had been in Mexico. "You must have been very young. You're Portuguese. Why did you join the Legion?"

The man chuckled. "I joined when I was eighteen. I needed to leave Portugal for a while." After saying that last part, his eyes shifted back outside to stare beyond the horizon.

Did he kill someone? Louisa wondered. Thinking better than to follow up on the point, she asked, "What made you want to join a medicant order, and what does the red ribbon mean?"

"Please stop pestering Brother Cruz," said Mère de la Nativité. She had placed her book in her lap and stared at Louisa.

"It's all right, Ma Mère." Brother Cruz smiled. "Her questions don't bother me. It's a welcome distraction."

The nun frowned but raised her book and returned to reading. Louisa could now make out the title, *Uma Alma de Mulher*, by Guiomar Delphina de Noronha Torresão.

"I've always lived simply. A vow of poverty isn't much of a burden. As to why I chose this life, I needed to get right with God." He tapped the red ribbon. "This means we are of the lowest rank in our small order." The man sighed, then flicked his eyes to her. "What about you? What do you plan on doing with your life?"

"Not becoming a nun, for one." Louisa suppressed her chuckle, and the Good Sister shot her a not-so-pleasant scowl. "I will be one of those annoyingly independent women who does whatever she can afford to do."

Friar Francisco's eyebrow shot up. "And how do you intend to pay for this independence?"

"With my brains, of course."

"Ah," he said in an incredulous tone.

Louisa squinted. "You doubt me?"

The friar raised his hands in mock surrender. "I would not dare to do such a thing, Mademoiselle."

With a harumph, Louisa leaned back, done with the conversation.

Then the friar asked, "What can you tell me about the man trying to kill you?"

João's cruel, sadistic smile flashed in her mind, and her face flushed. She intertwined her fingers to keep them from shaking. Invisible bugs crawled over her skin, and she clenched her jaws. The loathsome man disgusted her, terrified her, and, most important, had murdered her ability to dream of love.

Louisa leaned forward. "He is young, rich, and malicious. He is used to getting whatever he wants, can't handle rejection, and for some bizarre reason he is fixated on me." She leaned back, watching the clergyman's face, looking for any hint of the unusual man's thoughts. "When he attacked me, I thought I had caused him a major injury, and that is why he came after me again, but I must not have hurt him that much. I'm not sure why he is so obsessed. He talks about hurting me and loving me in the same sentence. The man is insane."

The friar's head cocked to the right, and he straightened. His attention became more intense than a moment earlier. "How did you hurt him?"

Louisa shrugged. "I could have sworn that I had stabbed him in the eye with a hair pin." She shook her head. "But I must have missed because I saw him less than a week later, and there was no sign of an injury. Maybe he has an equally crazy evil twin."

"Very interesting. What's his name?" A nub of a pencil and a small booklet appeared from under his cloak.

"João Lopes Gomes. Why?"

"It's probably nothing. When we get to Lisbon, I'll see what more I can learn. Is there anything else you can tell me about the man?"

Chapter 35
Convent of Christ

The tour traveled all day, stopping three times to care for their needs, eat, and change their horse teams. There had been few conversations after Louisa's brief discussion with the friar. As it was, when she described the three horrific encounters with João, she'd been careful not to disclose certain information.

Traveling with a nun could do that. Dampen a person's willingness to say too much. Instead, Louisa had spent the day wishing this once wonderful, glorious day would come to a merciful end. Each time a carriage wheel found a hole in the hardpacked dirt road, a jolt shot up her backside. Her bottom had had enough.

Two hours ago, after their last stop, her discomfort had gone from slight agitation to actual pain. After they disembarked in the sleepy village of Fatima to change horses, Mère de la Nativité insisted on stopping a short ride later to pray at what she claimed was a popular pilgrimage destination, the Sanctuary of Our Lady of Ortiga.

Louisa would have traded this torture seat for an hour of kneeling on the chapel's hard prayer benches. Maybe even two hours. The clatter of the wheels moving over cobblestones made Louisa smile despite the vibrations searing her from below. The blue skies darkened outside the door's small window, adding muted oranges and reds to its pallet. It was a pretty view, but Louisa was ready to see the road ahead of them.

Brother Cruz grinned. "We're here."

As soon as the carriage shook to a stop, the friar flipped open the door and jumped to the ground. He held his hand out, but Louisa paused, half in and out of the compartment. Her pilgrimage of pain had ended at the bottom of a stone mount. Bursts of sunlight from the sinking sun shone from between the crenels of an authentic medieval fortress looming above them.

Dreaming of fingers and toes crammed into mortar lines, cracks, and crevices caused her outlook to soar. *I knew this day was going to be special.*

Below the hulking castle, the road continued between two huge iron-banded doors that stood open within a curtain wall. A figure in brown and white waved from the walkway above the doors. Brother Cruz waved back to the sentry and once again offered Louisa his hand. She took it and stepped down, wincing. Moving her tortured muscles intensified her discomfort.

Maybe she would take a short nap. On her stomach. Definitely on her stomach. Then, she'd venture out to scale the walls and the towers that called to her. It would be nice if she didn't have to sneak out to do what she loved, but no self-respecting chaperones would allow their charges to risk their lives. Then again, slipping unseen through the darkness to climb high walls helped hone the skills she planned on using to fund her independence.

She collected her suitcase and joined the small mob that followed the colonel and the friars through the gates. The road sloped gently upward, passing long gardens with manicured hedges on either side. The defensive wall fenced in the garden on the left, while a long building, some of it in disrepair, walled in the garden on the right. At the top of the hill, wide steps opened onto a stone-paved landing, the porch of an ancient Gothic basilica. The enormous, rounded sanctuary doubled as a fortified tower with a bell.

"Welcome to the Convent of Christ. Let's get you settled." Brother Cruz waved a hand toward the church doors.

They passed under ornate moldings and statues of saints with Mary at the center. He continued speaking as he walked. "The Knights Templar created this castle in the twelfth century to guard against Moorish incursions."

The friar led them away from the impressive golden altar in the center of the rotunda and out of the church.

"When the Templars were destroyed in most of Europe, this stronghold survived, and the king of Portugal eventually took in survivors from all over the continent. He renamed them the Order of the Knights of Our Lord Jesus Christ. For many centuries, the martial tradition of the order continued here."

The group entered a multi-floor cloister surrounding a beautiful courtyard with trees growing in raised beds decorated by painted tiles. Weathered white stucco, arched openings, and red-tile roofs marked this section of the complex as newer than the castle's outer walls.

"The order was later made secular, though they still owned and managed all their former properties. Being knighted became an honor similar to your Légion d'honneur until the 1830s. That's when all of Portugal's monastic properties were confiscated by the state. Including this one."

Eugénie raised her hand. "Does that upset you?"

Brother Cruz shook his head. "It happened a long time ago. It's just the reality we live with."

Three friars, two graying and one barely older than Louisa, greeted them as they marched through a maze of luxurious courtyards and enormous hallways. The long walkways reminded Louisa of the grand hallways back in Saint-Denis.

Virginie asked, "If the government owns it, how is your order allowed to live here?"

The brother turned to walk backward. "We have worked out a lease with the government. We're allowed to stay as long as we spend a certain amount of time and money on the castle's upkeep. It is not cheap to keep this place from crumbling." He pointed toward a set of doors. "That's the dining hall. Dinner will be at seven bells."

After several more turns, the friar led them up two flights of stairs and onto a normal-size hallway. "Mère de la Nativité, you may use any of the rooms on this wing. The lavatory is on the ground floor to the right of the stairs. I'll meet you in the dining room for supper." He laughed. "Be sure to bring a hearty appetite. Brother Pinto is an excellent but touchy cook. If you don't ask for seconds, you don't get dessert."

Chapter 36
Out for a Knightly Climb

Louisa leaned into the night, away from the bell tower on top of the church. She did not look outward at the shadowy woods but inward, inspecting the sprawling convent. One hand anchored her to the steel pole that, on most nights, flew the order's distinctive flag: a white cross outlined in red on a field of white. Tonight, the banner hung limp, a corner of its cloth sticking to the sweat on her hand.

The need to perfect her skills was the excuse Louisa told herself—how she justified breaking rules to feed her addiction to exploring heights. Since she'd first fled from bullies to the cliffs as a small girl, she'd been hooked. The names, the jibes, the physical abuse, none of it meant a thing to a wall of stone. Up ten meters or a hundred, the immutable rock treated her no differently than the wind or the rain. A temporary visitor to be tolerated.

Louisa survived those first climbs, not by conquering the cliff but by mastering her fear, her anger, and her desperation. Empty of self, she became malleable like the wind and the rain, merging with the stone. In that state, the cracks and the crevices spoke to her, and there was nothing she couldn't do. Louisa was a savant, and her climbs, like Raphael's paintings, became personal expressions of surreal beauty. No rules could keep her from seeking that feeling. Not tonight, not ever.

The slick plaster walls of the tour's living quarters forced Louisa to sneak downstairs to begin her adventures. Virginie had fallen silent almost as soon as she placed her spectacles on the side table and laid her head on the pillow. Still, Louisa needed to wait until well after dark for the others to settle into bed. Only then did she ease into the hallway.

Thankfully, there were no friar-guards posted by their rooms. However, as Louisa crept through the complex, she discovered plenty of friars patrolling the grounds while others walked along the walls, staring into the darkness. At first, she had wondered whether the show of force was to protect the tour group, but they could have done that easier by guarding a smaller section of the convent. Besides, from up high, she could see the regular patterns of the patrolling guards. It wasn't for the tour's benefit; it was something the monks did all the time.

It had taken her a few minutes of skulking in shadows and avoiding the friars before she located an unobserved church wall. As she began her climb, Louisa said another merci to the kind parish priest who'd given her the magical balm after their escape from the barn. When they'd arrived at their rooms, she had rubbed some salve into the aching muscles on her posterior and the backs of her thighs. By the time she sneaked out, the stinging throb caused by the merciless carriage seat had subsided to a manageable level.

All the decorative detail on the Gothic façade of the church made her ascent simple. *If there were a slight breeze, this would be the perfect night,* she thought from her perch.

Despite all the guards, the many courtyards and buildings of the convent were dark except for an occasional lantern lit along the cloistered walkways. Louisa expected the old battlements over the fortress's entrance to be just as dark, but an intense glow emanated from the baily of the fortress. Even more curious to her were the distant sounds of metal on metal, like a blacksmith pounding away--hammer on an anvil.

She thought, *I should take a peek,* ignoring those Greek words of wisdom about cats and curiosity that popped into her head: *I periérgeia skótose ti gáta.*

After timing the guard rotations, Louisa crept down the basilica's ancient buttress toward the roof of the closest building. Seven hundred years of weathering had gouged large hand and toe holds into the mortar and the stones of the buttress, speeding her descent.

Several stories down, she leaped a short distance to the building's roof. She padded along the length of the building. Bending low, she kept her silhouette below the top of the roof and out of sight of possible guards on the other side.

At the end of the tiles, she lowered herself to her stomach and hid her face. A lantern-carrying friar walked down the dirt road between the gardens toward the main gates. The pings and clangs of metal on metal had become louder and more frequent, now happening at irregular intervals.

The outside wall of the building continued onward. Inside was the now-roofless building whose interior walls had crumbled. Weeds took root in every crevice as nature reclaimed the space. Three hands wide, the wall, complete with hollowed-out windows, ran until it connected with the curtain wall of the old fortress. Opposite the ruins lay the hedged garden the tour group had passed on their initial entrance.

Louisa watched the friar's lantern fade and started to stand when she heard something scrape behind her. Her body tensed. Her ancestor's words, *Ta matia sou dekatessera,* popped into her head. A glance over her shoulder found nothing. For another half-minute, she didn't move, listening.

When only silence greeted her, she stood and focused on the narrow, two-story-tall lane before her.

Arms raised to her sides, Louisa stepped onto the narrow path, putting weight on her foot a little at a time. Confident that the stone wouldn't crumble, she put her other foot on the wall, wiggling her feet and arms until her balance was perfect. She smiled as she took off, and a jolt of delightful energy shot through her. In seconds, her light-footed, fast walk took her to the first crenellation of the curtain wall.

Underfoot, the stones were older and even more worn as she reached the column and squatted down. The thick canopy of a large oak blocked her view but didn't hide the sounds of men grunting and steel clanging on steel from the other side of the courtyard. A man yelled in Portuguese, and the sounds stopped. He continued speaking a while longer before the activity started again.

This won't do, Louisa thought as she eyed the top of the wall.

The pillars, spaced a meter apart, would make it hard for her to work her way to the square tower on the other side. She could climb to the ground, but with her back to the people in the yard below, they'd spot her in no time. A large tree branch had grown close to two crenellations on the top of the wall. The leafy canopy could hide her movement.

Hugging the stone column, she stepped behind it until she was above the limb. After lowering herself with her hands, Louisa hung from the space between the two crenellations. She stretched out one hand And dug her fingers into the tree bark. Gripping it hard, she pulled down. It should hold.

Careful, she thought.

So much could go wrong with this next move. The bough might snap, and Louisa would tumble five meters. She put slow, steady pressure on the branch to prevent it from bending too much when she put all her weight on it. If it dipped too fast, someone might see her. At least, she didn't have to worry about being silent because of the noise the men made. She assumed they were sparring with swords, while their instructor shouted instructions.

Of course, this was not the first or even the tenth tree she'd climbed, using stealth to spy on someone. When the branch would move no lower, she let go of the stone wall with her other hand. The branch drooped a few centimeters under all her weight.

Hand over hand, she moved down the branch until her feet found purchase on another limb. She shimmied lower until she could see the yard through a thicket of leaves.

Amazing.

Still in their habits, five pairs of friars were sparring. Some held a single weapon, such as a short sword or a knife, while others fought with both. No more than two meters from the trunk of her tree, the instructor stood with his back to Louisa, his arms crossed.

Louisa admired the lethal grace with which the men moved. Blades flashed in the lantern light, slashing and thrusting as fast as a snake strikes. With the same speed and elegance, the opponents parried and dodged or skipped out of reach. One fighting friar––or were they warrior monks?––lost his knife from an overhead blow but stepped inside his opponent's next swing and grappled the man to the ground. Instead of a rough, out-of-control brawl, the pair writhed in a sinuous dance, each struggling to gain the upper hand.

True-life Knights Templar. They could be nothing else. She'd never heard of a modern Catholic order still teaching martial arts. The ramifications were enormous. No wonder they were practicing at night. No one could know. Her mind became a knotted mess, overwhelmed by questions as she watched the ballet of violence.

Engrossed in the action, Louisa hadn't seen Brother Cruz's approach until he stepped beside the instructor. Their conversation reached her as broken Portuguese. Louisa wanted to hear what they were saying, even if she only understood every fourth word. To hear better, she lowered her upper body and hung by her knees.

The friars' words were faint, but she heard, "*Um dos alunos disse que o Lopes Gomes mandou queimar as orelhas. Deve ser um dos bruxos.*"

He's talking about João. What is a bruxos?

Louisa strained her ears toward them. As the other man replied, she felt movement above her and forgot about the two men.

Back on Corfu, while she was training to be a thief, a squirrel had jumped onto the limb Louisa had climbed and perched on. The animal chittered its agitation at her, almost causing her to fall. She did not want a repeat of that near disaster. Her stomach muscles contracted as she brought herself up and grabbed another branch for balance. In the shadows above, two eyes popped open, cold and harsh—the eyes of a killer.

Even before she bit off her yelp of *sapristi*, cold steel pressed against her throat. Dressed all in black with his head and face covered, the man hissed, "*Descer devagar.*" Hard eyes motioned her to the ground as the knife eased away.

Louisa nodded, watching the blade the entire time.

This is bad. Very bad. Would the knights kill her to keep their secret? How did that ghost of a man sneak up on her so easily? Fear pushed the questions aside, and she focused on his demand.

Her eyes darted between the obstacles below and the blade as she moved down the branches using slow, deliberate moves. She squatted on the lowest limb that could support her weight and looked up. From a meter above, the man in black jerked his chin toward the ground.

With a gulp, Louisa dropped off the branch and hung from her hands. Exclamations came from two men on the ground as she let go. As she turned to face them, she found a short sword and a revolver pointed at her. Louisa raised her arms, and the man in black dropped to the ground behind her.

He said something in Portuguese. Frightened and speechless, she didn't even try to translate.

Brother Cruz lowered the barrel of the gun and said, "*Esta é ela. A rapariga que lutou com Lopes Gomes. Guarda as lâminas.*"

The name of her personal devil was all she grasped from what was otherwise gibberish, but it reignited the rage inside her. Standing taller, she pulled her shoulders back. The older man, who had a well-trimmed beard and mustache, hid his sword under his robes as Louisa hissed in French, "You mentioned João. What are you saying?"

Brother Cruz chuckled. "You are in no position to demand answers." He spoke to the man in black whose presence behind her made her more than a little uncomfortable.

The man's baritone reply shot over her shoulder, his citrusy breath stirring the few loose strands of her hair. Sweat plastered the rest to her head. She probably looked like a wet cat by now.

"Brother Bartolomea says you climb like a spider and slink in the shadows like an assassin."

Louisa spared the man in black a glance and shivered. "He's one to speak. I never saw him until his blade was at my throat. How long did he follow me?"

Friar Cruz chuckled. "Yes, he is like that." He translated her question into Portuguese.

The man barked a laugh and said, "*Na torre do sino da basílica.*"

"On the bell tower of the Basilica."

The entire time? Instead, she asked, "How close did he get?"

A heavy hand patted her shoulder, and she gulped as Brother Cruz said, "That close. But how is it that you are also like Brother Bartolomea?"

Louisa shook her head, not liking the implications of his question. "I'm not. I don't carry a weapon unless I know someone is trying to hurt me."

The brother nodded. "Alright, then explain."

That left a lot of wiggle room. Should she tell them why she was dressed in all black, climbing the castle walls and spying on them? Or just how she loved to climb? One axiom she tried to abide by held now: Never offer more information than necessary. At least, not until she got the lay of the land from these men.

After pushing down the rage that had edged into her voice, she said, "Climbing is my hobby. I learned to climb when I was young. I grew up on Corfu."

"Why were you spying on us?"

"I saw the lights and heard the noise. I got curious. When I got to that spot up there . . ." Louisa pointed to the first crenellation. "I couldn't see, so I climbed down the tree. I just wanted to take a peek. But then I heard you mention that man." She looked at the ground and shook her head. "I didn't plan on eavesdropping."

She brought her eyes up and locked them with the instructor's. "Are you going to kill me?"

The older man burst out laughing, and for the first time, Louisa noticed that the other pairs had stopped sparring. All the practicing friars watched them. When the instructor's laughter faded, he said in reasonable French, "What kind of monsters do you take us for?"

"You're Knights Templars," Louisa almost whispered, her hands still above her shoulders and getting heavier.

Then she added with more emphasis, "But I can keep a secret. I promise."

"Don't worry, child," the man scoffed. "Your guess was close, but the Templars ceased to exist five hundred years ago on that unholy Friday the thirteenth. We belong to the Order of the Knights of Our Lord Jesus Christ." He waved her hands down.

Louisa's fear eased while she lowered her arms, but she kept alert. It took only one of these warriors who wanted to see their secret remain hidden to end her life. "I thought they got rid of the religious aspects of the order."

"They did. When that happened, some in the Portuguese church decided it would be best to keep a small portion of the order separate from the government. The cardinal supports us, but we are independent and choose who we will help with the gifts the Lord has given us."

"So, you voted on Mère de la Nativité's request for protection?"

"Something like that." Brother Cruz looked toward the older man. "The small council did. Brother São Luís and I have little say on our missions, but we can refuse orders if our conscience prevents us." He pointed at Louisa's dress. "Interesting outfit."

Louisa undid the knot, and her skirt flowed out.

The instructor nodded with appreciation. "You are an impressive young woman, but I think it's time for you to return to your room." His eyes narrowed, and his voice grew stern. "And stay there."

"Yes, Monsieur. Before I go, will your knights help me stop that devil of a man? Lopes Gomes. He's tried to kidnap me or kill my friends four times now. He won't stop." Her jaw tightened. These men could be the answer. Desperate for the knights to understand just how evil and deranged the man was, she did the unthinkable.

Closing her eyes, she hissed, "He tried to rape me."

The instructor's eyes softened. "We will help if we can. The Church and our order are deeply concerned about the entire Lopes Gomes family."

Louisa tilted her head in confusion. "What concern?"

"From what you shared about the man with Brother Cruz, we suspect he and his family might be *bruxos*."

"*Bruxos*? What's that?"

The older man tapped his cheek for a second, then said, "I think the word in French is witches."

Louisa's lower jaw went slack. "Witches? Really?"

Are these men addled?

Brother Cruz shrugged. "We don't know what they are. What we do know is that there is a secret organization of rich and powerful people. They are pagans who worship the ancient Sumerian gods. *Bruxos* is the Portuguese name we use for them."

"And you think João and his family might be part of this coven––I mean, organization?" Louisa furrowed her brow at the incredulous story. Everything the friar said was so unexpected and strange that she didn't know what to do with the information except to think that it was nothing but foolish superstition. Then again, she needed to end the threat from João. If supporting the knights' delusions about this mysterious organization convinced them to help her, she'd play along.

The instructor answered, "That family might be part of the group. From your description, the young man causing all the trouble had the mark."

The mark? Louisa scrambled to understand.

As if reading her unspoken question, Brother Cruz said, "In the past, the leaders of the pagans all had scarred ears. Like they were burned or branded."

Louisa whispered, "Did they heal faster than normal?" Maybe it wasn't all nonsense.

The older friar nodded. "There are rumors of miraculous healing, but those were probably exaggerated."

She'd been positive she'd stabbed João in the eye, but it was more likely she'd struck his cheek than his eye, and it healed in a matter of days. Maybe he'd worn makeup to cover up the wound the last few times she'd seen him. *It has got to be poppycock. There's no such thing as witches.*

"The council will vote before you leave tomorrow. We are not allowed to kill except in self-defense." Anger blazed in his stare as he locked eyes with her. "It's hard, but there are other ways to deal with threats like him. If the council agrees,

I promise the Knights of Our Lord Jesus Christ will help you find peace and give him justice."

Louisa nodded. *I knew this was going to be a good day.*

Chapter 37
Decisions Delayed and Made

"Where have you been?" Virginie snarled as Louisa closed their bedroom door.

Louisa held up a hand. "Mon Dieu. I just went for a climb."

"Without telling one of us where you were going or what you were doing?" Virginie shook her head. "Eugénie and Catherine are out looking for you. I have been scared to death."

"I'm sorry. I didn't want to wake you." Louisa shrugged.

"Didn't want to wake me? We have some diabolical maniac trying to kill us." Virginie's voice cracked. "Trying to torture and kill you, and you don't have the decency to tell me where you are." Her eyes blazed with anger, and she shuddered. Tears streamed under her spectacle rims and down her face.

An ache deep in her chest gripped Louisa. She had been so into her problems she hadn't seen how much of a toll these last few weeks had taken on her friends. Fighting the normal instinct to pat her friend on her back, Louisa crossed the room and did the uncomfortable.

She pulled Virginie down into an embrace and rubbed small circles on her bent back. "I'm sorry." It didn't seem right to say anything else. She waited for Virginie to calm a little, then she said, "I wasn't thinking. Until we're home, I'll let one of you know what I'm doing."

"Good," Virginie mumbled as her heaving shuddered to a stop.

"No one needs to worry while we're here. We are as safe as we can be with the friars guarding us. They are much tougher than they look."

Nodding, Virginie lifted her head. "I'm sorry, too. I've just been so scared. When I'm not scared, I'm worried."

"We've been through a lot. Tell me." Louisa grabbed Virginie's shoulders and moved back to arm's length.

"When I'm not having visions of that monster choking me, I think about Simon. Have the police captured him? Is he safe? Is he really going to America?" Virginie bit her lower lip and fell silent.

"And? Are you going to go with him?" Louisa asked.

With her eyes drifting to the floor, Virginie clutched at her pink cotton nightgown.

Louisa kept her eyes trained on Virginie, intent on capturing her reaction. "Do you love him?"

Virginie raised her gaze and met Louisa's stare. "I do. When we were young, I loved Simon like a brother. He always had a good heart." She wet her lips. "God help me, but that boy has grown into a wonderful man."

Expert at lying, Louisa also excelled at reading people and the truth of their intentions. She winced at the one liar she hadn't been able to read. Despite that recent failure, she was confident in her ability here.

Virginie was sincere. Then why was she so troubled? Louisa didn't know, had never known, and was now sure she'd never know what it felt like to be in love. Like most things in Louisa's life, though, if she ever did fall in love, nothing would stand in her way of taking what she wanted.

Her friends didn't see the world the same way. Times like this reminded her of that. Maybe Virginie's problem was the speed of the upcoming decision.

"You don't have to go with him right away. You can finish school. Let him get established, and then join him after you graduate."

Virginie winced, her face clouding. "If I ask, Simon will wait for me, but that's not fair to him. Either I love him enough to share his dream, or I don't."

"What are you going to do?"

"I don't know." Virginie frowned. "I'll know when I see him. At least, I hope so."

"No matter what you decide, I am with you and Simon. When we get to Lisbon, I will make sure that you have all the resources needed to make a new life." A sinister thought came to Louisa. "As for the man in your nightmares. The one who terrifies me. I won't sit still and wait for him to seek me out."

The door flew open, and Catherine hurried inside, Eugénie on her heels.

"Thank God, you're fine," Catherine's songbird voice warbled with concern.

Eugénie closed the door. "Finish what you started to say. What are you going to do about him?"

After fishing in her pocket, Louisa held up the key to João's treasures. "Take something so valuable to him that he has no choice. Once I draw him out, hopefully our new friends will end the problem for us."

Catherine gasped. "The friars?"

"Why do you have so much faith in a group of poor monks?" Virginie tilted her head, a single eyebrow rising above her spectacles.

With a chuckle, Louisa replied, "They're not actually monks or friars. They are a militant order. The Knights of our Lord Jesus Christ."

Eugénie placed her hands on her hips and shook her head. "And if they don't solve our problem?"

"Then," Louisa sneered and pointed at the other girls, "we will end what we started."

Chapter 38
Lisboa Above the Sea

The day after Louisa had learned about the true identity of the two friars traveling with them, the tour headed toward the capital. It was too far from the knights' fortress to reach in a single day, so the caravan spent an uneventful night at a church in the small town of Santarém. The following morning, Louisa's luck ran out. Mère de la Nativité insisted that Louisa and the nun ride in the first carriage with the brigadier and the colonel.

The old general scowled at her as he sat on the bench seat across from her. Despite the look, he said, "*Salut, bonne sœur, Mademoiselle.*" He nodded.

"*Bonjour,* Brigadier," said Mère de la Nativité.

A curt nod was all that Louisa could muster.

The colonel pulled himself through the door using both hands. "*Mademoiselles, Brigadier, bonjour,*" he said to the occupants.

As he sat, Louisa acknowledged him with a nod and said, "Colonel. Your arm must be feeling better."

He smiled and rotated his shoulder a few times. "It feels much better. Merci." He nodded to the nun. "It is due to your ministrations that I am in such good shape." He smiled at the nun. "You must be excited."

The nun's cheeks flushed. "*Merci*, Colonel. Yes, I'm anxious to see my family." The nun's smile turned rueful. "It is always bittersweet, but I expect it to be more so this time."

The conversation reminded Louisa that they had come to Portugal because the nun's mother was ill. "Good Sister, may I ask about your mother's illness?"

"The doctors don't know. She's seventy-one. It could be anything. My brother's last letter said her mobility had gotten much worse and that her memory was beginning to slip."

"I'm sorry." Louisa didn't know what else to say.

"*Merci.*"

The colonel reached across the aisle and patted the nun's hand. "I just hope the five days we spend in Lisbon will be enough."

Mère de la Nativité placed her hand over his, her sad smile never leaving the colonel. "It will have to do, Adolphe. I truly appreciate all your concern."

Louisa felt her mouth gape open. *Can nuns do that?*

The nun had not only returned his physical comfort but also used the retired soldier's first name. The colonel must have noticed Louisa's reaction and pulled back, his cheeks splotched with pink.

A hand rested on Louisa's, and she flinched at the unexpected touch. Mère de la Nativité had twisted in her seat and now gave Louisa's hand a comforting squeeze.

The nun said, "I have been praying that we have no further trouble from that horrendous man." Her grip tightened, and her eyes filled with profound sadness. "Louisa, I've checked several times with your friends to see how you are handling all of this. I want you to know that Mère Sainte Adeline and I are here if you need to speak to anyone. Sometimes, it's hard to bare your soul to those closest to you. And you might want to speak with someone who has been in your shoes."

Louisa could only blink at the nun's invitation. A flush of heat crept from her chest up her neck until her cheeks blazed. Here was the *rulebook* personified, the anchor to Louisa's freedom, offering her comfort and counsel. The incongruency of it left Louisa speechless and more than a little confused.

Why would Mère de la Nativité speak so frankly in front of the men? Especially Brigadier Buffoon. Louisa glanced at the old general. He looked away, twirling his walrus mustache, just as chagrined as Louisa. Mère de la Nativité stared at the brigadier with a hardened expression. Then she returned her gaze to Louisa, jutted her chin toward the older man.

The silent signal shocked Louisa. She couldn't believe what the nun was prompting her to do. Had the nun just given Louisa permission to confront the old general? The blunt discussion about the attack on Louisa in front of the men set the stage for a confrontation if that was the nun's intentions. Louisa might have been wrong, but there were words she needed to say. She thought, *To hell with the consequences.*

Louisa took the nun's hand in both of hers. "I would like that. I'll speak with you on the ship home."

"Please do." Mère de la Nativité leaned in and whispered. "Child, I know you are proud. Don't let that keep you from taking a helping hand."

With a nod, Louisa whispered. "*Merci, beaucoup.*" Her emotions were still chaotic, but she gathered her thoughts, determined to take advantage of the onetime opportunity.

Mère de la Nativité let go and sat back in her seat.

"Ahem." The colonel looked uncomfortable and wiped his hands on his pants. "With the guards and our new friends, I don't think we will have anything to worry about from that scoundrel."

Louisa steeled herself and spun on the brigadier as if she had not heard the colonel. "Monsieur Gerard." The old soldier turned to her with a puzzled look. "I would hear your thoughts on João Lopes Gomez."

The brigadier's words caught, and he coughed. "Well. Yes. I might have made an errant assumption."

Errant assumption! Louisa seethed, anger storming inside her. She wanted to yell, "You pompous ass!" but she said with icy calm, "More like a catastrophic mistake that may cost a young man his future."

The military man drew himself straight, sitting at attention. "I apologize." He took a deep breath as Louisa's eyes shot flaming arrows at him. "Demoiselle, I may at times be an old fool, but I am a man of honor. When we reach Paris, I will do my best to make it up to the young man."

His contrition took Louisa off guard, dousing the flames fueling her anger, but she clung to a few embers to power her next words. "I don't need your apology. Simon Jupin is whom you owe an apology to, and I'll hold you to your word, Monsieur."

The brigadier lowered his head once in acknowledgment and placed his hand over his heart. Next to him, the colonel gave an approving nod to let her know that he had been in on the plan as well.

Leaning back, Louisa peered outside, her thoughts a mess. She didn't expect the old walrus's promise to mean much. The last time she saw Simon, the young man's determination made it plain to her that his decision to seek a new life in America wasn't made of desperation. Instead, she assumed the unfortunate circumstances had spurred him to turn what once had been a distant dream into an actual option. Louisa could only hope that the news that the brigadier was no longer a problem would divert Simon from his chosen course.

Louisa grasped at that sliver of hope as she watched the world go by. The news might let Virginie avoid making a hard choice—the decision that would lead to another friend leaving Louisa's life too soon.

What would Virginie do? For a moment, Louisa considered the issue from her friend's point of view. As long as Louisa had known Virginie, the reserved girl had wanted to teach in Paris. Even though Louisa planned on leaving France, Paris was just a short trip away, not on the other side of an ocean. It was hard for Louisa to see Virginie choose a different path, but, as with Marie's choice, Louisa needed to be happy for her friend's gain more than sad about her own loss.

Things never stop changing. Louisa's mother had always harped on this truism. The unspoken part her mother never shared was that change wasn't always pleasant or good. Many of the changes Louisa had faced had been negative, but she knew that without all that pain, she wouldn't be the woman she was today.

Her thoughts turned to the nun's offer of counseling and her recent wound by that devilish fiend. Now she needed to cauterize the source of that wound, and her thoughts turned to planning.

Around noon, their carriage stopped beside a park overlooking the city of Lisbon. Stretching her arms over her head, Louisa started walking across the park's semi-circle of grass. With a twist of her neck, she worked out the kinks while passing a gondola at the public gardens center.

She stepped over a curb lined by cypress trees to join her friends near a cobblestone-covered sidewalk where small white and black stones formed a mosaic.

"Beautiful view, isn't it? Too bad we won't get to explore," Eugénie said to no one in particular.

A jumble of white, yellow, and pastel-pink buildings with red tile roofs sprawled downhill almost to the sea. Ships with smokestacks, others with masts, anchored in the estuary of the Tagus River. The protection offered by that harbor was why men had taken up residence on these shores since before humans had begun to chronicle history.

Where Porto had the air of an old city trying to recapture its industrious past, Lisbon pulsed with youthful vigor. Smoke billowed from factories sitting along the water's edge, separated from the well-maintained city center by tenements housing factory workers and their families.

Brother Cruz stepped to the railing beside Louisa. "Mademoiselle Sophia, the council will support your efforts, but we must wait until he makes a move."

Louisa smiled but kept her eyes on the city. "Not a problem. I'll make sure he does."

"Is there anything you need from us?"

"I need to know where he lives and your help to leave our quarters at night to scout the location."

The friar looked at her. "You'll have to move fast."

Louisa turned to him. "We need to confirm he is there. When can you have the address?"

"Tonight," he said with confidence.

She felt Eugénie on her other side. The tall girl rubbed her lucky medal and shifted to hear Louisa's conversation better. Louisa smiled. *Don't worry, General Savant. I'll need your help as well.*

To Brother Cruz, she said, "Then we start tonight, but right now, I'm starving."

"I can help with that. Have you ever had a bifana sandwich?"

Louisa shook her head.

The friar's smile broadened. "Then all of you are in for a treat."

Chapter 39

A Soldier's Family

"I don't like it." Eugénie spun and jabbed a finger at the friar. "Not one bit."

Louisa gripped Eugénie's forearm. "I know you want to do more, but we have help now."

"I can drive the carriage." Catherine's soft, melodic voice grabbed everyone's attention.

How does she do that? Louisa had always been amazed when someone commanded a room with little more than a whisper.

"And I can be a lookout." Virginie pleaded with Brother Cruz, "Just give me a rifle or even a pistol. I'm a crack shot."

The friar furrowed his brow and pursed his lips. "I know that you are all competent young women, but my men have this well in hand. They are veterans who have been training in armed combat for years. You all know the plan and have your part to play."

"You don't understand. We—" Eugénie gestured toward the other three girls. "Are a family. Sisters. We can do more than sit here on our hands."

Brother Cruz shook his head in exasperation. "If Mademoiselle Sophia draws him out, you would only be in the way. I don't want any of my men distracted and worrying about you instead of focusing on the mission."

As empathetic as Louisa was toward the other girls, she needed her clan sisters to play a supporting role without being in danger. That night in Coimbra, when the Englishman almost killed Virginie and Eugénie, still haunted Louisa. The thought of losing any of them terrified her.

They're probably feeling the same way.

Louisa needed them to understand. The clan had done as much as they could. For the last three nights, they had ensured that the nuns and the colonel were none the wiser to Louisa's absence. On each of those nights, the friars had helped her sneak out to scout the target. The clan needed to cover for her one last time.

Everyone knew tonight was different. Louisa would be entering the devil's sanctum, and, if caught, there was a good chance he'd do unspeakable things to her. *Maybe reminding them of their part to play in the contingency will help.*

"But you do have an important job." Louisa added resolve to her words. "If I go in and don't come out on time, it will be up to you to rescue me."

Eugénie narrowed her eyes. "And by then, you might already be dead."

Louisa smiled. "I won't let that happen. I'm the only one who can get inside and break into his vault, so I need you to trust me."

That's it. Her line of thinking reminded Louisa of who these women were. They were part of the Légion d'honneur for a reason.

Louisa looked at each of them in turn. "Eugénie. Virginie. Catherine. What I'm asking is no different than when your fathers went to war. Think back." She paused, giving them time to reform those difficult memories.

A pallor fell over the three girls. Eyes drifted to distant times and places as thoughts turned inward.

Louisa gulped, her heart aching at causing her friends to relive such trauma. "I've never experienced that, but I bet it was one of the most difficult things you've ever done. No matter how scared you were, you were also proud of your fathers for doing their duty."

Catherine blinked away tears. Virginie had squeezed her eyes shut. Both had lost their fathers in the war. One's death had been quick, while the other's came after he'd suffered a year of pain. Eugénie saw the other girls' sad expressions, and her gaze dropped to the floor. Her father had gone to war many times and had always come home.

Louisa drew Catherine and Virginie closer and held out her hand to Eugénie, who took it. Brother Cruz became invisible as the Clan of the Dissipated huddled close, and Louisa said, "Knowing that you were going to be safe gave your fathers peace, but your love made all the difference. It gave your fathers courage." She tightened her arms around her friends. "That's what I need. You *are* my family. I know it's dangerous, but I'm the only one who can do this. More than anything, right now, I need that same courage. I need to know that you are safe, and I need your love."

Chapter 40
The Thief's Codex

Through the gap in her black head covering, Louisa once again examined the roof of the *modest residence* that the Lopes Gomes family called home. Had the mansion and its lush gardens been built in Paris, the French would have dubbed it a *hôtel particulier*.

Although the palace was the supposed location of the Lisbon Literary Guild, the cardinal's contacts described the building as a front. Inside the luxurious mansion, the clergy suspected the Lopes Gomes family of leading pagan rituals for a coven of so-called *bruxos*. For the last year, special clerical investigators had recorded the comings and goings to and from the residence.

Because of those efforts, Brother Cruz had brought Louisa the address of the wealthy family the same day they'd reached Lisbon, along with even more vital information––that João had arrived a day earlier. Less critical specifics about the unique history of the Palácio Quintela also impressed the friar, who relayed it in detail.

Her tormentor lived in a building of some repute. Count Farrobo, known for his lavish parties, was one of its earliest owners. The count's extravagance spawned the Portuguese term *farrobodo*, which translates into "to party wildly."

Fitting, Louisa thought. If she had her druthers, a *lopesgomes* would soon translate into "a sadistic cretin."

When she'd first begun her scouting of the location, she'd had to fight off frequent yawns, given the late hours. After three days and nights turned upside-down, her body moved to a nocturnal clock. She hoped it would give her an edge against anyone she might encounter except the regular night duty guards.

Tomorrow, their trip would end, and they would board a steamship bound for Le Havre and home. Louisa had one last chance. Tonight, she'd gather the bait and lead João into the trap to end this nightmarish threat. The alternative did not sit well with her.

She couldn't comprehend what drove João's obsession with her, beyond that she had pummeled his fragile ego at each turn, and now his reputation lay in tatters. The *lopesgomes* would never stop coming for her. How long would it take for her sanity to crumble from peering over her shoulder every day, expecting to be kidnapped or get a knife in the back?

Even more important than for her safety, Louisa had to stop João, or the only people who loved her would continue to be in danger. That madman had already preyed on them just to get at her.

As she peered down at her target, the spiritual presence of her clan helped solidify Louisa's resolve. She pictured Eugénie touching her father's medal and leading prayers for her with Virginie and Catherine huddled close. With her heart full of love for her sisters, Louisa ran through her breathing exercises, centering every thought on the mission.

Most people thought a burglary consisted of nonstop bursts of energy and constant danger-fueled fear. Even some thieves believed that. They were either foolish or daredevils who sought out life-or-death situations. People glorified crime because of the perceived excitement. They never considered what it took to be good at the job.

Trained by an expert, Louisa considered any theft that took place with too much fear or excitement a failure. There was no denying that she loved the rush of climbing and the thrill of getting away with her crimes. She even loved keeping the secrets that came with her career, but she seldom let her joy override the rules of a well-executed burglary.

This mission was different. This job's circumstances required Louisa to break *A Thief's Cardinal Rule--The Reward Must Be Worth the Risk, and There is No Reward Worth Your Life.*

Three days of observation and surveillance were not enough to reduce the risk. If she were caught, she might be killed. Still, given her constraints, she had done as much as possible to minimize the danger. Her eyes roved over the target, and she reviewed again what she knew.

Built toward the bottom of one of Lisbon's many hills, the palace was taller on the lower side than on the uphill side. The entrance fronted a prominent street with a view of an oval park, while behind the house's enormous walled garden ran another primary avenue.

At that moment, Louisa stood on the roof near the rear of the eighteenth-century church, Our Lady of Incarnation. Like many buildings in Lisbon, the church's back wall abutted the side of its neighbor. In this case, it shared a wall with Palácio Quintela. A carriage house and a garden wall separated the devil's palace from another mansion and its extensive grounds, completing the target's perimeter.

Olive oil–powered lamps, hanging from poles, cast the vast, lush garden in brassy hues. Louisa eyed the two guards leading a ferocious-looking dog around the large fountain at the center. Two nights ago, she had seethed while watching that *kópanos*, João, host a party in that garden.

Beautiful women in extravagant dresses and handsome young men in formal attire ate and drank all night while being entertained by quintets of musicians, singers, and acrobats. Given the knights' accusations about the Lopes Gomes family, Louisa half-expected to witness the guests dancing around a witches' cauldron. By the middle of the night, she'd seen no animal sacrifices, but the actions of half of the attendees who remained had devolved into the most feral of behaviors. The height of her hiding spot had provided a small mercy in that regard.

Louisa shook her head, pushing the vile memories from her mind.

Time to find a lock for my new key, Louisa thought. She moved to the edge of the church's roof, squatted down, then hung from her hands and dropped the half-meter to the palace's roof.

That she now violated *Rule Number Two--Don't Rush* didn't mean she had to be foolhardy. She'd mitigated as much risk as possible by following *Rule Number Three—Make Plans with Multiple Contingencies.* A diagram formed in her mind with all the possibilities.

Confirm the status of the most significant threat, Louisa thought as she skirted around the domed skylight that, during the day, added natural light to João's office. At night, her black shadow would be easy to see against the city's diffused glow. After padding down the slanted roof, she checked inside a dormer window overlooking the garden.

A man-shaped lump moved under the duvet, changing positions on a massive four-poster bed. To make sure João was asleep, Louisa glared with hatred at that lump for several minutes. With a shiver, she pushed those feelings away. She needed to be in complete control, a cold, calculating thief and, when necessary, a shadow.

She moved away from the window and crossed the roof. *Always start a search in the most likely places.*

At the center of the residence, a small tower in the shape of an octagon protruded skyward. It gave the ballroom its grandiose height. Hunched over, she crept around the tower's windows.

Once past them, Louisa made her way to the two dormer windows on the far side, the ones overlooking the carriage house. The dormer windows sat three meters off the floor. She squatted beside one, peering down into the room. When nothing moved, she strained against the wood frame to push it upward.

After listening for several minutes, she slipped inside the building and hung from the windowsill before dropping. Her opanke-like shoes, made of supple black leather and lined with soft padding, cushioned her fall.

Rule Number Four--Always Have an Escape Route.

Louisa kept an eye on the door as she unlocked the standard window below the dormer and raised it to get her fingers under the frame. Her exit ready, she examined the room in detail. Floor-to-ceiling bookshelves lined most of the walls except one. A massive portrait hung there of a man wearing a Renaissance-era jerkin standing next to a woman in a golden dress.

It can't be that easy.

Louisa crossed to the painting and ran her fingers along the edge of the frame. Reaching as high as she could on tippy toes, she checked for anything that might be a latch or a trigger to a trap. Nothing felt suspicious. She stood to the side and tried to lift the painting away from the wall, pulling harder a little at a time but without success.

So heavy. Louisa grasped the gilded frame with both hands and tried again. Two-thirds of the way up the frame, large hooks on either side held the portrait in place. The only option was to lift the bottom of the painting, which defeated the purpose of hiding a secret door. Still, she gritted her teeth, her arm straining against the weight while she held the frame away from the wall and felt the smooth wood paneling behind it.

Hardly ever comes easy. Louisa frowned and examined the man and the woman in the portrait in detail. Nothing suggested that these people were devil-worshiping witches. The ridiculous accusations made her think the knights were making whole cheese from a bit of milk.

Anytime she thought of *Rule Number Five--Be as Meticulous as Time Allows*, her uncle's alternate phrasing always came to mind. He would say, "Move with a sense of urgency, but do not rush."

Louisa lit a small candle to help her inspect the rest of the room. Without finding anything promising, she put the candle away and pulled a meter-long string from her pocket. Her uncle had taught her early on that a mark's hidden vault is where to find the greatest treasures. One of the few ways to ferret out a vault's location was to identify hidden spaces between rooms.

She spread the string wide and glided around the room with quick, practiced movements, measuring the library's width and length. A separate process calculated the distance from the wall to the door. After memorizing the tallies, she moved to the door, placing her ear against it. A little light leaked under the oak portal, highlighting one of her matte-black slippers.

This next action was the most dangerous part so far. As Louisa twisted the doorknob, she tensed, preparing to rush for the window. The crack let in more light, and she peeked one-eyed into the corridor. A few olive oil–burning wall sconces cast the hallway in low light. She'd only seen João on this floor in the past and breathed a sigh of relief to find the passage empty.

Louisa cringed at the slight creak when she stepped out of the library onto the corridor's wooden flooring. She left a crack in the door and turned toward his parents' quarters. If the safe wasn't in there, she doubted it would be in the deranged man's rooms. A guarded basement would be the only other logical location.

Too many people had access to the rest of the home, and if the value of the goods in the vault was accurate, Louisa doubted the owners would even let guards know it existed. Men became idiots when seducing a woman, so she had no reason not to believe João's loose tongue about the treasure room's contents. If it were her, she'd prepare false hiding places and traps while hiding the safe in a location where she spent plenty of time.

Louisa moved down the hallway, one string-stretch at a time, keeping the numbers in her head. At the next door, she put the string away and turned the knob but found it locked. Her lock picks danced in her hands until there was a soft click.

With one ear to the door and the other seeking approaching footsteps, she stayed still for a count to ten. After a turn of the knob, she gave a light push and peered into the near darkness. Wan light filtered through gauzy drapes hung on the room's two windows.

She slipped inside, closed the door, used her lockpicks to secure the entrance, and then turned to the room. A match, a candle, and a small candle holder came out of another pocket. One big step away from the door, she struck the match and lit the wick.

Louisa stood in front of a massive desk made of rich hardwood. There were two normal-size portraits on the left wall. The same man and woman looked down on her with a regal air. In an odd turn, their clothing was from this century. She wondered whether vanity ran in the Lopes Gomes line. Why else would they have dressed up in almost Medieval-style clothes for the other portrait?

She shook her head at the pomposity of these people as she moved to open one of the windows and began the search. Stands lined the other walls, displaying an ancient sculpture, a weapon, or eons-old pottery decorated by long-dead master artisans. There were no hidden compartments in the stands, nothing out of the ordinary in the desk, and only blank walls behind the paintings.

Louisa finished the examination, set her candle on the desk, and made more measurements. She retrieved a nub of a pencil and a piece of paper from another hidden pocket and sat in a leatherbound desk chair big enough for two of her. She sketched out the two rooms. After double-checking her numbers, she pinched out her candle and put it away with the paper. Her internal clock told her time was running out. The next room needed to give her something.

For a heartbeat, her fear of not succeeding made her resent all the silly authors who made heroes out of dashing, devil-may-care thieves. Their stories never spoke to the frustration and the failure that are often the thief's only reward for days or even months of planning.

It's all Robin Hood's fault.

With tempered haste, Louisa moved back into the hallway. Down she went, stretching her string to the turn before measuring the distance to what should have been the door to João's parents' bedroom. The lock on this door had dual keyholes, one regular and one abnormal.

Louisa thought, *The prize must be somewhere inside.*

Fighting to suppress her excitement, she picked the first lock. Her attempt at the unique lock was as impossible as she'd first envisioned it. She took João's key from another pocket. It went in the keyhole, and when Louisa twisted, the key's decorative handle spun on the shaft.

She hesitated, chastising herself for not seeing the key's unique attributes before now. If she did not manipulate the key the right way, it might spell doom. After a little more thought, she doubted this was the door to the vault. Time dwindling, she had to take risks. A complete turn counterclockwise and a snap signaled the mechanism unlocking.

Her hopes confirmed, she finally exhaled. Yet, she might have just activated a trap. Her chest tightened as she placed her back to the wall and stretched her arm as far as she could. She turned the knob. Ready to jump away, she squatted low and pushed. The door swung open. Nothing happened.

Penguin-style, she waddled to the doorway. Using a firm palm, she pushed against every centimeter of the rug for a meter beyond the threshold. With muscles tensed, she stood and twisted the key clockwise until the handle at the top stopped spinning.

Here we go again. Louisa eased the key out of the hole. She blinked in relief, and the growing tension in her back eased. Stepping inside, she closed the door without bothering to relock it--too much risk.

Before she put the key away, she twisted the top of the handle. Extra ridges popped out from the shaft, going in multiple directions. *Impressive.*

Louisa swapped the key for the candle and began her inspections. A plush leather couch and several antique settees formed a U-shape in the sitting room. There was a door to the left and another to the right.

She crossed the room and unlatched the double doors in the corner that led to an outside balcony. She performed a hurried inspection of the room. There weren't many good places to hide a safe. Disappointed, she made her measurements.

The corner of the building contained a lavatory full of sparkling marble and porcelain tiles decorated with blue Portuguese designs. There were no possible exits, so Louisa left the door open wide before starting a search that turned up nothing. Her despair swirled faster as she removed her string and stepped off more dimensions.

One more room.

Less cautious, she almost jogged to the door on the other side of the sitting room. As she reached for the doorknob, she stopped and shook her hands to release her nervous energy.

With her emotions reined in, she went through all her security checks before opening the door. Light from her tiny candle caused gold to pulse in the room's many mirrors. Like an opulent room at Versailles, baroque gilded flowers and filigreed patterns sparkled on every surface, including the golden cherub finials topping the four tall bedposts.

Louisa almost gagged at the over-the-top display. *Is this what a witch's room looks like?* She laughed at the silly thought and added, *How could anyone sleep here?*

Thoughts of the vile garden party suggested a different use for the bedroom, and Louisa saw the mirrors in a whole new light. *Gross!*

Where to begin? The double doors on the far wall led to a Juliet balcony overlooking the back gardens. She unlatched those and defaulted to her standard search pattern for the rest of the room. From the inside out, she circled counterclockwise. Sometimes one, two, and even too-many-to-count black-clad reflections followed her around the room.

After finding only wood, silk, and down, Louisa moved from the bed to the matching armoires. She tapped every surface, seeking a false compartment. No secret bolt holes or levers were revealed, but she discovered a small fortune in hanging clothes. João's mother's armoire contained gowns threaded with gold and silver, but nothing Louisa might take would force João to chase after her. Besides formal wear, the father's armoire held several jewel-encrusted pocket watches and cufflinks.

Those went into a small pouch for her secondary mission. The jeweled watches and cufflinks would be safe for Simon and Virginie to sell once they reached America. They only needed to find a trustworthy buyer. It was not enough. Louisa owed them much more and desired to see the couple off with enough cash to fund a first-class voyage, along with six months of living expenses.

Fear of not finding the safe pushed Louisa back to her primary mission. She had a soul-deep ache to see João's head on a platter, and these other thoughts were dangerous distractions.

On the bright side, the job was going according to plan.

The ideal caper consisted of conducting a tedious search while alone in the dark with no real excitement other than relieving treasure from those who could afford it. Louisa had never been anything but a realist, and she began to measure the room without much hope of finding what she had come for.

Back in the sitting area, she sat on a windowsill, drawing out the rest of the measurements. With the floor plan filled in, her irritation boiled over. It had to be here somewhere. Her eyes darted to the candle, and her thoughts turned to dark visions of burning drapes. Fists clenched, she dismissed the idea.

Lifting the holder, she assessed her drawing one final time and noticed an error. She'd forgotten to draw the lavatory. Drawers within her mental filing system flew open, and she perused the contents until she located the numbers. Resuscitated hope surged inside her. Two meters were missing from a wall. Tilting the pencil, she shaded in a gap between the sitting room and the lavatory.

Louisa smirked. *They may never put me in a book, but someday, they'll write about me in the papers.*

Chapter 41

The Key to Satan's Heart

Buoyed by detecting a possible location for the vault, Louisa inspected the walls with renewed diligence. The wood paneling in João's parents' sitting room was as she had found it the first time. Inside the spa-like room of marble, porcelain, and tile, she stepped into the claw-foot bathtub to reach the wall in question. She ran her palms over the floor-to-ceiling mural, seeking any unusual bumps.

Like others she had seen, the panorama showed the flow of time. Land battles against the Moors and the Spanish dominated one side before transitioning to sailing ships fighting on the high seas and ending with plantations in tropical locales from the New World. A small detail she hadn't noticed the first time hit her like a thunderclap.

In each scene, banners were flying the same emblem. At its center was a symbol shaped like a wheel with unbalanced spokes. It had four stick-figure arrows lying crisscrossed on one another so that the arrows' fletching pointed in four directions on one side and the sharp ends pointed in four different directions on the other.

Looks like a compass. Louisa shook her head at the knights' foolishness. *Not just a compass but directions for a coven of witches.*

She chuckled in silence as instinct made her reach toward the flag of a sailing ship whose cannon blazed against another sailing vessel. Her fingers grazed the star on the tile, finding grooves. All three flags on the mural had the same small indentations.

She brought forth the unique key and twisted the handle. She fiddled with the mechanism lining up the little prongs based on how far she twisted the top. When the prongs matched the flag pattern, she pushed the key against the tile. It didn't budge a bit. After trying each flag, she sat on the lip of the tub in consternation.

What did I miss? Louisa's gut told her that the symbol held the answer. It could be anywhere in this room. She lifted a leg to step out of the tub and kicked the stopper loose.

She shook her head at her clumsiness and thought of *Rule Number Seven—Leave No Trace of Your Presence.* She bent to put the plug back in place and saw it. The stopper had come to rest upside-down, its cork stamped with one of the symbols.

Heart hammering with excitement, Louisa squatted over the open drain. Half of the opening went down a pipe, but metal with a keyhole covered the other half.

What is this? Louisa grinned. She had expected to find a hole in the same shape as the symbol. After she reflected on how a thief would utilize the key, the lock's puzzle unraveled in her thief's mind. No one could unlock this door without understanding the key's relation to the symbol. Even then, other variables made using this key dangerous.

Louisa practiced twisting the key to the correct shape on top of one of the flags. Listening for an alarm, she pushed the key into the hole a millimeter at a time until a slight shudder signaled that the key was as far down as it would go, but it was still not fully inserted. With a precise twist of the handle, she opened the prongs to the correct position. When nothing happened after ten seconds, she pushed. The shank sank until the bow of the key touched the metal of the keyhole.

Louisa licked her lips, trying to calm her nerves in this moment of truth. Fifty-fifty propositions violated every rule of good thievery. She'd always known those were the odds. Anyone creating such a complex key must have had the foresight to trigger an alarm or, in the worst case, shoot poison-tipped darts from above, based on the direction in which she twisted the key.

Her eyes darted to the ceiling. She found only flat plaster. She checked to make sure the lavatory door stood open. *Don't want to suddenly be locked in.*

Blowing out a deep breath, Louisa spun the bow of the key clockwise. Tumblers fell into place, and wires inside the wall whirred over hidden pulleys. She popped above the tub's edge, eyes darting toward the sounds. The floor jerked, and the tub tilted toward the wall. She had only a second to decide––stay or flee.

Louisa curled into the porcelain bowl, accidentally snuffing out her candle as the tiles of half the wall fell inward, exposing a dark hole. It took only seconds for the tub to be on its side and to slide into the gaping maw until any hint of light inside the lavatory disappeared.

A pleasant woody-citrus smell greeted her as she lay inside the tipped-over bathtub. She doubted João could have heard the noise on the far side of the mansion, but just in case, she got moving. She groped around her, seeking her candleholder. Brass bounced off glazed ceramic when her search pushed it over the edge of the tub. As loud as a bell, she snatched for it as it spun. The holder was empty. It took her a few moments to retrieve and light her next-to-last candle. She crawled out and stood on the tiles from the wall, which had become the flooring in front of the tilted bathtub.

Lined in cedar, the two-by-five-meter room had shelves running the length of the longer wall. Small statues, crosses, scrolls, and books covered that wall. A shadowy mound stood to her left. She stepped in that direction, and her mouth gaped. A pyramid of stacked golden bars glinted in the candlelight. Moving close, she made out Spanish stamps on the long, irregular bars the width of three of her fingers and about one finger high.

Incredible.

Pirates had lusted after these bars for centuries, but the weight of gold was problematic for tonight's robbery. Disappointed, Louisa left the bars and inspected the shelves. On the floor below the first shelf sat several boxes containing Bank of England notes bound in small stacks of different denominations. Louisa grabbed one bundle of fifty-pound notes, two twenties, and four fives.

If they contained one hundred notes each, it was more than enough money for Simon and Virginie to land on their feet. After a pause, she took a stack of five-pound notes for herself. It would serve as her nest egg once she got to England. Given the vast wealth in this room, she doubted anyone would know anything was missing. Yet, she needed this theft to be noticed.

Although they were more challenging to see along the dim shelves, Louisa found enough rings, earrings, and necklaces made of rare gemstones to rival many a monarch's crown jewels. Again, she ignored them. Anyone selling those jewels would become a target.

Her eyes lit upon a hand-size cross with a pedestal. Encrusted with small diamonds holding giant rubies that formed an inner cross, the religious artifact sparkled red and white even in the dim candlelight. She picked up the heavy cross.

People need to see this.

Despite Louisa's flexible views about personal property, she believed only the worst kind of person would hide such a beautiful cultural icon. *Who should I give this to so that it won't put them in danger?*

After settling on the only logical choice, she slipped the cross into the small bag, which sagged under its weight.

The knights were adamant that their help required no reward, but Louisa hated being indebted to anyone. The cross would be a small token of thanks, and only a fool with a death wish would try to take it from them.

Even stealing such a valuable piece didn't guarantee João would come after her. She needed more. *What would draw him out?* Given the man's ego, she doubted he had shared the loss of the key with his parents.

Once again, Louisa wondered what kind of people had raised such a monster. Given his vile demeanor, she assumed they would not be happy if they discovered the loss. Was it enough if he knew she had the key and the ability to break into the vault? She doubted that. It might take years for anyone to discover that the cross was missing, and he would have a replacement key made. *I need something personal.*

Louisa's inspection continued until she reached a small chest with the same compass-like symbol burned into the wood. She moved to the side before lifting the lid. When nothing happened, she peered into it and drew out a stack of four ledgers. She flipped open the one on top and furrowed her forehead.

Written in discernable groupings were slashes, dots, and lines. Some marks were individual versions of those used to form the compass symbol. She flipped through several pages, and all contained the strange code.

Spells? Louisa chuckled. *It's probably illegal accounting ledgers.* Her uncle had kept notes using a secret code that only he could read.

Spells or not, since they were in this vault, these books had real value. How much was this information worth? Could it force João to confront her? Time would tell.

The tempo of Louisa's internal metronome quickened, signaling her to increase her pace. She'd begun stuffing the books into the bag when the feel of vellum caused her to pause on the final tome. It was old. Older than the calfskin copy of the book she'd stolen in Coimbra.

Louisa flipped through the ancient volume, her eyes widening at the passing pages. Each contained a portrait of a man or a woman with more of the strange code below each picture. *Is this a family album or the coven roster?*

Perusing the book was like walking through the galleries of a museum exhibit, showing a timeline of art from the Medieval to Romantic periods. Pages five and six contained pictures of the same man and woman she'd seen earlier in the two sets of portraits, which she assumed were of João's parents. They wore even older styles of clothing in these drawings. With another turn of the vellum, Louisa stared in shock. The pretentious, predatory eyes of João stared back at her.

But these brown eyes belonged to a young woman who could pass for Louisa's older sister. She peered close. The woman's King Louis XVI–era ball gown only added to Louisa's growing queasiness about the unnatural resemblance of the woman to her. But the woman's stare was the same look Louisa had seen in her nightmares. It made her fear what she might see next.

She turned away and flipped the page. She gazed at the pile of gold in the corner. She knew what she would find; bile rose in her throat at the thought of it. *You must make sure.*

Every muscle in her body tensed. She twisted her head and gagged, dry heaving. João's smug countenance filled the next page, his lascivious eyes ensnaring her own. His obsession, his revolting desires were never about Louisa; they were intended for this other woman.

Was she João's sister? Her outfit placed her as a long-dead relative. None of it mattered. No one could make sense of crazy. All Louisa knew was that a sickness like his never ended. He would pursue her to the end of the earth, his mental substitute for the woman in the book.

After she pushed down the impulse to disfigure his face, she pulled out her small knife and sliced his visage free. She placed the book and the folded picture in the bag and slung it over her shoulders.

He'll come for her, Louisa thought with a stern nod and headed for the bathtub.

Curled inside the sideways porcelain tub, she blew out her candle and put the holder away. After crossing herself and sending another small prayer, she spun the key counterclockwise. Hidden wires ground inside the wall. The tub rolled into the lavatory and tilted itself upright.

She poked her head up for a quick look about the empty room, then pulled on the key. When it stopped coming up, she twisted the bow in the opposite direction to collapse the prongs forming the witches' symbol. She tried to pull it up. It would not budge.

Wires whirred, and gears turned.

"*Sapristi,*" Louisa hissed as her head whipped toward the lavatory door.

The portal was swinging closed. A steam-powered whistle, like a locomotive's, exploded inside the room. Instinctual as a cat, Louisa jumped straight up and pushed off the bathtub's edge, hurling herself toward the doorway. As her feet touched the marble flooring, she lunged feet-first for the threshold and slid across the marble flooring. Her right foot slipped through the opening, and the door rammed into her ankle.

Ears ringing from the whistle's shrieking, Louisa moaned and wedged her shoulder into the gap and pushed. It took all her effort to pry the door open. Like a champagne cork, she popped free. The door slammed shut behind her. With a hobbled shuffle, she made for the unlocked double doors leading outside.

Her jaws tightened as she ignored the pain in her leg and the overwhelming urge to clamp her hands over her ears. She pushed the doors open and stepped onto a small balcony attached to the carriage house roof. The entire top of the stable was used like a large porch with steps down into the garden. The faint, whining bark of the guard dog and almost inaudible shouts from the guards came from the direction of the garden.

Louisa ignored the instinct to panic, focusing on acting out the steps of the escape route that she had practiced in her mind earlier. Wincing in pain, she climbed onto a wrought iron railing. She jumped toward the lip of the molding over the window to the office a meter away. Her fingers grabbed the ledge at the top. She hand-hopped over to the other side and began to swing. She let go, flying to the next window, then with another swing, she launched herself to the next. After bringing her swaying to a stop, she used her good foot to shove open the two panes of the library's unlocked window.

A louder shout came from the direction of the carriage house. Louisa kicked back, then forward, her feet disappearing inside. She let go at another gun blast. The glass pane beside her shattered, shards ricocheting past. She landed with most of her weight on her uninjured leg and hopped to a one-legged stop. Another bang and a bullet ripped into the window frame.

The whistle went silent, echoes of its shriek ringing in Louisa's ears.

"*Na biblioteca!*" the guard shouted as his footsteps faded.

Louisa peeked outside to see him disappear down the steps toward the garden. Each time she moved her foot, a stab of pain lanced through her ankle. She gritted her teeth and climbed onto the windowsill. She stood up inside the room, then squatted and jumped with both legs. A sharp sting knifed through her entire leg as she grabbed hold of the dormer window's frame.

Thoughts of what João might do drove her to move faster, and she hauled herself up, ignoring the hurt. With an elbow on the sill, she shoved the window up. Using only her arms, she scrambled through the window as someone opened the door leading to the hallway. She slithered onto the terracotta tiles, only a few centimeters from the roof's edge. Light spilled into the room from the corridor. Louisa stood and looked down into the library.

A long shadow led the way as a shirtless João stepped inside, a revolver in his hand. Louisa moved to the side of the window.

This is it. Time for the fox to give the dog a scent.

She swung the bag off her shoulder and pulled out the folded page before securing the bag again. As she glanced around the corner, a bullet blasted the glass. She yanked her head back. With a smirk, she yelled in a mix of English and Greek, "Missed me again, *kólos*!"

"You," he said in a husky whisper.

Louisa needed to wrap this up before a guard returned to the carriage house and saw her. Her voice dripped sweetness. "I found your key and came to make all my dreams come true."

João chuckled. "And failed. I have the key."

"Did I?" She wadded up the page and, staying out of sight, tossed it through the window into the library.

Steps came closer. His voice took on a conciliatory tone. "Why don't you come down? I can still make your dreams come true. I won't hurt you. Promise."

Louisa peeked with one eye.

The devil's stomach muscles rippled as he bent to pick up the paper. His eyes darted toward her, and he wore an uncomfortable grin. "We don't need to drag this out." He unfolded the vellum page. There was a sharp intake of breath. Then the timbre of João's voice changed to icy cold. "Give it back."

"No," Louisa quipped. Every second she dragged this out was dangerous, but she had to know. She focused on his face, trying to capture even the most minute reaction. "Who is she? Your sister?"

His olive skin reddened, and his jaws flexed. "Shut up!" He glared at her, veins bulging in his neck. "You don't know anything. You're just a worthless whore!"

She spit out her response: "You disgust me."

The tension in João's body gave way, and the tone of his voice collapsed into contrition. "I'm sorry. It doesn't need to be like this. I love you."

Louisa cringed. "You love her. Lunatic."

His eyes hardened. "You will be mine. I'll find you in France if I need to."

I'd rather be fed alive to pigs, she thought, then said, "Come get me."

In a bear crawl, she moved up the incline toward the roof's ridgeline.

Still favoring her leg, she shuffled across the top of the mansion as more shouts rose from the garden. Moments later, guards yelled from the street in front of the palace. As she reached the wall abutting the church, she jumped, the agony in her ankle reigniting.

Can't get hurt, Louisa thought as she clambered onto the church roof. Tears threatened as she made it up one last incline to a small window.

A grim-faced Friar Cruz leaned forward with arms outstretched. Callused, sturdy hands grabbed her and pulled her inside. Louisa gasped, trying to catch her breath.

The knight frowned. "Are you hurt?"

"My ankle."

He stood, scooping her up to cradle her in his arms. "Did you bait the hook?"

Louisa nodded and then tried to wriggle free. "I can walk."

He shook his head. "We need to go fast." The big man jogged out of the room, and she wrapped her arms around his neck.

They moved down several flights of stairs and then through the sanctuary lit by hundreds of candles. Louisa stared upward, admiring the pink, green, and blue rococo ceiling as she bounced along with his strides.

"Did it work?" Brother Cruz asked as they left the church.

Louisa was about to answer when he lifted her onto the bench of an open-air buggy. Brother Cruz sat beside her while Brother de São Luís took the driver's seat. On her good leg, she half-stood and looked behind them.

"Don't go yet." She thrust a hand, palm out, toward the driver while keeping her eyes trained on the corner of the church in the street.

Two men rounded the building and skidded to a stop. One turned away, cupping hands to his mouth, and shouted something in Portuguese. The other lifted his revolver and fired. Wood splintered off the back of the carriage.

Louisa flinched, ducked down, then peered back over the seat.

João screamed as he rushed into view next to the men. "Stop shooting, you fool! I need her alive!"

Brother Cruz transitioned into his knightly form and leaned over the back of the buggy, aiming his revolver. He squeezed off a shot that sparked against the cobblestone street. The three men dove for cover.

A warning shot? Really? Louisa thought and frowned.

The knight chuckled. "Looks like you did it."

Louisa faced forward, placing the loot sack at her feet as she sat. "Go. But do not lose them."

"Haw!" Brother de São Luís yelled as he snapped the reins. The horses jerked forward.

Brother Cruz settled down beside her and rattled off something to the driver in Portuguese.

Louisa locked eyes with Knight Cruz and whispered, "It's in your hands now."

Chapter 42

Heroes Never Lie

The carriage's two-horse team nickered and neighed as they pulled away. Kneeling, Louisa leaned over her cushioned seat to keep an eye on their pursuers. The final part of their plan gave control to the knights. Louisa struggled to mentally relinquish the responsibility for what came next. João's guards dropped farther behind as the carriage horses picked up their pace with long, loping strides.

Brother de São Luís yelled something from the driver's seat, and the carriage listed left. The wheel under Louisa lifted off the cobblestones. Stomach lurching, she leaned toward the outside and felt Brother Cruz shifting his weight toward her. The steel-wrapped wheel bounced back to the ground with a jolt as they climbed one of Lisbon's seven hills. The carriage slowed even though she felt the strain of their steeds' greater efforts pressing her harder against the cushions.

The tension in her shoulders eased, then tightened as relief and apprehension skirmished as prevailing emotions. At least, the throbbing from her ankle had lessened to mere nuisance levels.

Brother Cruz's other planning concern turned out to be unfounded. Neither Lisbon's municipal guards nor the more recently established police force interfered in the night chase. They met only empty streets and heard only the uncanny clops of their horses' shoes on stone.

Louisa was about to tell the driver to slow down when four horsemen rounded the turn. João had acquired a loose-fitting white shirt, and it billowed around him as he leaned over his mount. The other three riders wore the same gray uniforms she'd seen on all the Palácio Quintela guards. Their horses surged forward, closing the gap with the carriage.

Louisa's apprehension turned to fear. As if sensing the danger, their horse team stretched into a full gallop. They raced by occasional gas lamps casting shadows on the buildings along empty sidewalks. The pursuers closed to within three carriage lengths, and Louisa looked at Brother Cruz, her uneasiness soaring.

He gave her a wink. "Don't worry, Mademoiselle. I'll take care of this." The warrior monk replaced his revolver with a short cudgel.

"Why don't you shoot them?"

The knight grinned. "*Put your sword back in its place, Jesus said to him, for all who draw the sword will die by the sword.* We must not kill except in self-defense of ourselves or an innocent."

This is not the time for turning the other cheek, she thought and grabbed his forearm. "I'm an innocent. Shoot them."

Knight Cruz laughed. "Can you drive the team?"

He's truly crazy. "I don't know the streets."

"Good point." He lifted the cudgel toward her. "Want this?"

Louisa shook her head. She pulled her loot sack into her lap and removed the encrusted cross. "I've got this." She held the jeweled icon up, gripping the shaft with the pedestal on top.

The friar laughed. "*Draw your strength from the Lord and from his mighty power.*"

The closest horse gained a stride, the animal's nose running even with the buggy. Brother de São Luís yelled a command in Portuguese. The buggy slewed to the left, and a guard pulled back to keep from being forced onto the sidewalk.

The buggy shifted right, and another rider veered onto the sidewalk on that side. They turned right, the slope disappearing as they raced across level ground.

The attackers made another attempt, and both riders moved up beside the carriage. Louisa gripped the railing tight with one hand. The smooth gemstones became slick in her palm, and she grasped the cross tighter. The man nearest her leaned away from his saddle, reaching for the side of the cabin with his fingers stretched open. Eyes bulging, the guard's mount shifted to within two hands of the carriage.

The guard grabbed the edge of the cabin and shifted in his saddle, preparing to jump. Louisa slammed the pedestal of the cross down on the man's hand. He howled and snatched his hand back. Gathering himself, he glared straight at her. Louisa shook the cross at him.

The guard kicked his mount and raced forward, the horse running even with the carriage team. The buggy swerved left again, the wheels rubbing against the animal, which had to hop onto the raised sidewalk. A store sign suspended over the mosaic pavers hit the guard in the shoulder. With a smack and a groan, he flew from the horse.

"Hah!" Louisa bellowed.

She turned in time to see another guard swing a saber across his saddle, the blade glinting. Knight Cruz twisted his wrist, his cudgel swiping the blade down and away. The friar used his other arm to follow the sword's trajectory, snagging the wrist of the bewildered man. A yank unsaddled the guard and pulled him screaming head-first toward the buggy's spinning wheel. A quick bap, bap, bap, cut off his scream, and the man's face slapped against one spoke after another.

That's going to leave a mark. Or three. Louisa chuckled until she looked behind them and saw that three new riders had joined João and the remaining guard. Their attackers pulled back, content to keep them in sight.

Brother de São Luís slowed the horses to a trot as they made a curve that started them going downhill. Whenever the pursuers closed the distance, the friar sped up, keeping the gap. With some distance still to go before they reached the cardinal's church, Louisa decided they were safe enough for her to show Brother Cruz why they were being chased.

She opened the bag and handed the regular ledgers to the friar. "I think these are important." She placed the vellum tome on top of the stack. "And he's desperate to get this one back."

The friar placed the stack in his lap, pulled the book from the bottom, and flipped it open. He whistled and said, "*Mãe de Deus.*"

Louisa tilted her head toward him. "Does that coded writing mean something to you?"

The man's head bobbed up and down. "Every *bruxos* communication we've ever captured used this language." He looked up, his expression hard. "If you don't mind, I'll give these to my superiors. It may help shed light on this mysterious group."

With a shrug, Louisa said, "I can't use them. Look at the other one."

Brother Cruz pulled the vellum book to the top and opened it to the first page.

Louisa said, "Keep going."

He moved through the drawings until Louisa jabbed her finger on a picture of a woman. "That's his mother." She waved a hand, and he flipped the page. "His father."

She began to thumb through the pages until she reached the second to last one. She paused to make sure she had his full attention. "This next one is his sister." She turned the page.

Brother Cruz hissed and crossed himself. His eyes darted from the portrait of Louisa's doppelganger back to her.

She grimaced. "Now you understand."

"This is Satan's work." He slammed the tome closed.

"I thought your order might use this in your ceremonies." Louisa twisted to show him the jeweled cross right side up. "Do not think of refusing this gift. It is the least that my friends and I can offer for the order's assistance."

She placed it on top of the books.

The brother licked his lips. "I will give it to Grand Officer da Costa."

"Wait until our boat leaves." She raised a single eyebrow, the same mannerism that her mother had used to demand young Louisa's compliance.

The brother gave a playful smile. "Sim, Senhora." He laughed and placed the ledgers and the cross in a small compartment under the driver's seat.

After twenty more minutes of the subdued chase, the buggy clip-clopped into a small piazza and pulled to a halt in front of stairs leading to Igreja de São Vicente de Fora. The cardinal of Lisbon kept his offices at the church, and the attached monastery acted as the tour's final residence in Portugal. Six more knights waited in the shadows around the trapezoid-shaped plaza.

The two knights with Louisa hopped to the ground. Brother de São Luís took up a position behind the horses while Brother Cruz stayed at the back of the carriage with Louisa to his rear.

Their pursuers stopped their horses in the open space and dismounted. They spread into an uneven line, approaching at a slow walk. Louisa waited until João and his men were in the very center with no easy escape route before shouting in English, "Halt!"

The approaching line came to a staggered stop, and more than one man put his hands on his knees.

João stepped forward. "Mademoiselle Sophia, how about a truce?" He took one more step forward. "Return my books, and I'll walk away."

"It's too late for that. You'll never stop." Louisa leaned around behind Brother Cruz to look at João. "It's time for justice. Put your guns down, you're surrounded."

João shook his head. "Ridiculous. You're outnumbered. But I will accept defeat. If you give me back what is mine, you will never see me again."

From darkened corners and from behind trees at the edge of the piazza, six figures in brown tunics stepped into the moonlight. Six rifles were aimed at the five men in the middle. The guards with João turned in slow circles. One of them raised his hands while another bent and set his pistol on the ground. João went silent, but even from a distance Louisa could see frustration in his eyes.

The hoofbeats of a two-horse team preceded the port chase carriage that appeared from a side street and pulled to a stop almost in front of their buggy.

The door of the carriage opened as Brother Cruz waved his arm at the driver and yelled, "Saia agora!"

The startled driver looked around in confusion as the brigadier half-stumbled down the carriage steps to the street.

"Unbelievable." Louisa muttered to herself. The timing of General Buffoon was, if nothing else, regimentally impeccable.

Almost falling, the old soldier righted himself with the use of his cane. When he was stable, he pointed the business end of the walking stick at Brother Cruz. "What is the meaning of this?"

Louisa smelled his sweet-and-sour port wine breath from several meters away and cringed. Ignoring the question, Brother Cruz waved and yelled to the driver again. The driver's eyes widened as if seeing the friar's short-barreled revolver for the first time.

He cracked his whip, and the horses snorted and jerked the carriage forward. As the general's carriage raced away, Louisa was astounded to find the men in the middle hadn't moved. Four of them had arms raised high while João scowled in her direction, his revolver hanging at his side.

"Of course, I'd find you in the middle of trouble, Demoiselle."

Louisa glanced at the brigadier. His walrus mustache had constricted around his pursed lips as he jabbed his cane toward her.

She locked eyes with João again. His tanned face had turned a menacing plum shade. Then he looked to the side, and his expression transformed into a cruel sneer.

"Louisa, it's good to see you."

She whipped her head to the side to see a flushed-faced Simon jogging toward them. The brigadier turned and stepped toward the young man as if to meet him.

What is he doing here? Her mind raced, and her eyes darted to João. His arm rose.

Too late, she screamed, "Simon, look out!"

Fire burst from João's revolver, followed by several eruptions from around the plaza. Louisa's tormentor spun to the side, his arm going limp. His pistol clattered to the cobblestones. The men around him yelled for mercy, one of them dropping to his knees.

Louisa turned and ran toward Simon, on his knees propping up Brigadier Gerard. The soldier looked up at the young man as a dark wetness spread across his formal white shirt.

Louisa knelt beside them, and Simon asked, "Why?"

His voice quavering, the old soldier replied, "Because. I am a general of France." The walrus mustache arced into a rueful grin. "I misjudged you, son. Forgive me."

Anguish wracked Simon's body. "*Merci*," he croaked.

The brigadier's smile grew broad. "I can't wait to tell this story to the lads." His voice trailed off as the life in his eyes faded to nothing.

For all his faults, Brigadier Etienne Gerard had died a hero at the hands of a demented coward. Simon began to weep, mumbling incoherent words while tears of rage flowed down Louisa's face.

That animal. That demon.

Hands clenched, she jumped to her feet and ran toward João. The murderer had hung his head, the resignation of a whipped dog in his eyes.

The pain in her ankle flared but faded to nothing as her fury grew. A primal need to kill, to murder, to destroy consumed her. Something guttural came from her throat as a strong arm pulled her back, lifting her feet off the ground.

"No!" She kicked backward and was rewarded with a grunt. With no rational thought, she leaned forward trying to bite her way free as a second arm enveloped her. A soothing "Shh" whispered into her ear as the human blanket brought her to the ground. The gale of her storm weakened, along with her strength. All the while her eyes tried to burn João to ash.

When she was still, Brother Cruz asked, "Can I let go?"

Louisa's voice cracked. "He deserves to die."

"He does, but he surrendered." He loosened his grip.

She went limp as sudden weariness washed over her. *I'm so tired. Why am I so tired?*

Several friar-knights led João to the buggy. As four of the friars drove him away, she shook herself free and sat up. She tried to stand but had to lean on Brother Cruz for support. The buggy disappeared into the night, an unfitting end to her travails.

She looked at the friar, her eyes pleading. "He has to pay."

Brother Cruz stood ramrod straight, and the Knight of Our Lord Jesus Christ rumbled his answer to her plea: "For his crimes, the council has command-ed that João Lopes Gomes be deprived of his manhood and exiled to the most primitive of places."

Chapter 43
Never Fear the Future

A fishy, salty wind whipped her sash back and forth, forcing her to hold it in place as she stood in line to board the ship. Louisa had thought she'd be happy once she got her revenge on João. If not happy, at least she should have been relieved. Instead she felt empty, guilty, and scared in equal measure.

As the coffin approached, Simon joined the line of seven somber girls, two solemn nuns, and the colonel to pay respects. With a crisp salute, the colonel snapped to attention. Mère Sainte Adeline sniffled as six sailors carried Brigadier Gerard's French flag–draped, pine coffin past them and up the gangplank.

As his remains went by, Louisa asked the brigadier for forgiveness. She'd thought he was nothing but a pompous braggart. With his death, the man proved to be every bit the heroic soldier his stories had claimed. It felt fitting to her that he would be buried in the country he'd served his entire life. There was one small consolation for her in his death. She thought the old soldier had been proud of how he met his end.

It had been unfortunate that the brigadier returned to the monastery when he did, and worse luck that Simon showed up right behind him. An oversight on Simon's part, but the young man had never learned where the tour group was going to stay in Lisbon. Desperate to find Virginie before the tour left Portugal, he had followed the old soldier from a business meeting. Simon had remembered arranging that meeting when still employed by the man.

At least, the chaperones never learned about Louisa's part in the events. The friars constructed a cover story, claiming that João had shown up with armed men and tried to kill Simon. The brigadier had stepped in front of the bullet meant for the younger man, and the friars had dispatched the murderer.

The coffin disappeared onto the ship, and Louisa's heart tightened with dread. She didn't want to say goodbye to Virginie, but the time had come.

The colonel spoke to the group, "Mademoiselles, time to board."

Virginie caught the colonel's attention, "Colonel, a moment please." She went to the man and whispered in his ear.

"I understand, Mademoiselle Ghesquiere." He bowed and walked away to help Mère de la Nativité onto the gangplank.

Louisa grabbed her friend's elbow, and Virginie turned around with tears in her eyes. Louisa handed the black bag to Virginie. It was full of British pounds, jeweled watches, and gem studded cufflinks. Louisa's voice cracked. "This is for you and Simon. If it's not enough. I'll get more." She drew Virginie into a hug.

Sniffling, Louisa said, "I won't say goodbye. I love you."

Virginie hugged her back and laughed. "I love you, too."

Louisa turned away and moved to stand beside Eugénie, needing her last best friend's strength to get through this loss.

Simon stepped up and took Virginie's free hand in his. "I know how much I'm asking of you. I promise to love you from the bottom of my soul and with every bit of my strength."

Virginie leaned in and placed a gentle kiss on his lips. She straightened. "I know you would." She licked her lips and swallowed. "I can't go with you."

Parbleu. Louisa's mind raced. Her eyes flashed to Eugénie and then to Catherine. Neither one seemed surprised.

"But—" Stunned, Simon opened and closed his mouth, seeking words that would not come.

"This isn't my dream, Simon. It's yours." She reached up and wiped a tear from his cheek. "You deserve someone who shares that dream. That's not me."

"Is there nothing I can do?"

She handed him the bag. "Make your dreams come true. I'll try to do the same."

He stared at her with unspoken words. At last, resignation flashed across his face, his composure coming back. "I'll make you proud, but I can't accept this." He held up the bag.

Yes, you can, Louisa thought, her indignation ignited.

Favoring her hurt ankle, Louisa took two quick hops and slapped Simon's back. "Do you know what I went through to get that? If you don't take it, I'm going to break your arm."

Simon turned to her with a laugh. "*D'accord, d'accord.* I'll take it." His eyes sought Virginie one more time, and he nodded before stepping back to address them. "I'll never forget this. If any of you come to America, find me. My home will always be open." Stiff and looking as if he was about to lose control again, he gave Virginie an abrupt hug. "Goodbye."

He broke his embrace, looked down, and rushed away. Virginie watched him go until he disappeared into a crowd of passengers and dockworkers.

"Pleasure. You could have told me." Mad that her friend had hidden her intentions, Louisa glared at Virginie for a long moment. The pain on her friend's face made Louisa soften her next words. "Are you sure?"

Virginie pulled off her spectacles and wiped away tears. Tight-lipped, she replied, "If I had gone, I might have had a wonderful life, but there's no use dwelling on it. I've chosen my path."

Louisa smiled. "I'm proud of you. You know my philosophy: you should feel no shame in loving yourself above all, but how did you know that you made the right choice?"

Like a wise woman dispensing her most sage advice, Virginie said, "I don't. But as my mother told me before she passed––*if you accept the responsibilities that come with your choices and do the work, you'll live a full life. Live life like that, and there are no bad futures.*"

She adjusted her spectacles, then put her arm around Louisa's shoulders. "Let's go home."

Epilogue

João jerked awake. The ship lurched and rolled to one side as it slewed downward into the trough between waves. With his sharpened hearing, the howling wind and the crashing waves boomed in his head. The sounds kept him from thinking straight, but it was his stomach that truly betrayed him. It tried to jump into his throat again.

He fought to keep from throwing up. With nothing left inside, each dry heave had him tasting bile. He jerked the chain between his shackles and used the back of his sleeve to wipe his mouth. Even more dried blood covered the cuffs of his shirt and the legs of his pants than the last time.

The elven magic in his veins healed any ailment, but it took time. Within a few hours after he dropped into his last exhausted, dreamless sleep, his wrists and ankles—the source of the blood—were once again flawless. He had rubbed them raw, fighting against his manacles. That same healing power would soon catch up to the queasiness in his stomach.

The ship tilted and reeled upward, rocked at the peak, and staggered down another storm-fueled wave.

Just need to endure.

After several more ups and downs driven by the squall, João's heaving stopped, his mind and stomach rolling in harmony with the ship. He regretted no longer having the distraction of seasickness. *This is harder to endure.*

Feeble rays of golden light flickered between the bars. Bolted to the ship's bulkhead, a single lamp almost kept the darkness at bay. The floor of his cell was covered by the vomited contents of his last meal and filth that had sloshed out of the corner bucket nailed to the deck.

He shook his head, not wanting to remember. Still, he had to confirm that it was real. That this wasn't just a nightmare. When he moved one hand downward, the chain running through the metal ring on the wall and attached to his wrist shackles pulled his other hand upward. He felt between his legs. Finding his search incomplete, João closed his eyes and thought, *It's true. I'm a eunuch.*

Scenes from his last night of freedom flashed by. After the chase through the streets of Lisboa, he'd tried to kill that idiot Simon. Then came the pain of bullets ripping through both of his shoulders. He'd never experienced physical pain like that.

With no more fight left in him, the monks bound him and hauled him away. By the time they'd reached a small cottage by the sea, the bullets inside him had dissolved, and the wounds were nothing but fading scars. The friars had called him a witch, and some spoke of burning him at the stake.

Instead, they knocked him out and did something much worse.

The magic in his blood healed the castration cut within a day, but, like the points of his ears, his powers could not bring back what was destroyed. He woke in the hull of this ship. None of his jailers had spoken to him. He had no idea where they were taking him.

Being immortal gave a man a different perspective on life. At least, that was what he'd been told by his sister and a few other older elves. João's problem was that this was the beginning of his long life. He hadn't yet gained the wisdom that multiple lifetimes would afford him. Maybe in a thousand years, he wouldn't regret his actions that night. He pushed his self-pity aside and focused on the only goal that mattered: how to gain his freedom.

When Tiamat finds out I've been taken, she'll come for me.

Thoughts of his sister brought Louisa's face to mind, and that same searing hatred flowed through him for the ten thousandth time.

The ship lurched again. The light on the wall guttered and blinked out, leaving João's prison in total darkness. He gave in to the black, imagining what he wanted most. To still be whole. To still be a man. Time and his pain stopped in that abyss of midnight.

A crewman stumbled into the hold and lit the lamp. The light twinkled back to life, bringing João the cruel gift of reality. His illusion fled, the flames exposing the injustice done to him.

Fueled by his hatred of Louisa, he yanked and kicked. He fought against the iron bands welded around his wrists and ankles, thrashing his skin raw and bloody. The pain numbed his actual wound. João's self-flagellation continued until, through exhaustion, he fell limp. Sleep claimed him after one last thought: *Louisa, you will pay for this. I don't care how long it takes. I'll kill you. Then I'll kill everyone who ever meant anything to you.*

Thank You for Reading

If you enjoyed *Louisa Sophia and a Legion of Sisters*, please consider leaving a review on Goodreads.

Louisa's Book
Page on Goodr
eads.com

Please try Russell Cowdrey's other books starring Louisa Sophia:

Ancient Civilizations, Lamentations and Magic Book 1

Echoes of Ancients, Lamentations and Magic Book 2

Coming soon – Harvest of Ancient Sorrows, Lamentations and Magic Book 3

The Lamentations and Magic series takes place when Louisa is twenty-six and transports the reader across 1880s Egypt to the other side of the universe were magic is all too real. The series includes some great new characters with elements of science fiction, fantasy, romance, and found family.

Coming in late 2025 or early 2026 – *Louisa Sophia and The Clan of the Dissipated* – Twelve year old Louisa's world has turned upside down. Her mother is dead, and her uncle awaits his date with the gallows. Join Louisa's epic journey from Corfu to the Legion of Honor school in Saint-Denis where she first meets Eugénie, Virginie, and Marie.

To keep up with the latest on my writing adventures signup for my newsletter at RussellCowdrey.com.

If you would like to read about the research I put into this book and others, subscribe to my substack at www.HistoryIsMagic.com.

Please follow me on Amazon, Facebook, Instagram, TikTok.

Thank you again for joining me on this journey,

History is Magic,
Russell Cowdrey

Historical Notes

The Inspiration: Les maisons d'éducation de la Légion d'honneur

The schools are officially part of the Légion d'honneur organization and not the Department of Education. The school superintendents are managed by a retired general whose boss is the president of France. At 213 years of age, these state-supported, all-girls boarding schools also have an unusual hereditary aspect to their attendance.

To apply to one of the schools, an applicant's parent, grandparent, or great-grandparent must have been awarded France's highest medal, the Légion d'honneur, similar to the United States' Medal of Freedom. In addition to being educated at one of the top schools in France, the students live in an actual eighteenth-century abbey that reminds visitors of Hogwarts.

This is a great starting point for any novelist, but the magic I found in the history of real people associated with the school has added so much to the book. During my research, I discovered a dissertation written about European women's education during the late 1800s. Part of Professor Roger's paper incorporated a diary written by Eugénie Savant, a student who attended the Legion of Honor School at Écouen from 1875 to 1880. In her diary, Eugénie discussed how she and her friend, Virginie Ghesquiere, formed a secret society along with other students, the Clan of the Dissipated, to help bring them joy amid the school's demanding class schedule and unflinching rulebook enforced by a staff of strict nuns.

I am proud to have included fictional representations of Eugénie, Virginie, and the Clan of the Dissipated within the following pages. Two chapters in the book are my take on a story from the diary, while another was shared with me by current students at Saint-Denis during my visit to the school in December 2023.

After speaking to six classes of young women attending Saint-Denis, I became invested in capturing the students' female-centric esprit de corps. The young ladies I interacted with were intelligent, well-mannered, and confident. They are fantastic representatives of the school and of France.

The Author's Journey: How the book came to be.

Louisa Sophia is 99 percent fictional but is based on the real-life illegitimate daughter of the 1st Earl of Cromer, <u>Evelyn Baring</u>. The only factual aspects of her fictionalized life are her relationship with her father, that her mother was Greek, and that she was born on the Greek island of Corfu.

While looking for a high-end boarding school to be part of the Louisa character's background for my historical science fiction series, <u>Lamentations and Magic</u>, I came across the Maisons d'éducation de la Légion d'honneur, which took me on a research binge.

The best English-based research I found on the schools was a synopsis written in the early 1990s by Professor Rebecca Rogers. Her thesis on women's education in the nineteenth century extensively referenced the diary of a young woman who attended the Legion of Honor school at Écouen from 1875 to 1880.

Eugénie Savant was that young woman's name. Through her diary's translated words, I learned of her best friend, **Virginie Ghesquiere**; the rulebook; the nuns who ran the lower-level schools; an extraordinary classroom story; and the two girls' secret society, the **Clan of the Dissipated**. The two primary nun characters in the story, **Mère de la Nativité,** and **Mère Sainte Adeline,** were mentioned by name in the diary. "Chapter 4: A Pyrrhic Victory" is my take on a diary entry describing a militaristic classroom competition.

My wife and I traveled to Portugal in March 2022. I outlined a plot with a younger Louisa Sophia as the lead protagonist during the trip. The story uses many historical locations we visited in Portugal and includes a supporting cast of nuns and students from the Saint-Denis branch of the Legion of Honor schools.

I chose the Saint-Denis branch because Écouen is no longer a functioning school and because of Professor Rogers's connections. She put me in touch with teachers and administrators at Saint-Denis.

Our Portugal trip took place at the tail end of the Covid lockdowns, and before flying home, we tested positive. I completed the plot outline while quarantining at the seaside town of Sesimbra, an hour south of Lisbon. Best illness ever.

In December 2023, I was invited by an English teacher at the Saint-Denis school to visit. My stepson and I attended six of the teacher's classes where we spoke to current students. We confirmed that today's students were not so different from the teenagers who attended in the 1870s, secret societies and all. You can read my article about the school, *A Singularly Unique School*, on my blog, HistoryIsMagic.com.

Characters and events mentioned in the book, as well as their historical significance, are discussed in the following sections. If a character is not listed, he or she is 100 percent fictional.

The Characters

Louisa Sophia (clan name: Audacieux/Daring)––Based on the real illegitimate child of the First Earl Cromer, Evelyn Baring, who became the Egyptian consul-general or British citizen in charge of occupied Egypt after the invasion of 1882. Her age and almost all other details of her life in this book are fictional. I do not know whether Louisa Sophia was her full name or her first and middle names.

Eugénie Savant (clan name: Gaité/Gaiety)––The very real author of the diary, she never married or had children. Her niece donated the diary to the Legion of Honor upon her death.

Virginie Ghesquiere (clan name: Plaisir/Pleasure)--Eugénie's best friend, as written in the diary. I was unable to find any other historical details about Virginie.

Marie Coffinières de Nordeck (clan name: Joie/Joy)--The fictional daughter of the real and (in)famous <u>General Grégoire Coffinières de Nordeck</u>, who was accused of cowardice during the Franco-Prussian War of 1870–1871. I chose to use General Coffinières de Nordeck as Marie's father because of his tangential relationship with General François Achille Bazaine, who later became the scapegoat for the loss of the war. I used the political details about the rumors and the trial as the primary reason for Marie being an outcast like Louisa.

Catherine Denault (clan name: Ravissement/Rapture)--An utterly fictional character.

Mère Sainte Adeline--Eugénie mentioned the nun in a positive light in her diary. She was not the teacher who held the actual militaristic academic contests. Unfortunately, that teacher/nun's name was Mère Sainte Eugénie, which caused confusion, so I made Mère Sainte Adeline the teacher. All other details about her were fictionalized except for her name.

Mère de la Nativité (Ana)--She was mentioned in the diary, where she was referred to as a strict disciplinarian. All other details about the nun were fictionalized.

Madame Le Ray (Buttons) --The actual and very real headmistress of the school at Saint-Denis in 1874. All her other details have been fictionalized.

Colonel Adolphe Theuvez (1816–1874)--Commander of the 74th Infantry Regiment during the Franco-Prussian War. He could have known General Coffinières de Nordeck, but there are no other known details of his life. Everything else about the colonel is fictional.

Simon Jupin--Virginie's childhood friend and potential mate is 100 percent fictional.

Major General Joseph Vinoy––The actual grand chancellor in charge of the Legion d'honneur in 1874.

Gabrielle Chanzy––Her father, Antoine Eugène Alfred Chanzy, known as Le Général, was the best and most successful general in the Prussian War. I chose Gabrielle to play the part because being the daughter of this war hero would have given her the clout to be at the top of the pecking order at Saint-Denis. I have no idea whether Gabrielle attended Saint-Denis, and all other details about Gabrielle in the book are fictional.

Julie Paley (Jeton Un)––100 percent fictional.

Joséphine Maneval (Jeton Deux)––100 percent fictional.

João Lopes Gomes––100 percent fictional.

Brigadier General Étienne Gerard––An homage to one of Sir Arthur Conan Doyle's famous short story characters, the braggart and seducer <u>Brigadier Etienne Gerard</u>.

<u>Antónia Ferreira (Ferreirinha)</u>––One of the most influential and revered women in Portuguese agricultural and wine-making history. Married to a cousin who was uninterested in the family business, she inherited her father-in-law's love of the land and the people working it. The Portuguese wine industry survived the phylloxera blight of the late nineteenth century in part because of the work of Ferreirinha. She is so famous that a new bridge connecting Vila Nova de Gaia to Porto is named after her and is set to be inaugurated in 2026.

Paulo Ferreira da Fonseca (Marie's fiancé)––The fictional young second cousin of Ferreirinha. The only factual part is that the Ferreira da Fonseca family was closely tied to Ferreirinha's family and had a vineyard in the Douro Valley.

<u>Gustave Eiffel</u>––Yes, the man who built the tower had an office in Bolsa Palace during the 1870s while he designed Porto's first major bridge. You can see his office if you visit the palace today.

Brother Francisco Rodrigues da Cruz––100 percent fictional character.

Brother Francisco de São Luís--100 percent fictional character.

The Knights of Our Lord Jesus Christ--The martial sect of knights in the book is fictional. The details of the secularization of the order and the confiscation of the Church's properties in the 1830s are the facts. When I visited the Convent of Christ at Tomar, I heard the story of the surviving Templars coming to Portugal and being renamed. After that, I knew I would create the possibility of a rogue part of the order existing at the time of Louisa's visit.

Major Events Before and During the Book

The Siege of Paris--The book takes place in the years following this major event in French history. The defeat of the French by the Prussians in the <u>Franco-Prussian War</u> had vast ramifications across French society. The Commune of Saint-Denis would have been on the front lines during the battle. While visiting the school, I met with one of the Legion of Honor archivists who showed me the daily entries for the school superintendent at the time, which revealed that Prussian generals visited the school in the months following France's surrender.

The Great Wine Blight--The wine blight that devastated many of the European vineyards was caused by a North American bug (aphid) to which the European vines had no resistance. To solve the problem, hardy American varieties were identified and imported to Europe to be grafted with European varieties. In an ironic twist, a Texan, Thomas Volney Munson, was consulted and provided native Texan rootstocks for grafting. Because of Munson's role, in 1888, the French government sent a delegation to Denison, Texas, to confer on him the French Legion of Honor Chevalier du Mérite Agricole.

Translations

The following translations are provided in the order they appear in the story.

Dieu merci: French for thank God.

Skatá: Greek for crap.

Mère de la Nativité: French for Mother of the Nativity.

Ma Mère: French for My Mother.

Sapristi: French for heavens or good heavens.

Mon Dieu: French for my God.

Terminale: French feminine noun that refers to the upper sixth year, the oldest year in French secondary schools.

Surveillantes: French for lady supervisors.

Père: French for Father.

Mère de l'Adoration: French for Mother of Adoration.

Garde impériale: French for Imperial Guard. These were Napoleons most elite troops.

Professeure: French for Professor or Teacher.

Mademoiselle: French for Miss.

Demoiselle: French for young lady.

Couilles: French for balls.

Zut: French for damn.

Décimes: French for 1/10th of a Franc or equivalent to 10 cents.

Merci: French for thank you.

Merci beaucoup: French for thank you so much.

Muito obrigado: Portuguese for thank you very much.

Com licença: Portuguese for excuse me.

Con fluidez. Muchas gracias: Spanish for with fluency. Thank you very much.

Kólos: Greek for ass.

Compreender: Portuguese for understand.

Sim, obrigada: Portuguese for yes, thank you.

Gios pórnis: Portuguese for son of a whore.

Parbleu: French for good Lord.

Minha linda menina: Poruguese for my beautiful girl.

Santuário de Nossa Senhora dos Remédios: Portuguese for My Lady of Remedies.

Carre: French for a cloth held over the heads of the bride and groom during a wedding ceremony.

Ela é a única: Portuguese for she is the one.

Onde ela está: Portuguese for where is she?

Fils du diable: French for son of the devil.

Mon dieu, non: French for my God, no.

Kópanos: Greek for jerk.

Pare: Portuguese for stop.

Desculpe: French for excuse me.

C'est de la merde: This is crap.

I periérgeia skótose ti gáta: Greek for curiosity killed the cat.

Ta matia sou dekatessera: Greek for your eyes fourteen. Similar to the English phrase to have eyes in the back of your head.

Um dos alunos disse que o Lopes Gomes mandou queimar as orelhas. Deve ser um dos bruxos: Portuguese for One of the students said that Lopes Gomes had his ears burned off. He must be one of the witches..

Descer devagar: Portuguese for go down slowly.

Esta é ela. A rapariga que lutou com Lopes Gomes. Guarda as lâminas: Portuguese for, This is her. The girl who fought with Lopes Gomes. Put the blades away.

Salut, bonne sœur: French for hello, good sister.

Bonjour: French for good morning.

Na biblioteca: Portuguese for in the library.